## "I MIGHT AS WELL
## WEAR A SCARLET LETTER."

"For a kiss?"

"Look at my brothers." Whistles and catcalls came from the front porch, where Tom and Bernie were making kissing motions. Samantha gazed at Jake and shook her head. "You've done it now. Aunt Phoebe will go into shock. Wanda is probably on the phone, and by ten o'clock it will be all over town. Next Friday when I get my hair done, I'll get a lecture about loose morals."

"On the other hand," Jake added softly with devilment dancing in his eyes, "for a ruined reputation, I should get to do more."

"You can work on it," she teased, flirting with him and turning to climb into the truck before he could take her up on her statement.

He caught her wrist. "That's a challenge, lady."

"It was meant to be," she retorted.

# SARA ORWIG
# Lightning Season

**ZEBRA BOOKS**
**KENSINGTON PUBLISHING CORP.**

ZEBRA BOOKS

are published by

Kensington Publishing Corp.
475 Park Avenue South
New York, NY 10016

First Printing: January, 1993

Printed in the United States of America

*To Hannah Elaine Slater*

# Chapter One

"Night, Granddad. I'll be along soon," Samantha Bardwell said as she stood at the back door of the Bardwell Café. A single bulb burned overhead, and it shed a circle of light on the ground. The faint sound of music came from a jukebox in the pool hall at the end of the block.

"You work too hard, darlin'." Asa Bardwell patted her shoulder before he turned away.

Shaking auburn curls back from her face, she smiled and wondered how many times they had gone through this ritual. As he went down the wide dusty alley, she felt a squeeze in her heart. His shoulders were becoming more stooped, and his step was a shuffle. His old felt hat sat to one side of his head, white hair sticking out beneath it, and she was filled with love for him. She wished he didn't have to work so hard. At eighty, he should be retired and enjoying life.

With a sigh she went back inside and closed the door. Thinking about the mountain of bills on her desk at home, she counted money from the cash register. Feeling worried, she stared at the piles of crumpled bills and the stacks of coins. They had taken in forty-eight dollars and twenty-three cents, and Asa had given her the lease payment from the pool hall. Altogether the amount wasn't enough for both her brothers' dental bills. She couldn't make ends meet. Samantha bit her lip and brushed her damp eyes. There had to be a way to drum up more business, yet every idea came to nothing. She had developed a barbecue recipe. They had a new menu. They had low prices and served big portions. The Bardwell Café couldn't conjure up customers where none existed, and Salido had long ago become a town of very few people.

She put the money in a packet to take to the night depository at the bank on her way home. One thing—she felt safe walking around at ten o'clock on a Thursday night with forty-eight dollars in her hand. Salido, Oklahoma, was listed as a ghost town—although to the 764 people who occupied it, Salido didn't feel too ghostly.

She went to the walk-in pantry to put away a jar of pickles. With a squeak the door swung shut behind her. Samantha placed the pickles on a shelf and looked at their meager supplies. They didn't need a large storage area; a small cupboard could hold what they had on hand. She remembered when she was a child and Asa would bring her to the café. She would come into the pantry and run her small fingers over the bright jars. She recalled containers of red tomatoes, yellow corn, green watermelon pickles, golden peaches—an endless array of tempting food.

With a sigh she turned to the door and tried to open it and couldn't. Frowning, she tugged on the brass knob.

She was locked inside. She had meant to have the door fixed, but it was another expense she'd put off. She jiggled the tarnished knob harder, and it fell out into her hand.

"Oh, no . . ." Frustration and anger mingled. Her feet hurt from standing all day, she was worried about money, and now she was trapped in the pantry.

The closest people would be the men in the pool hall on the corner, but they would never hear her yell over the noise of the jukebox. Besides, there was an empty building between the café and the pool hall. She looked at the tiny window high above the shelves. She was slender with narrow hips, but the window was barely larger than an air vent. It was hinged at the top—a single pane of glass that opened out at an angle. Could she crawl through it? She knew it hadn't been opened in years—if ever.

Holding to a support post and moving carefully from shelf to shelf, she climbed up and shifted jars out of her way. The top shelf was dusty, rarely used, with only a few cans of beans on it. It was four feet lower than the ten-foot ceiling of the café that had been built in 1890. The window looked too small, but she didn't want to spend the night in the pantry.

Prying the pane open, she turned on her stomach and wriggled backward. Cool night air blew into the stuffy pantry. She inched her legs farther out until her hips met the window jambs. It was going to be difficult to get through.

Samantha pushed, and then she realized it was too tight. Her hips were squeezed uncomfortably in the narrow space. She would never get her shoulders through. She tried to go back inside and couldn't. She was stuck!

"Help," she called. "Hey, someone!" she shouted louder, wriggling and gripping the shelf, trying to pull herself forward. She couldn't move in either direction. She struggled, sweat breaking out, her legs getting tired as she pushed and tugged to no avail.

She heard a motor and kicked harder. Maybe someone would see her legs. She knew if she yelled, no one would hear her over the car motor. The rumble grew and then stopped.

"That's a hell of a way to go home," a man's deep voice remarked. "Or are you trying to burglarize the place?"

"I'm stuck."

"I'll come inside," he called.

"You can't get in, the pantry door's locked," she cried, relieved to know she wouldn't spend the night wedged in the pantry window. There was no answer from the man. Where did he go? Suppose they had to call Ward Connors and the volunteer fire department to get her out? She heard a rattle, and then someone kicked the pantry door and it crashed open, flying back against the shelves with a bang.

A tall, dark-haired man entered. His broad

shoulders dominated the pantry, while his lively dark eyes danced with amusement. She felt a blush start at her collar and burn its way up to her eyes. Worse yet, without effort he had an unmistakable male presence that made her aware of her appearance just when she didn't want to be reminded. It took a second to recognize him as one of the local ranchers and to think of his name — Jake Colby.

Stepping up on a box, he grinned. Warm hands closed around her waist, and with a jerk she was free.

"Thank heavens!" She rubbed her hips, closed the window and twisted around to climb down. He gripped her narrow waist again, and he swung her to the floor.

"Thank you. I thought I could squeeze outside."

"I don't think I could even get my leg through that little window," he remarked, laughing.

She smiled in return, feeling foolish, aware of her tousled hair and the dust all down the front of her red shirt and jeans. "The door swung shut behind me and locked. When I tried to push and pull on it, the doorknob fell off in my hand. I didn't want to spend the night in here, so I tried to climb out."

He grinned and shook his head. "You're one of the Bardwells."

"I'm Samantha. And you're Jake Colby."

"Right," he affirmed, offering to shake her hand. She glanced down at her dust-covered fingers. She turned her palm up, and he flicked one

11

quick appraising glance over her with open male curiosity. With a grin, he took her hand in his in spite of the dust. His grip was firm and warm as he shook with her. "I'll get your door fixed, because I finished off the lock when I kicked it open."

"You don't need to do that." She gazed up into compelling black eyes with thickly fringed dark lashes.

"I insist on paying for repairs." He tilted his head to study her. "I'm trying to remember . . . seems like you were at college not too long ago."

"More years than you think," she remarked dryly. "It's been three years since I finished. I stayed to get an M.B.A." She was aware of the closeness of the tiny pantry . . . the quiet. Jake Colby standing only a few feet away. His eyes looked full of curiosity. She remembered hearing that he was divorced. "We don't see you in town much."

"Nope. I seldom come in. This is the first time this month. I didn't see a car outside."

"I walk home. We don't live far, and there's no danger in Salido."

"You're safe but I'll give you a ride." He stepped aside for her to go ahead of him. He pulled the door closed behind him and knelt down to squint at the knob. Faded jeans pulled tautly over muscled legs. His black boots were dusty and scuffed. His broad-brimmed Stetson was pushed to the back of his head as he poked at the splintered wood. He stood up. "I'll send someone by tomorrow."

"Really—"

"I insist. C'mon. How about a beer on the way home?"

She wondered when she'd last had an invitation like that. Suddenly her tiredness vanished. "Yes, thanks. I have to stop by the bank's night depository," she explained, holding up the bag with the money.

"Sure thing."

As they left, she locked the door and climbed into his navy Ford pickup. He closed her door and went around to his side. His hat was still pushed to the back of his head, a mass of black curls showing. She had been rescued by a sexy, appealing man, while she felt as if she looked like the two-year-old peaches bottled on the pantry shelf. Fuzzy around the edges.

"I'm surprised you came back here from college." Light from the dash highlighted his prominent cheekbones and accented the hollows in his cheeks. Her gaze shifted to the wide, cobbled main street, lined with empty, turn-of-the-century buildings that made it look like a movie set. The one wide main street was also the highway. Three more streets ran parallel to it on the east, and six streets ran parallel on the west, all with tall shade trees—elms, oaks, sycamores.

"Settling in Salido wasn't what I'd planned." She lifted her hair off her neck and enjoyed the crisp March wind. As she turned, she caught him studying her. "Someday I'll move to a city. When I graduated, my family needed me. I help Granddad run the café. All through college I dreamed

13

of a career in marketing or advertising—instead I sell barbecue."

"And who's the man in your life? He must not live in Salido."

"There isn't time for one," she answered instantly, thinking about the hours she worked and momentarily forgetting Jake Colby.

"That's a damn waste," he stated softly in a voice that cajoled her back to an awareness of him. "What did your family do while you were in college? They got along without you then."

She shrugged. "They got deeply in debt, actually. My father ran up big debts before he was killed in a car wreck. Mom died of hepatitis when I was in high school. Granddad can't do what he used to, and Bernie, my seventeen-year-old brother, tried to help, but he couldn't do a lot. The other two were too young then to work except for running errands and sweeping. Tom is sixteen and Myra is fourteen."

"That's quite an age gap between you and the others."

"Mom lost three babies between when I was born and Bernie. I feel like a second mother now. They try to do as much to help as they can. All of them work part-time and buy their own clothes. The boys keep the yard mowed. Myra does a lot of the cooking at home."

"Do you need to call home and tell them you're with me?" He held out a cellular phone.

"No," she answered, laughing at the thought.

"They won't think someone carried you off on your walk home?" he asked, flicking her a glance that was a mixture of curiosity and assessment.

"Nobody is going to kidnap anyone in Salido, and sometimes I stay very late at the café. Granddad and the kids are sound sleepers and wouldn't wake if we had an earthquake. They'll never miss me. Dad's sister, my widowed aunt, lives with us. Uncle Charley died eleven years ago. Aunt Phoebe is a movie junkie. She watches old movies on late-night television and loses all track of time."

Jake swung the truck into a parking space in front of the three-story sandstone bank that towered over the one-story office buildings along the rest of the block. The bank was built in 1890 and three years ago had had a night depository installed. Jake Colby held out his hand. "I'll drop your deposit in for you."

With a long-legged stride he crossed the walk and slid the packet into the opening. A lean, handsome man, he wore a plaid shirt with sleeves rolled back, revealing strong forearms. Who was the woman in his life now? Samantha wondered. He climbed onto the seat and glanced at her. "The nearest place for a beer at this time of night is in Monroe. Willing?"

The college town of Monroe was twenty miles away, and with its population of nineteen thousand, Monroe was a big town compared to Salido. She gazed into Jake's dark eyes and nodded. "Why not? Sure."

He grinned, revealing white teeth and a slightly crooked eyetooth. He turned to swing the truck back into the street, and in seconds they were headed north on Main. Beyond the blocks of businesses, they drove past two-story houses, most with lights out. The tall Victorian homes had seen better days yet still held the grace of an earlier period. They passed the street that led the two blocks to the train station, where only one train a week came, now, carrying freight only.

"When I'm home, I always feel like I've fallen back in time. This is a small town out on a wide prairie where the pace is slow. The world seems pretty far removed from Salido."

"You ought to come out to my ranch. There the world is aeons away. I need the quiet. I suppose you don't, working in a café all day."

"I like working with people. Some days I don't get out of the kitchen if I do all the cooking."

They sped through the night with a crisp wind rushing through the windows. Stars were bright overhead, and greening fields stretched for miles in the silvery moonlight. Samantha felt contentment, relaxing momentarily, forgetting the bills for Bernie's and Tom's recent fillings, the bills owed by the café, Granddad's need for new glasses. She suspected Granddad wouldn't have dropped the timer in the fryer today if he'd been able to see clearly what he was doing.

As Jake drove, he switched on the radio. "Like country music?"

"Sure," she answered, thinking about her collection of Bach and Beethoven and Chopin. Waylon Jennings's voice came on and she relaxed more.

"I know what we can do—how about a little two-stepping?"

She smiled and shook her head. "I haven't danced in so long—"

"No kidding?" Jake's brows arched, and he sounded dubious. She received another assessing look, as if she were an oddity he hadn't encountered before. "We have to remedy that, Miss Workaholic."

"I'll step on your toes."

"I won't feel it through these." He pointed his booted feet. Minutes later he turned into a long metal building, set a few yards back from the highway. Cars filled the lot, and the overflow lined the road. A lighted sign said: Bill's Place. Beer and Music.

When she climbed out of the truck, she could hear loud music. They entered a long building that was smoky, dark and filled with college students. At the far end was a combo with an electric guitar, drums and bass. People were crowded together, dancers circling the room as they did the two-step. Without obvious effort Jake acquired a table for them, and as soon as cold beers were in front of them, he took her wrist to lead her to the dance floor.

He placed one hand on her hip. Her fingers rested lightly against his warm back, and she became conscious of the slight contact. Once again she was aware of her disheveled appearance. Her clothes were rumpled and dusty, her hair slightly tangled, while he looked fresher than crisp lettuce. He danced with a fluid grace, and she followed him easily.

His gaze caught hers and held as he gave her a

quizzical look. She noticed the shifting of his hips and the action of his long legs as he watched her. He was sexy, virile. The combination of his height and his dancing ability drew attention. The slight sway of his narrow hips, the graceful glide to his steps, drew the notice of other women. Enjoying herself more than she had in a long time, she relished the evening. It held a touch of unreality for her. The day had been long and tedious, and now she was dancing, something totally unexpected, physical, and fun—and as far out of her routine as flying to the moon.

After three songs Jake took her hand, and they sat down. He leaned closer over the table. "Liar. You've been dancing, and you didn't step on my toes once."

"I haven't done a two-step since I can't remember when. I *live* in the café."

"Every day?"

"Seven days a week and six nights."

"What time do you have off?"

"If I get free, it's on Sunday night."

"Go to dinner with me." He gazed at her with a direct look while he waited.

She stared at him. There was no room in her life for dating. When she'd climbed into the truck with him she hadn't thought about anything beyond the next few minutes. She knew the Colbys and had known Jake for a long time, but not well. "You're divorced?"

"Yes. I have a little girl. Melody," he said, and his voice changed. A tender note of warmth came into his tone that made it obvious Melody was special in his life. "She's four years old." He reached into his hip pocket to get his wallet, flipped it open and held it out. "Here's the most recent picture. I had it taken two months ago."

She looked at a smiling child with dimples and black hair like her father's. She had black eyes like his, too. "She's pretty. She looks like you."

"The two statements don't fit together."

"She has your dark eyes and curls."

"I have a nanny, Mrs. Latham, who's home with Melody." He took the billfold from Samantha, his warm fingers brushing her hand again. She was aware of the slightest contact with him. "Will you go to dinner?"

"Yes, I'd like that," she said, feeling a flutter of excitement as she gazed into his eyes. He had a disturbing way of staring at her that made her feel he was caught up in erotic speculation. Or was his directness triggering a response in her that caused her imagination to run rampant?

The music changed from country western to a fast rock. Jake jerked his head toward the dance floor and stood up. "Like to dance?"

"Sure . . . I'm always game," she teased, standing, moving toward the floor. He stepped closer, blocking her path.

"What are you game for, Samantha?" he asked in a soft, husky voice that carried a lazy Southwestern drawl.

She heard the sparkling challenge in his question, knew he was flirting, and she enjoyed it. "For anything away from the restaurant," she answered, wondering about him. What kind of man was he? What was he like? She couldn't remember hearing much about him from any of her friends, but it was probably because he was older.

He touched her collar with a faint drift of his hands on her red shirt. She was as conscious of the contact as she would have been a caress on her bare flesh. Animal magnetism seemed to be an apt description for the power he had. "We can get you away from the restaurant Sunday night."

"Anything out of the café is extraordinary for me," she replied, looking up at him. She turned toward the dance floor.

She liked to move to the faster beat, dancing around him, feeling exhilarated. His belt rode low on his narrow hips, the wide buckle glinting dully in the light. She turned, spinning around. When she faced him again, she caught his gaze on her hips. Then his eyes rose to meet hers, a sexual speculation unmistakable. Her pulse was caught in an arpeggio run. Jake Colby was a sexy, sensual man.

They stayed on the floor for over an hour. When they returned to the table, she was breathless and hot. He caught her arm. "Ready to go?"

She nodded, glancing at the clock behind the bar and surprised to see that it was half past one. The time had flown. Outside, the music was muted as he turned the key in the ignition and they sped away, heading back to Salido. A cooling wind blew her hair, and she rode quietly, enjoying the night, catching the smell of new wheat, keenly aware of the man beside her.

"I live in the four hundred block on Oak."

20

"I know where your home is."

"I guess we all know where everyone else lives."

"Your grandfather and mine were friends. They used to take me fishing with them when I was a kid."

"Is that right?" she asked, not recalling ever seeing him at their house. "I don't remember you."

"Thanks." He gave her a grin, and she laughed. "Sorry. That was a while back."

"I'm teasing. You were a baby then. I'm far older."

"Grandfather Time. I'm twenty-seven, and you must be all of four years older than I am."

"Nope, more than that. I'm thirty-three, so when I was seven and going fishing with them, you were just toddling around."

He was too masculine, too thickly muscled for her to conjure up an image of a seven-year-old boy. He pulled to a stop on the street in front of her tall, two-story Victorian house. The porch ran around the entire structure, with a swing hanging in front. Lights blazed in the wide downstairs windows that were raised.

"Your family watches television this late?"

"Yes, Aunt Phoebe watches the late movies every night. Come in if you'd like. On weekends Bernie and Tom, my brothers, stay up with her. Granddad is a morning person, so between the late nighters and the early risers, we seldom have all the lights off at this house. Want to come in?"

"Thanks, not tonight. I have to drive back to the ranch, and it's forty miles." He turned in the seat to face her, stretching his arm out across the

21

back to catch a lock of her hair and turn it in his fingers. "I had fun tonight."

"Thanks, Jake, so did I."

"How early do you open the café tomorrow?"

"I usually arrive around six o'clock. We have some customers who come in for breakfast," she answered, aware of his fingers twisting a curl of her hair, his knuckles brushing her ear while he studied her.

"You started that early yesterday morning?"

"Yes, I did. Sometimes I take off, and Granddad manages things if I have to run errands."

"I think it's time you get out and have a little fun."

She shrugged and looked away, her thoughts shifting back to the bills and problems. "I'm too busy to worry about getting away."

His finger trailed along her cheek and throat in another slight physical contact that brought her back to awareness of him. She turned to find him watching her solemnly, and all her thoughts about the restaurant faded. Her pulse quickened as she felt caught in his dark gaze. His expression was curious as he looked at her mouth, and his purpose was obvious, breathtaking.

His hand slipped to the back of her neck and drew her gently forward while he leaned closer over the gear shift. There was a momentary hesitation as they looked at each other. She wanted his kiss; her heart drummed in anticipation. His lips brushed hers, lightly, briefly, a faint friction that stirred her senses and made her want more, a gentle tug on her lips that awakened nerves.

With her heart pounding, she closed her eyes as he slipped his arm around her waist. His mouth covered hers, his lips a firm pressure as he held her.

His tongue played over hers, touching, stroking, and her mouth opened beneath his. With its heated touch, his tongue slid into her mouth. Warmth flowed in her veins, unfolding deep inside her, and she felt an aching longing to be loved. It had been so long since she had been on a date, and she knew she was vulnerable.

His kiss deepened, becoming insistent. Finally she pulled away. He gazed at her with the same speculative look she had seen before.

"I'd better go inside," she whispered.

He stared at her intently as if he was going to pull her into his arms again. Instead he inhaled deeply, then turned to climb out of the truck and come around to open the door for her. He draped his arm casually across her shoulders to walk her to the door.

"I hate to say I'm glad you were stuck in the pantry window, but I am."

"Thanks for rescuing me. It was fun to go dancing."

"White knight to rescue fair damsel."

"Thanks, Jake." At the foot of the front steps she turned to face him.

"Sunday night at six? Shall I pick you up at home or at the restaurant?"

"Make it seven and pick me up here, and I'll look a little better than this."

He arched his brows. "You look pretty nice to me right now," he said as he touched a lock of her hair, his voice conveying an intimacy that set her heart fluttering. "See you at seven." He opened the screen door, and she stepped inside the house. He turned away, and she watched him stride down the front walk.

"My goodness! Who is that?"

Aunt Phoebe had her nose pressed against the glass at one of the long windows in the hall. Her face was framed by her hands so she could peer outside.

"Aunt Phoebe, please don't stare at him as if it's a total phenomenon for someone to bring me home."

She didn't move. "Well, who is he? Gracious, he's tall."

Samantha gave up and went down the hall. "He's Jake Colby."

"The Colby boy who's divorced? How do you know him?"

"He got me out of the pantry tonight because I was locked inside."

"Why did you do that?" Phoebe asked, turning from the window. Samantha looked at her thin aunt whose auburn hair was thickly streaked with white. Her blue eyes were round behind her bifocals as she stared up at Samantha, and Samantha knew she was in for a dozen questions.

"It was accidental, Aunt Phoebe. He heard me calling for help and came to get me out."

"Where was Asa, for heaven's sake?"

"Probably here at home in bed."

"You were at the restaurant all this time?"

Accustomed to telling the truth, Samantha knew if she told what time Jake got her out of the pantry, she would have to account for every minute. "It wasn't bad."

"You poor thing. The Colby boy. I'm sure he's a father."

"He has a four-year-old daughter named Melody." Samantha glanced in the living room at the flickering scene on the television screen.

"Are you going out with him again?" Phoebe asked, trailing after Samantha as she started to climb the stairs.

With a sigh Samantha turned, bumping the newel post that fell off. She knelt to pick it up and put it back in place. Another one of the hundred things around the house that needed fixing. "I'm going out with him Sunday night," she admitted softly, realizing now she wouldn't get to bed for another twenty minutes.

"Oh, my word! He's older than you, Samantha. And he's a father."

"Aunt Phoebe, he just asked me to dinner. He didn't ask me to marry him. I barely know the man."

"Every marriage started with a first date. You aren't acquainted with eligible men, Samantha, but he is not the type for you."

"Yes, ma'am. I'm going to bed, Aunt Phoebe. Bernie's home, isn't he?"

"Yes. All three children are asleep and so is Asa. *The Attack of the Killer Bats* comes on in eleven minutes, and I'm going to watch it. Want to put on your pajamas and come down and watch with me?"

"Not tonight," she declined, thinking Aunt Phoebe was lucky. She couldn't add two and two, and she didn't worry about bills. She had a tiny gift shop where she sold knickknacks and the occasional quilt she made. She brought home her paycheck and never gave a worry as to how they would get along. Samantha went upstairs while Phoebe returned to the living room.

As Samantha lay in bed, she went over the bills, pondering about what they would do. She had to think of something to bring in more business. She couldn't transfer the whole family to a bigger town; she couldn't move away and leave them. She turned over to gaze out the window at the stars, remembering dancing with Jake. Memory of his kisses brought an intense longing and an aching void. Restlessly she turned over. Sunday night couldn't come too soon.

## Chapter Two

In the middle of the afternoon the next day, she was cleaning a table when she paused to look around the café. The room was thirty feet long with aged, stucco walls and the same decor it had had for the past forty years. Maybe it needed a coat of paint. Three dark brown fans were suspended from the high ceiling. She thought about the college hangouts in Monroe. Salido was an easy drive from Monroe. If they could attract college kids to the café, business might increase appreciably. She glanced around the room again, and the more she thought about it, the more the idea appealed. Bernie, Tom and Myra could help paint.

She raised her chin, staring out a smudged window and thinking about possibilities. With a glance at the big clock over the door, she hurried to the kitchen.

"Granddad, I'll be back in two hours." She untied her apron and yanked it off, her enthusiasm building.

27

"Ellie going to take extra-long today?"

"No. I need to run an errand." Kissing his cheek, Samantha picked up her purse to hurry outside and stride down the buckled walk. She glanced at her image, which was reflected in dusty plate glass windows of vacated shops. Her auburn hair fell free over her shoulders. For a moment she wondered if the pale blue cotton dress was the proper thing to wear to the bank or if she should have worn her Sunday best. Too late to worry—she didn't have time to go home to change.

Three blocks away on First Street, she went around the side of a frame house and opened a door. Smells of shampoo assailed her as she let the screen close softly behind her.

"Hey, Samantha," Ellie Hanlon greeted her, turning around, her eyes sparkling while she combed Mrs. Parson's hair.

Elvira Parson peered at Samantha through thick glasses. "Afternoon, Samantha."

"I'll get to you in just a minute," Ellie promised. Ellie's thick cap of black curls framed her pixie face, the same hairdo she had worn since her freshman year in high school.

"No hurry." Samantha watched Ellie work, thinking how much this hour meant to her out of her days at the restaurant. She couldn't afford to pay to get her hair done, but Ellie was her best friend and did it free. She wanted Samantha to take the time to come visit once a week. In turn, Ellie could eat free at the restaurant—a bargain that was better for Samantha, because Ellie seldom ate out.

"You're dating Jake Colby, we hear," Ellie teased, with a grin.

"Aunt Phoebe's been on the telephone." Samantha laughed. "He helped me get out of the locked pantry at the restaurant and gave me a ride home, so according to Aunt Phoebe we're an item."

"There you are, Mrs. Parson." Ellie stepped back.

Mrs. Parson paid Ellie and stood up, patting her gray hair, and turning to Samantha. "There aren't many eligible men here. I told Phoebe to stop worrying. The man will be a good catch and he will take care of you just fine. Course, the Colbys are ranchers, so you'd have to live out of Salido."

"Yes, ma'am."

Mrs. Parson studied Samantha a moment. "You might wear a little makeup, Samantha. Not too much, just a smidge. And drink more milk. Men like women with more meat on their bones. See you next week, Ellie."

She swept out the door and Samantha looked at Ellie and grinned.

"C'mon, tell me. It's all over town you're dating him."

"You know Aunt Phoebe." Samantha sat down to get her hair shampooed while Ellie turned on a spray of water. It's just what I told you. I got locked in the pantry. I tried to climb out the window and got stuck. He saw my feet sticking out the window and he rescued me and drove me home."

"And you're going out with him Sunday night. And your aunt thinks he's too old for you and he's a father. I think he's a hunk. What's he like, Samantha? He doesn't come into town much and they say the ex-wife was gorgeous and a model. She was a snob deluxe—would hardly stop in town and never said hello. I didn't like her."

"Maybe she was shy."

"You always give everyone the benefit of the doubt."

"It's easy enough," she replied with a smile, her thoughts shifting to problems. "Ellie, I've been thinking about the café. I have to do something—the bills are about to bury me—I'm going to redecorate and advertise in the Monroe paper to see if I can draw the college crowd. What do you think?"

"Draw them to Salido? They won't come. Why drive over here?" she asked as she rinsed Samantha's hair.

"It would be something different."

"You'll waste your time and effort." She helped Samantha sit up. Ellie began to comb the curly, wet strands of auburn hair.

"I'm going to give it a try."

"What do you think you'll do with Jake Sunday night? It's great you're going out with him."

"I don't know what we'll do. He really didn't say."

"You can bring him by the park and introduce him around. I'd like to meet him. We're playing softball with the team from Monroe."

"You and Vernon?" she asked, thinking about the stocky blond farmer Ellie had dated since her freshman year in high school.

"Yes. I'm going to put my foot down with Vernon. If he doesn't agree to get married this summer, I'm going to threaten to give back his ring."

"You did that last summer, Ellie."

"I know." She raised the chair to blow dry Samantha's hair. "Vernon is a man terrified of marriage. And I can't guess why. His momma and daddy have been married thirty-one years and they're as happy as peas in a pod. He's getting so he stutters if we talk about marriage. What are you going to wear Sunday? You can borrow my red dress if you'd like."

"Thanks, Ellie. I might do that. I haven't decided yet what I'll wear because he didn't say where we're going."

Conversation changed to Ellie's softball team and the movie playing in Monroe until Samantha was through and headed for the door.

"Samantha, call me Monday and tell me if you had fun with him Sunday night — foolish question! He's the best looking man in the county except Vernon."

"He is kind of cute," she admitted, thinking

cute was not the right description of Jake Colby. Just thinking about his sexy bedroom eyes made her pulse quicken. "Thanks, Ellie."

"Call me! I want to hear all about it."

Samantha walked in hot sunshine to the bank and stepped into the quiet lobby. Glancing around, she recognized everyone. Gerald Bison was at the teller's window talking to Lori Foster; Samantha's close friend Nedra Thompkins's head was bent over her desk. Samantha walked to Nedra, and when Nedra looked up, Samantha smiled.

"Hi, Nedra. I'd like to see Mr. Yarrell."

"Hi, Samantha. Sure. Just a minute, and I'll see if he's busy. I hear you're dating Jake Colby."

"Yes, I am," she replied, giving up, realizing Aunt Phoebe must have spread the word like sunshine.

As soon as Nedra returned to her desk, she motioned Samantha to go into the president's office. As she entered, he leaned back in his chair. His black hair was parted neatly in the center of his head and combed down smoothly on both sides. "Good afternoon, Samantha. Have a seat. What brings you to the bank? A school raffle for Myra? Or to catch up on late mortgage payments?"

One worry at a time. She sat down across the desk from Wilson Yarrell and crossed one knee over the other. "Mr. Yarrell, I'd like another small loan."

He blinked and arched his brows. "Whatever

for?" he asked, causing her to feel a touch of annoyance. Why should he sound so surprised that she would ask for a loan?

"I want to redecorate the café, because I think I can draw more business if I do."

"Don't be ridiculous, Samantha. You couldn't draw more business in Salido if you gave the food away free. We just have so many people here, and there isn't any way to change our population. Heaven knows, redoing the café won't make people move here."

"Mr. Yarrell, I've thought this over," she stated, remaining patient. Mr. Yarrell always fought relinquishing one penny of the bank's money unless he knew for certain he would get it back twentyfold or better. She had come prepared to argue. She opened a folder and placed a sheet of paper in front of him. "I've stopped at Treadwell's Light Shop and priced fixtures this morning. Then I went to Unger's Hardware and checked the cost of paint. Bernie can print signs, and I called a T-shirt place in Monroe. I think if I refurbish the café, get an appealing T-shirt and advertise in the Monroe paper, I can draw the college crowd."

Wilson Yarrell glanced at the paper and pushed it away, holding it out to her. "They'd never drive over here."

"I think they will. A lot of them don't worry about the price of gas, and it would be something different to do. Look at the amounts. I'm not asking something astronomical."

"Samantha, I think it's nice you're trying, but this won't do any good, and it's a frivolous waste of money."

"Perhaps it is, Mr. Yarrell, but I think I can make the café appeal to that crowd. I'm not asking for a giant loan. I'll use the café for collateral."

He peered at her through his glasses and rubbed his chin. "I advise against it."

"I'd like to do it," she persisted, feeling caught in a contest of wills. "The café does make some money, and if I can't make payments, you'd become owner. If so, you'd own almost all of Main Street."

"Lot of good it would be to me if we lose much more of our population." He sat back in his chair and picked up her paper and studied it. "You know the bank's interest rate."

"I'm willing to pay it."

He studied the paper again and then peered at her intently. "Do you think you can pay the bank back at the rate of four hundred dollars a month?"

"Yes, I do," she promised firmly, feeling her heart beat faster, because she didn't know if she could or whether she would lose everything with this scheme.

"All right, Samantha, I'll have the papers drawn up for the loan."

"Can I get it today?"

"Yes, you can." He shrugged. "Maybe you'll succeed. God knows, you and Asa try." He

34

peered at her. "You're dating Jake Colby. Smart move, Samantha. The man is solid. As substantial as they come."

"Yes, sir." Solid, sexy muscle, she thought, but she didn't think that was what Mr. Yarrell had in mind.

She sat back feeling enormous relief, because she knew how tight Wilson Yarrell could be with the bank's money. He lived in a small frame house that had been in his family for generations. He walked to work and seldom drove his 1953 Cadillac. He kept it polished and in the garage, taking it out on holidays and when he drove his wife, Imogene, out of town.

Samantha prayed she could repay the loan, and she felt butterflies in her stomach over what she was about to do. If she didn't succeed, they could lose the café and everything they owned.

She pushed the fears aside, because they would overwhelm her if she gave them much thought. Sitting back, she waited while Wilson Yarrell left the room to get the papers drawn up and have a check cut for the money.

She glanced around the spartan office, which held a functional oak desk, a file cabinet, two worn leather-covered chairs that were probably as old as the bank. A brass spittoon was in one corner—another carryover from bygone days.

When she left the bank, fears threatened to engulf her because of what she had done without consulting Asa or anyone in her family.

Over dinner when she broke the news, she

35

tried to put as much enthusiasm as possible into her voice.

"Me, paint? I'm playing baseball!" Bernie exclaimed, shaking long brown hair away from his face, an earring glinting dully in one ear.

"I'm playing ball, too," Tom echoed. "We don't have time to work on the café."

"That's ambitious of you, Samantha," Phoebe noted, "but it hardly seems necessary."

"We have to do this," she declared, feeling frustrated and exasperated. She leaned forward. "All of you are going to help. I took out a loan at the bank, and if this doesn't succeed, we'll lose the café!" she blurted.

"She's right," Asa stated quietly, looking at the boys. "Bernie, you and Tom will juggle this with your ball playing. School's out—"

"And I gotta work at the gas station, besides helping at the café." Bernie's lower jaw thrust out.

"And I bag at the grocery!" Tom added.

"I baby-sit," Myra piped up, shaking her red curls that were tied in a ponytail behind her head, short strands springing loose and curling around her face.

"You'll all help," Samantha declared, "or we'll lose everything and have to sell the house and leave Salido." She hadn't intended to scare them. As she looked at their startled expressions, she felt a mixture of anger that they wouldn't willingly help, and she regretted that she had to frighten them into it.

"Well, I'll help you, Samantha," Phoebe interjected. "When I close up at the gift shop in the afternoons."

"Thank you, Aunt Phoebe. I'll work out a schedule with each of you. We'll start after dinner."

"Aunt Phoebe says you have a date with a real old dude who has a kid. Is that true?" Myra asked, studying her. Instant quiet settled while all eyes turned to Samantha.

"I'm going out with Jake Colby Sunday night. I'll probably never see him again, and he's not some old dude with a kid. He's barely older than I am and he has a little girl who's only four years old."

"Is he cute?" Myra asked.

"Jake Colby?" Asa asked, squinting at her.

"Yes, Granddad."

"She couldn't get out of the pantry, and Mr. Colby rescued her," Phoebe informed them, and Bernie choked on his potatoes.

"How did you do that?" Bernie asked and Samantha knew she would get questioned until she told them all about it.

"You didn't tell me—is he cute?" Myra persisted.

"He's absolutely adorable," Samantha replied in exasperation.

"How did he know you were in the pantry?" Bernie continued. "Was he a customer?"

"No, he was driving down the alley."

"What in heaven's name was he doing there

in the middle of the night?" Phoebe inquired.

"He had been at the pool hall."

"Oh, my Lord. He hangs out with the men at the snooker parlor!" Phoebe exclaimed. Bernie and Tom exchanged a glance.

"How did you get out of the pantry?" Myra persisted.

Samantha put down her fork to tell them, her mind drifting to her plans to redo the café while she answered their questions. Finally dinner was over and she could plan a schedule to start on the café.

Sunday night she hurried home, showering and changing swiftly to jeans and a turquoise shirt. Jake hadn't said what they would do, so she was uncertain how to dress. But most everything around Salido was casual and Western. All the worries concerning the café melted away as she thought about going out with him again.

At five minutes to seven she heard the doorbell and went downstairs, turning the corner at the landing. Bernie, Tom and Myra pushed each other out of the way to get to the door while Aunt Phoebe was only steps behind them. Watching everyone, Asa stood in the living room doorway.

As the boys pushed each other, Myra slipped past them and opened the door. Samantha closed her mouth and bit back the words she had started to say to them. It was just one evening, and Jake might as well meet her family head-on.

Myra opened the door, and Samantha's pulse raced faster when she looked at Jake. The hat was missing, and his thick black hair curled above his forehead. He wore jeans and a red and blue plaid shirt. His gaze roamed over her family, returning to Myra as he smiled at her.

"Hi!" she greeted him. "I'm Samantha's sister, Myra."

"Hi, Myra," he replied easily. "I'm Jake Colby."

"Hi, Jake," Samantha greeted him as she descended the steps. His gaze met hers, and her heartbeat revved another notch as she looked into his dark eyes. "Come in and meet my family if they'll let you get in the door."

"I'm Phoebe Bardwell Ruffin." Aunt Phoebe extended her hand, and Jake shook hands with her.

"Glad to meet you, ma'am."

"I knew you when you were a little shaver. Now you're all grown up and you must be every bit of thirty-eight years old."

As he laughed, Samantha hurried down the last few stairs.

"Not quite, Mrs. Ruffin. I'm getting there. Some days I feel thirty-eight."

"You rode a bull in the last Monroe rodeo, didn't you?" Bernie asked.

"That's right. You like bull riding?"

"I haven't ever ridden one."

39

"Gee, bull riding is cool," Myra cooed, scooting closer to him. "I haven't ever known a real bull rider."

"Sure, you do," Bernie corrected her. "You go to school with Tolley Frazier and he rides 'em."

"Tolley's subhuman," she muttered under her breath to Bernie. She turned to smile at Jake.

The boys and Myra and Phoebe blocked Samantha from getting to Jake. She put her hands on Tom's shoulders. "Jake this is my little brother Tom, my brother Bernie. You met Aunt Phoebe and Myra." She felt like she was in the crush at May's Dry Goods Store at their annual white sale. While she talked, she moved Tom out of the way as Jake shook hands with the boys. Samantha stepped to Jake's side and took his arm, steering him toward Asa. "This is my grandfather Asa Bardwell. Everyone, this is Jake Colby."

Asa and Jake shook hands. "Good to see you Jake. I haven't seen you in a long time. You still fish at Lake Lewiston?" Asa asked. "That's where your grandfather liked to fish. We caught some beauts there. We used to take you along with us when you were a little fellow."

"I was just there last weekend. Caught a dandy bass."

"Is that right?" Asa jerked his head toward the living room. "Come in here. Let me show you the lure I just made."

"Granddad—"

40

Jake grinned and took her arm. "Sure. Let's look at it."

Phoebe's lips firmed, and she peered through her bifocals at Jake. They all streamed to the living room where Jake bent over Asa's tackle box while the boys perched on chairs. As Phoebe sat down with her quilting, Bernie and Tom looked down at the tackle. Samantha wondered if she would spend the evening home with the family. Myra had suddenly become interested in fishing equipment, something she had never shown a flicker of interest in before. She stood close to Jake, looking at Jake more than the lure Granddad was describing. Myra at fourteen was keenly interested in boys, and Samantha had resigned herself to some battles over dating. She never guessed she would have to worry about Myra slavering over a thirty-three-year-old man.

Samantha watched Jake as he squatted down in front of Asa's tackle box and looked at various lures. His jeans pulled tautly on his long legs while he discussed bass and bluegill fishing. Finally he stood and Granddad motioned toward the frayed blue wingback chair. "Have a seat. You don't need to rush off."

Jake turned, winked at Samantha and glanced at Phoebe who was glaring at him. "That's a fine quilt," he remarked easily, strolling over to look at it and picking up a corner.

"Thank you. I'm doing all the states' flowers in this quilt."

"You sure are. Here's our mistletoe, Texas's

41

bluebonnet, Colorado's columbine. My grandmother loved to quilt and I treasure all of them. My favorite is one that's all shades of blue."

"Aunt Phoebe taught me how to quilt," Myra added, moving around to face him. "Aunt Phoebe's won prizes at the county fair."

"Is that right? I'll bet I've seen your quilts on display then, because I always go look at the quilts. Last year the winner was one that was red, white and blue."

"You remember my quilt?" Phoebe asked, blinking and looking at him with arched brows.

"Yes, ma'am. That was a mighty fine quilt."

"Well, thank you, Mr. Colby."

"It's Jake. You just call me Jake." He flashed her a grin that was warm enough to ignite kindling.

Phoebe blushed and smiled at him, and Samantha knew that she had heard the last argument from Aunt Phoebe about Jake Colby. And Myra was practically drooling over him. When Samantha gave her a fierce look, Myra turned her back. Half an hour later Jake stood up.

"Well, I promised to feed Samantha, so I guess I'll take her out and keep my word. It was nice to meet all of you."

Once again the whole family followed him across the room, moving with them to the door and out onto the porch. As Samantha and Jake went to the truck everyone waved except the boys, who disappeared around the side of the house.

"I don't have a date often, as you can tell," Samantha noted with amusement. "You're as much a novelty as a Martian."

"It's time to reverse that." Arching his brows, he glanced at her.

"Change my not dating? I'll tell you, right now in my life, I don't have time," she stated, thinking about renovating the restaurant and the extra hours that would take.

"You sound like a woman with a worry."

She shrugged. "I'm going to forget the café for the next three hours."

"I don't mind if you talk about the café. And I won't object if you forget the café. Whatever you like. You have a nice family."

"You won over Aunt Phoebe." Samantha studied the width of his cheekbones and the flat planes of his cheeks, deciding he was handsome enough to cause Myra's drooling. Samantha felt a bubbly eagerness for the evening. It was mid-March, and in the last dusky rays of day he turned the truck onto Main Street toward the highway.

"I really do remember her quilt. My grandmother quilted and I always thought it was great. She made a special one for Melody, and Melody still sleeps with it every night."

"Is your grandmother living?"

"No. All my family are gone."

"There's just you and your daughter and a nanny?"

"That's right."

"Does Melody stay with her mother part of the year?"

"No, she seldom sees her mother." He stared straight ahead. "Diantha is a model and she's been in her first movie. She grew up in Los Angeles — and the Full Moon Ranch is a far cry from Los Angeles. I interfered in her career, and when she decided she preferred it to me, she also felt Melody was a hindrance. She sees Melody about once a year and calls about four times a year. At four years of age Melody hasn't realized yet that her mother really cast her aside."

"I'm sorry." Samantha hurt for him and his little girl. "Our family is close, so it's difficult for me to imagine."

"I try to make up for it, try to be both mother and father."

"You're probably marvelous at it."

He grinned and looked as if he relaxed slightly. "You couldn't know whether I'm good or bad or a real catastrophe."

"You're too interested in people and patient with them to be a bad father. After the way you treated my family, I'm sure you're wonderful to your own."

By the time he drove through Monroe, it was dark. Street lights were on, and as they passed the campus with the long, one-story red brick buildings that comprised Monroe College, lights glowed on the buildings and walks. Samantha watched a couple stroll across campus. "That's what I'm aiming for."

"Excuse me?"

She waved her hand toward the college. "I'm redoing the restaurant and changing the name from the Bardwell Café to Salido Sam's. I'm having a T-shirt designed with what I hope is a catchy logo. Then I'll advertise in the Monroe College newspaper. I hope students will drive to Salido to the café."

She braced for the usual skepticism or amusement or a flat denial. Instead he cocked his head to one side as if he were giving the matter consideration. "Why do you think they would drive that far? They won't realize the decor is changed. You'll have the ad but what's the inducement?"

"I hope the logo, the T-shirt and simply a new place will draw them. I'm getting a karaoke and ordering lots more beer."

"There aren't any karaokes in Monroe as far as I know. Maybe you have something."

"You're the first person to think so," she remarked dryly.

"Sounds as if you're fighting some battles alone," he stated as they left Monroe and night closed in around them again.

"No. Granddad is right there beside me. He works so hard, but the café is dying on the vine."

"I didn't ask—how about hamburgers? If you want something fancier, we can go somewhere else. I promised something extraordinary."

"Just being out on a date is extraordinary."

She would have fun with him anywhere because he was easy to talk to. She had few people to discuss anything with except Granddad and Ellie and occasionally Nedra Thompkins.

Jake drove to Sangley, north of Monroe, and stopped at a log building on the edge of town. Trucks and cars were parked in front, and the smell of woodsmoke and charcoaled meat filled the air. When they walked inside, Jake draped his arm casually across her shoulders. It had been a long time since she had been out with an appealing male, and she was acutely conscious of each brush against him.

As they crossed the dimly lit café, she was aware of his height; she came only to his shoulder. They ordered hamburgers and sat close to a small, empty dance floor. After the burgers were eaten Jake settled back into the corner of the booth while he had a beer and she had a glass of tea. He propped his foot on the seat, and talk returned to the topic of the café.

"You're renovating the café yourself or hiring it done?"

"We're doing it. I've worked out a schedule when Bernie and Tom and Myra can give me some hours."

"I knew your grandfather and I've seen all of you at one time or another, but I don't get into town often."

"You've been into town twice this past week," she observed with amusement.

"There's a good reason for the second trip,"

he replied, and she felt her cheeks grow warm.

"I wasn't fishing for something."

"I know you weren't. Do you like rodeos?"

"Yes. Sometimes Bernie is in the bronc riding, but he's not very good at it. I hate to watch him, because I'm scared he'll get hurt."

"Monroe's having their annual rodeo a week from Saturday night. Want to go?"

"I'd love to, but I work Saturday nights."

"Couldn't you, just once, get someone to work for you that Saturday night?" he asked, his dark eyes intent on her. She gazed back with the same directness, feeling her heart beat faster. There was an electric tension crackling between them. She felt it and she knew he did, too. She could see it in his eyes, yet she had no time in her life for a complication of any kind. Least of all a breath-stopping, sexy male.

She thought about all the work she had to do Saturday night. Weekends were the busiest time at the café. Myra couldn't cook. Aunt Phoebe . . . impossible. Granddad would work all day Saturday and all night, anyway. Bernie might do it, but he would fight about having to give up his Saturday night. "Just once . . ."

She gazed into Jake's dark eyes that urged her to agree. "I'll get a replacement."

"Good," he replied and flashed a wide smile that softened his features and made her glad she had accepted his invitation. Appealing creases bracketed his mouth and tiny crinkles from being outdoors fanned from the corners of his black

eyes. It was a winning smile that was as irresistible as a friendly puppy. "I'll pick you up about
six, and we'll eat first. You'll have to sit alone
part of the time—you won't mind will you?"

"You're riding that night?" she asked in surprise.

"Yes. The last event. Bull riding. But it
shouldn't be scary to you like it is with your
brother, because you don't know me well enough
to worry."

"I'm frightened for every bull rider."

"Aw, shucks. For a minute there I thought you
were going to say you're concerned about me."

She smiled, knowing he was teasing her, looking into his eyes and realizing that she would
worry because it was him.

"Who was he, and why did you break up?"
Jake asked quietly.

"You don't know there's ever been a man in
my life." She felt amused by his assumption.

"Yes, I do," he answered without smiling.
"There was one."

She was curious. What made him think there
had been a man? She thought about Devon as
she looked down at herself. "Something about
the way I dress or the way I wear my hair?"

"Samantha," Jake answered, still sitting back
in the corner with his elbow on his knee, the
longneck in his hand, "with your big blue eyes
and your red hair, there's been a man."

She blushed then, thinking she must have
sounded like she wanted a compliment. "His

name was Devon Smith. We started dating when I was a freshman in college and we dated all through college. We broke up because he didn't want me to come back to Salido to help my family. He wanted me to move to Houston with him. He didn't like my family. You should understand. You wouldn't want to marry someone who doesn't like your little girl."

He looked away and the harsh, shuttered expression showed fleetingly in his features. It was gone when he turned back to her. "I won't marry again." He took a drink of beer, and she watched his Adam's apple bob as he swallowed. He lowered the bottle to look at her. "I'm surprised you don't mind being buried in Salido."

"Men can't ever understand women who don't want to get married."

"Maybe they just don't believe what they say."

"It isn't that I don't want to get married. I just wasn't ready to abandon my family when they needed me. Anyway, that's over. Devon seems like part of my life that happened a very long time ago."

"Do you ever hear from him?"

"No. It was over three years ago, and I haven't met anyone since."

"Or given anyone the time of day," he added, his eyes twinkling again.

She expected another evening of two-step and country western music, because the building was made of logs with a rustic decor. Instead the pieces were old favorites.

"Let's dance." Jake stood up and reached across the table to take her hand. He drew her to him, his arm going around her waist, pulling her close. They moved together in step and he was easy to follow. She was conscious of the warmth of his body, the scent of woodsy after-shave and the faint sharp tang of beer on his breath.

The next piece was fast, and he moved away from her, holding her hand to turn her and then releasing her. Watching him move with a fluid masculine agility, his slender hips gyrating rhythmically, she felt warmth coil low inside her. His lean body was graceful, sexy.

In minutes she was hot. Jake unbuttoned another button of his shirt, and her gaze drifted down to the dark hair curling on his chest.

The next number was another slow one. Wrapping his arms around her, he pulled her closer. They moved in unison as if they had danced together for years instead of minutes. His waist was narrow, his body lean and hard. A rancher, a bull rider. And a man bitter over his divorce. Yet he was fun, and it had been so long since she had enjoyed the company of a virile, appealing man. He had made it clear there would be no entanglement, no commitment, no deep involvement. Those ground rules were all right at this time in her life. Lord, what fun it was to be with him!

When the number ended, they applauded with the other dancers, and then another slow one started. This time he held her away from him slightly as he had the first dance, and he gazed down at her with a faint smile on his face. "You haven't lost your knack for dancing while you've worked in the café."

"I like to dance." His lips were slightly full, sensual, and as she gazed at them, she remembered his kisses. She was aware of his hands holding her, of the occasional brush of their legs.

They sat out the next dance, but then got up again and danced for an hour, fast and slow. As she moved with him, the tension built between them. The teasing and light banter were gone, and she knew he felt the same stirrings she did.

It was almost eleven as they danced to a slow blues number, a sexy rhythm that was deliberate, the sensual wail of a cornet floating in the air. Jake was watching her, and her heart was beating fast as she gazed back at him.

He wrapped his arms around her and drew her to him. She felt his body, hot, hard, aroused. Desire burned in her, a searing urge that made her want to thrust her hips against him. They stopped in the middle of the dance floor as others swirled and moved around them, and she looked up at Jake.

"Come on," he urged.

She nodded. With his fingers on her wrist, they crossed the room to go outside into cool night air. Holding her hand, he walked around the corner of the building into the shadows, and her heart slammed against her ribs. Her breathing came erratically as Jake leaned against the wall. Spreading his feet, Jake pulled her up against his body and wrapped his arms around her.

His gaze searched hers, and then her eyes closed as she tilted her face up. His mouth covered hers, his tongue thrusting over hers, wet, insistent. She returned his kisses, her hips twisting against his hard length while she moaned softly and felt desire shake her. This shouldn't be happening—his melting kisses and her deep response—yet he was irresistible.

Wanting him, she wound her arms around his neck. His hand slid over her hip, pushing beneath her turquoise shirt to cup her breast. His thumb flicked over her taut nipple through the cotton blouse and filmy lace bra.

It had been aeons since she had been caressed, and her body responded wildly. Heat thickened her blood with an ache burning low in her, making her move against him. His body was hard, so good against hers, his hands a delicious torment.

She pushed away from him slightly and felt as if she were in a steam room that held no air. She gasped for breath, gazing up at him. "I have to stop. I can't go so fast."

"Go home with me." He stroked her nape, sending fresh ripples through her. His black eyes held seductive promises, coaxing her to yield.

"I can't." She suffered an inner battle of longing and caution. "I can't ask you in at home and I can't go with you. You know how conservative Salido is. My family is twice as traditional, and the whole town would gossip. They'll talk about where I am now and what time I get in tonight."

"Oh, hell . . ."

"At present I have to devote everything to taking care of my family. We're just barely staying afloat. I can't complicate my life."

"I don't want that, either. I won't interfere with your family."

"They take all my efforts. And it isn't just them," she admitted. "I can't go that fast, Jake. I'm not casual. I've only known Devon and that was years—almost like a marriage."

Jake leaned back and closed his eyes. "Okay, Sami." He looked at her and traced her lips with his thumb, stroking her lightly. The drumming in her pulse started again just by the warm, sensual drag of his thumb over her lip. She wanted to close her eyes and yield to him. "You're a very desirable woman, Samantha. C'mon, I'll take you home." He took her arm, and they strode with long steps toward his truck.

She felt foolish and prim and at the same time, she was shaken and certain in what she told him. They would be bankrupt and lose the restaurant if she didn't give it her all.

She couldn't accept a casual relationship, either. She would shock her family and the town if she went home with him. And she could never take him home at night with her. Not unless they wanted to sit up until sunrise and watch *Attack of the Killer Bats*.

As he thrust the key into the ignition, she caught his hand. He looked at her quizzically.

"I can't be casual, but I wish we had some other choices." She reached out to touch his lips with the tips of her fingers. With a narrowing of his eyes, he drew a deep breath and crushed her to his chest across the gear shift for another long, wet, passionate kiss that left her gasping again as he released her and leaned back.

Jake studied her. She was doing the sensible thing, following the course he should follow. Lord knows, when he pulled her out of the window, he had no intention of any kind of involvement. He looked into those big, luminous eyes. This one would want commitment from her baby blues right down to her pretty little toes. What was it about her that was so hot? When he met her, she was dusty, disheveled and rumpled. Her mind was on her business and her family, and she didn't date or flirt. Yet she was all woman, and when he danced with her, the looks she gave him stirred erotic fantasies. She moved with a sensual abandon, and the few kisses they'd shared had all but fried his tonsils.

*A narrow escape there, Colby.* If she had gone home to the ranch, what a complication in life it would be. Be grateful. He couldn't summon up a shred of relief. He didn't want involvement, although it sounded as if she truly didn't want any, either. Impossible to imagine, but from all

54

he had heard and seen, that seemed to be the truth.

She was refreshing to be with. He didn't like being chased and there had been too many over-friendly women. Samantha Bardwell had her mind on other things, and it took an effort on his part to catch her attention, a challenge he found he enjoyed. She was wasting her life shut away in Salido, and the jerk from Houston had given up too easily.

And when she let down the barriers and returned his kisses, she held promises of unbelievable sex. She was totally responsive, sensual and unaware of her effect on him. He wanted her, to feel her give in completely. Dream on, Colby. The lady won't unless there is a trip to the altar, and at that he would balk. The most fantastic woman in the world wasn't worth disrupting Melody's life again.

He shifted on the seat, feeling a heaviness in his groin, trying to force his thoughts away from Samantha's kisses.

She was looking straight ahead, her profile to him. He let his gaze slide down to her slender throat where a patch of moonlight splashed her skin with alabaster rays. He longed to lean the short distance and kiss her there, to hear her swift catch of breath and see her body respond.

Instead, he reached down to start the motor. Be calm, be sensible, and be thankful tomorrow. But right now, taking her home and keeping his hands to himself wasn't what he wanted to do.

"Home it is."

Along the way they discussed the Monroe football team, the café again, the movies Phoebe watched. Jake told her about his Cessna.

"You have your own plane?"

"Yes. I have a pilot's license, and I do a lot of business in Dallas. My broker and my attorney and my accountant are all in Dallas."

"Not Oklahoma City?"

He shrugged. "Dallas is about as close as Oklahoma City, and my accountant is a friend, so I go to Dallas."

As they talked, Samantha glanced at Jake. Aching to go home with him and knowing that she shouldn't, she looked out the window, letting cool wind blow over her heated skin. She was vulnerable and she could lose her heart effortlessly to this lean, easygoing man and be hurt as badly as she had been when she had broken up with Devon.

Jake turned into the drive at her house and cut the motor. The tall Victorian house was dark except for a dim glow that came from the living room.

"They must have all the lights off except the television," Samantha said, aware Jake turned toward her. "Aunt Phoebe is probably peeping out to see us. The last time you brought me home, she watched us."

"I know." Jake stroked Samantha's jaw, trailing his finger down her throat. "I saw her looking out the window."

"Oh, Lordy, did you!" she exclaimed, startled that he didn't seem to mind.

"You have an interesting family." There was a pause, a silence that was filled with longing so tangible it was like a pull of ebb tide as she looked up at him. His fingers caressed her arm while his gaze drifted to her mouth.

"We might as well give her her money's worth," he said in a husky voice, leaning forward as his arm tightened around Samantha. He kissed her, his tongue thrusting deep. Any protest about Aunt Phoebe was forgotten. All thoughts vanished as Samantha ran her hands across his broad shoulders and clung to him. His mouth was a pressure on hers, his tongue went deep as she kissed him back.

A long time later she pushed away. "We have to stop."

He didn't answer, but turned and stretched and inhaled, making his broad chest expand. He glanced at her. "I want you to meet Melody. Will you let me pick you up and take you out to my place for dinner next Sunday after you close?"

"I'd like that very much," she answered solemnly, surprised and pleased, feeling their relationship just became less casual with his invitation to meet Melody. Little tinkling mental bells of warnings to avoid complications in her life went unheeded.

He climbed out to walk her to the door. "What's your schedule in the morning?"

"We're starting the redecorating, so I'm going

in at five and begin to get everything ready. All of us will work after closing tomorrow night."

He nodded. "Sorry I can't help, but I've got to run a ranch."

"I understand. I wouldn't expect you to. It's nice you didn't tell me it's a ridiculous thing to do."

"I think it's a good idea."

"You and I are the only ones. Even Granddad is skeptical, although he won't say so. He wouldn't want to discourage me. I had fun tonight, Jake."

He stroked her jaw, touching the corner of her lips. "I did, too. I'll see you this week."

"Good night." She stepped into the open doorway and turned to watch him stride back to his truck. Her gaze went down the long length of him, and she could remember being pressed against his muscled legs.

"Did you have a good time?" came a whisper.

Samantha turned to see Phoebe in her flannel pajamas that she wore whether it was ninety degrees or twenty degrees. Her hair was in curlers and she had on her pink cotton robe.

"I had a very good time."

"Are you going out again with him?"

Samantha debated whether she wanted to stir the town gossip to a frenzy or put Aunt Phoebe off for a few days. The frenzy was inevitable if she had two more dates with Jake. "I'm going to dinner with him again."

"Oh, my goodness! He is the nicest boy and

so handsome. I talked to Wanda this evening, and she said he's quite wealthy."

"He also stated he would never, ever marry again."

"Men always say that until they're standing in front of a preacher."

"I think this man means it."

"Pshaw. He succumbed before. He will again."

"Well, this woman won't. I'm already married —"

"My Lord, Samantha," Phoebe exclaimed, clutching her robe. "Did you marry that Devon —"

"I'm married to the café. And I have to open it at five in the morning. Good night, Aunt Phoebe."

"My goodness! You had me going there — married to the café. Mercy. I'm watching a Tarzan movie. Want to — no I guess you don't — but the ape is almost too good to miss."

"Not tonight, Aunt Phoebe."

"Samantha, your mama's wedding dress is packed in a big box in the attic."

"Please don't tell people I'm marrying Jake Colby! I've only been out with him twice." Samantha went upstairs and spent the next hour remembering Jake, feeling as if she would melt with memories, relishing them and thinking about the next time she would be with him. Suppose Melody didn't like her?

# Chapter Three

"I won't be home until late, because I'm going to his ranch with him," Samantha said, knowing Phoebe was already planning the wedding with her friends. She glanced at the clock over the mantel. Usually punctual, Jake was five minutes late. She straightened the sack in her hands, feeling foolish for taking the new T-shirt with her, yet wanting Jake's opinion.

"See, Samantha, he wants you to know his little girl," Phoebe said with a wistful expression. "That means he's serious. I think a September wedding would be just lovely. You can have Ellie as maid of honor and Myra and Nedra and your friend Genny for bridesmaids."

The front door banged and Bernie appeared. "You'd better rescue Jake from Myra." He jerked his head toward the front. "She says her shoe is caught in her bicycle wheel, and Mr. Marvel is getting it loose."

"Oh, no." Samantha rushed to the front door with Phoebe trailing after her.

Wearing a navy T-shirt and jeans, Jake was hunkered down on the driveway, working over the bicycle wheel. Myra was stretched out by him, her foot on the wheel. Myra laughed at something he said.

"Get me the scissors," Samantha told Bernie. With a grin he handed her a pair of shears, and she marched outside to the bicycle.

"Trouble?"

"Her shoelace is caught in the wheel," Jake explained, glancing up at Samantha. His gaze raked over her shorts and shirt in a swift appraisal that almost made her forget the problem. Then she looked at Myra who was watching Jake like a two-year-old studying a cherry lollipop.

Samantha bent down and snipped the shoelace Jake was struggling to unravel. "Now, Myra, you're free."

"Hey! You cut my shoelace."

"There are more in the linen closet upstairs." Handing the scissors to Myra, Samantha smiled at Jake as he stood up and grinned. "I'm ready to go."

"Great. Bye, Myra, Bernie." He took her arm and glanced at Myra and shrugged. He turned toward the truck, and Samantha heard Bernie snicker behind them.

"Nyaa, she threw rain on your parade!"

"Bernie, you're a dork!" Myra snapped.

"I didn't know you were out here until Bernie came in and told me," Samantha said. "I should protect you from Myra. I wonder how long it took her to get her shoe caught in the wheel."

61

He chuckled and draped his arm across her shoulders. "It's hormones at work. Thank God I'm not a teen anymore."

"I still feel guilty about taking the time off from the restaurant, but this is nice."

He opened the door and paused, blocking her path. "Leave the guilt behind. That's an order."

"Yes, sir. I usually forget the restaurant when I'm with you."

"That's a real compliment." He looked at her and suddenly sounded solemn. She climbed into the truck and sat down, Jake standing at the open door, watching her. "You look like a million."

"Thank you," she replied, feeling a rush of pleasure. "You said to dress for a picnic."

"That's right." Jake closed the door and went around the truck to climb beneath the wheel. It was the first time he had seen her out of jeans, and her legs were shapely, long, gorgeous. She wore a pale blue knit shirt and blue shorts with sneakers and ankle-length white socks, and she was a knockout.

"It's a long drive to the ranch."

"I told them I'd be late getting back tonight."

"How's the restaurant?"

"We're getting the painting done. The new fixtures will be put in Monday, because that's our least busy day. I brought my new T-shirt to get your opinion. I'll wait until you're not driving."

"Get it out. I can glance at it and watch the road."

She opened the sack, pulled out the T-shirt and shook it. Jake glanced at it, looking at a woman in a Stetson standing next to a grinning buffalo. The buffalo's hoof was around the woman's shoulders and above them was the name Salido Sam's in bright red letters.

"It looks good. Salido Sam's?"

"Yes. I have my new barbecue recipe and a new name and the restaurant has been redone."

"It sounds great, Samantha," he enthused, looking at the hope in her expression and making a mental note to tell his friends to eat at the restaurant.

Since their last date he had called her every night, and he had learned that she went to work at five in the morning and stayed until midnight. He suspected all kinds of schedules had been juggled for the date tonight.

"How about I send a paint crew over Monday? Maybe we could go out more often," he said as they took the highway out of town.

"Thank you," she declined, smiling at him, "but this is a Bardwell problem, and I can't let you do that."

"You can if I want to do it."

"No. Not if we're going to date. Things get all tangled that way. If you send a paint crew, I can't go out with you again."

"Put it that way . . ." He glanced at her. "But I would like—"

"I'm sure you would." Placing her hand on his knee, she turned toward him. Her touch was like the sudden lick of flame from a torch and just as volatile to his system. He turned toward her, the truck slicing onto the gravel shoulder, and he jerked his attention back to the road. She yanked her hand away and straightened.

"Put your hand back," he urged, "and I swear I'll keep my eyes on the road." He risked one quick glance and saw surprise in her expression.

"I do that to you?" she asked softly.

He groaned. "Yes, you do that to me," he answered gruffly. "You look gorgeous and all I want to do is pull you close. Put your hand back on my knee. I promise I'll watch the road."

He was having a more difficult time each date with her. She was huggable, kissable, approachable. Keep your hands to yourself, Colby. And pray she doesn't. Since when had he gotten so keenly aware of a female? From that first night when he had seen her legs flailing the air from a high window. He didn't have this kind of reaction to other women. He liked women and he liked sex, but he didn't want involvement in his life, and he usually could keep things in perspective. . . . Until Samantha Bardwell, who warped his perceptions and set his nerves quivering and was taking up an inordinate amount of his attention. And she didn't seem to notice or care.

He put on a Garth Brooks tape, turning it low and rolling up the windows so they could talk.

An hour later as they came over the rise that gave a view of the ranch house, he glanced at her. Her eyes sparkled and she leaned forward slightly, and he felt a clutch inside. "There's the house," he informed her softly.

"This is beautiful, Jake," she whispered.

Agreeing with her, he looked at the sprawling

meadows, the meandering line of emerald where cottonwoods and willows followed the creek. In the distance on a rolling hill was his long ranch house. He loved the ranch and gained his strength and peace of mind from the solitude and spaciousness, and he wanted her to like it, too. For just a moment he remembered the first time he had shown it to Diantha. She had looked as if he were ushering her into a prison.

"We're going to live out here?" she had asked him. A tiny part of him died right then, because he knew their love would never be as good as he had hoped or expected. He just hadn't realized how bad it could be.

He didn't need another mistake. He couldn't afford one, emotionally, and he didn't want one for Melody's sake. He didn't want entanglement, yet he was safe with Samantha. He looked at her again, his gaze drifting down, mentally whisking away the blue shirt and shorts and feeling a tightness come inside. She was relaxed, natural, living an ordinary life with simple pleasures, and it was an enormous relief to him to know her. He wanted no more to do with glamorous, sophisticated women. Diantha had been enough for a lifetime.

"I like it here," he stated quietly.

"I see why you don't come into town often. I don't think that I'd ever want to leave," she admitted, and then blushed as she turned to him. "I sound as if I'm ready to pack my bags."

"Any chance?" he asked lightly, hoping to ease her over the moment, yet half wondering about her answer.

She smiled and looked away as if the question was too ridiculous to answer. His gaze slid down again over her pale knit shirt that clung and outlined her full breasts. She was all woman, delicious, independent, a challenge. And he suspected she had no idea how much of a temptation she was to him.

As he slowed to a stop at the back of the house, Melody came bursting out, followed by Mrs. Latham. He held the door for Samantha and turned to scoop Melody into his arms.

"Samantha, this is Melody. Melody, meet Miss Bardwell."

"Hello, Melody," Samantha greeted the bright-eyed child who looked scrubbed and beautiful in a plaid shirt and shorts. She wound her arm around Jake's neck, her small fingers playing with his dark hair. Her hair was as black and curly as his, and dimples showed in both cheeks when she smiled. When Jake glanced at her, the love he felt for her showed in his eyes.

"Meet Mrs. Latham," Jake said, continuing the introductions. "Mrs. Latham, this is Miss Bardwell."

"It's nice to meet you," said the tall, gray-haired woman. "It's a beautiful day for a picnic, and Melody has been counting the minutes. Everything is packed and ready."

"We'll load the Bronco and we're off." Jake set Melody down. "Let's get the things."

He took Samantha's arm, and they crossed a shaded patio that ran the length of the back of the house. Hanging pots were filled with philodendron, and pots of ferns were scattered along the porch. "I'll give you a tour of the house when we return, because I know how much she wants to go on the picnic."

"Sure. She's beautiful," Samantha stated, looking at the curly-haired child who resembled her father in her dark coloring. Her features weren't his, and she had smooth creamy skin and a saucy turned-up nose and rosebud mouth.

"I think so. Thanks."

They carried baskets to the Bronco. "Are you sure we're not staying for the week?" she asked on the second trip, watching the flex of Jake's biceps as he hoisted an ice chest and basket on top of blankets.

He grinned and winked. "Melody likes to take lots of things on a picnic."

"There's enough food for my family and yours."

As soon as they were in the Bronco on the winding graveled road away from the ranch house to the west, Jake began to sing and Melody joined him. Listening to Jake's baritone, seeing a mellow side to him with his daughter, Samantha sang with them. The land was lush and rolling, greening in spring. Horses grazed in a fenced pasture, and as Samantha looked at the wide spaces, she felt a sense of peace.

Jake forded a shallow, rock-bottomed creek. He turned to drive parallel to it and stopped beneath spreading limbs of a tall tree. The cottonwood's leaves shimmered in the slight breeze, and as they climbed out, Samantha heard the melodic cry of a mockingbird.

Beside the creek they unpacked baskets. Jake spread two large blankets and in minutes Melody was wading in the creek.

Samantha couldn't resist, removing her shoes and socks, wading in with Melody, feeling sharp rocks and mud beneath her feet. She climbed out and dried her feet on a towel Jake had brought from home. He knelt to build a fire, piling brush in a heap, and soon he had a roaring blaze going. They grilled burgers and ate in the shade of the cottonwood.

"We ought to hire you to cook at the restaurant. The hamburgers are delicious." Samantha smiled at him. "I'm glad you're not competition."

"No worries there. I'm not cut out to be a cook."

"You might be pleasantly surprised."

"Daddy cooks fish and spaghetti," Melody added. "And sometimes he makes me a chocolate milkshake."

"And there is my entire repertoire."

"Well, if you ever get tired of ranching—"

He laughed, touching her cheek with his fingers. "And if you get tired of Salido Sam's. Or if it's enormously successful, what do you dream about doing?"

She shrugged. "I'd like to move to a big city—I think Dallas or Houston. I'd like to work at an ad agency. I did an internship at one while I was in college, and I loved working there. It's exciting to think about doing ads for big companies and helping on promotions. And if I were really well fixed, I'd like my own agency."

"Maybe you'll get your own someday. You'll have to give up all the peace of Salido for a hectic pace."

"I'm ready for it." Samantha smiled at him, enjoying Jake and Melody. His daughter was easy to have around.

As Jake was dousing the fire with sand, Melody scooted close to Samantha and tugged at one of her curls.

"Your hair is red. It's pretty."

"Thank you."

"Do you have a little girl?"

"No, I don't. But I have two brothers and a sister—Bernie, Tom and Myra."

"Do you have a mother?"

"She's not alive. I have a grandfather."

"Daddy says I have him and I'll always have him."

"I'm sure you will."

"Will you read to me?"

"Sure," she said and waited while Melody fished a book out of a bag and returned to sit on Samantha's lap. She smelled like lilacs and she was soft and loving, her plaid shirt and shorts now wrinkled. While Samantha read *The Cat in the Hat,* Melody turned a silken curl in her fingers and leaned back in Samantha's arms.

"Do you like to read, Miss Bardwell?"

"Call me Samantha, all right?"

"Yes, ma'am. Samantha."

"Yes, I love to read to little girls." She looked into unfathomable dark eyes as Jake folded a tablecloth and watched her.

While the sun disappeared in the west, Samantha read the third story to Melody. Jake stretched out on the blanket, and once when she turned a page, she glanced at him. Her gaze ran down the length of him, the tight jeans that hugged slim hips, his long legs. Her breath altered, desire stirring. With an effort she returned her attention to the book.

When they finished reading, Melody wanted to ride on his shoulders. He swung her up, carrying her to the creek, lifting her up on a branch of a tree and letting her climb. With ease he grabbed a branch and pulled up into the tree, climbing with her, his navy shirt straining over the muscles in his back. He was handsome and appealing, gentle and caring with his daughter. Samantha felt a need for caution. She hadn't known Jake long, yet she was drawn to him more each encounter. Seeing him with Melody was another appealing facet to him and his daughter was adorable. In minutes they came down, Jake dropping to the ground and swinging Melody down to put her on his broad shoulders again.

She laughed and clung to him as they came back to the blanket. "It's time we start for home."

They loaded the Bronco and it was twilight by the time he turned onto the road. Night had fallen when they reached the house.

"Let's go tell Mrs. Latham you're ready to take a bath." He took Melody's hand and disappeared down the hall. In minutes he was back, taking a basket from Samantha.

"Mrs. Latham is in charge now. Melody will

come back to say good night," he said, moving around the kitchen that was long, filled with new appliances, with cabinets of gray ash.

"Melody is precious, Jake."

"Thank you. I think so, too. I feel fortunate that she's so easygoing. It makes my life easier."

Scrubbed, her hair damp, Melody reappeared dressed in yellow pajamas. "One story, Samantha?" she asked, holding up a book, and Samantha nodded.

"One story and then bedtime." Jake picked Melody up. "Let's go into the family room."

Samantha followed as he led the way through a wide hall to a spacious room with a beamed ceiling and wide stone fireplace and white plaster walls. The room was masculine, relaxed, and welcoming. The colors were bright and cheerful, and Samantha liked Jake's home. She wondered what he thought about the clutter and confusion at her house. She sat on the sofa, and Melody climbed onto her lap and settled as Samantha opened the book to read.

As she turned the pages, she looked down at the child in her arms. Melody was soft, a beautiful, bright-eyed child. She twined a lock of Samantha's hair in her small fingers and looked up to meet Samantha's gaze. She smiled at Samantha and pointed to the page and Samantha commenced reading, but glanced again at Melody as she turned a page. The child was part of Jake, bearing a faint, feminine resemblance to him. Samantha stroked her curls, remembering when she used to hold Myra, wondering if she would ever have a little girl to love.

"You're not reading," Melody reminded her.

"I'll read," Samantha replied, looking at the book.

Jake moved restlessly around the room, leaving to speak to Mrs. Latham and to turn down Melody's bed. He returned, standing in the doorway and looking at Samantha reading to his daughter. Melody had taken to Samantha as naturally as a bird learning to fly. One of Samantha's curls was caught in Melody's fingers and he felt a crunch in his heart. Samantha was filling too many gaps in his life. He leaned against one of the posts to watch them, his gaze drifting down over Samantha, and his body responded, heat filling him, thickening his blood. He went to the kitchen to lock the back door and turn down lights, returning in minutes.

Aware of Jake moving around behind her, Samantha read softly. Halfway through the book, she noticed how still Melody had become and looked down to see her dark lashes feathered over her full cheeks. She glanced at Jake who smiled and crossed the room to pick up his daughter.

"You're good with her." His dark eyes studied her.

"I have a little sister. It's been a long time since I held Myra and read to her."

"Come see Melody's room."

She stood to follow him along the hall to a room that was unmistakably Melody's. He placed his daughter in a canopied bed surrounded by teddy bears. The white furniture was covered with dolls and bears. A white rocker held a rainbow of cushions.

Jake bent over the bed to cover Melody with the sheet. He leaned down to kiss her cheek, and Samantha wondered about the woman who had given both of them up for a modeling career. Jake looked strong and tough, yet with his daughter, Samantha saw a vulnerable side to him as he became a gentle father who adored his child.

He straightened up, crossed the room to take her hand and switched off the light as they left the room. "Come here." He moved down the hall to knock on a closed door.

"Yes?" It opened and Mrs. Latham appeared in a maroon velvet bathrobe.

"Melody is in bed, Mrs. Latham."

"Fine. I'll check on her." She closed the door quietly and Jake pulled lightly on Samantha's arm.

"I want you to see my room." Moving down the wide hall, they turned a corner. In a wing to the south, they entered a large bedroom and sitting room. She looked at Prussian-blue leather furniture, a king-sized bed. The polished oak floor was covered by Navajo rugs, and Western art hung on the walls. It was another masculine room, yet warm and appealing and comfortable.

Jake opened sliding glass doors. "We can sit out here."

She went outside with him on the darkened enclosed patio where a sprawling yellow bougainvillea grew. He turned to face her, an intent look in his eyes as he reached out to take her hand.

"I've wanted to do this all day," he said, drawing her to him.

Her heart thudded while he looked down at her, and then his head dipped down and his mouth covered hers and he kissed her, wrapping his arms around her to pull her close. His hands slid down her back to cup her bottom and pull her up against him.

She slipped her slender arms around his neck, her heart pounding fiercely. She ached to kiss him, to feel his hands on her and to touch him, yet she had to be careful, because neither of them wanted commitment. Slow down, slow down before it's too late, she counseled herself, even as she pressed against him and returned his fiery kisses.

One hand was a warm, intimate pressure, holding her hips against him, and she felt his hardness. His other hand slid to her throat and then he shifted, releasing her slightly, so his hand could move to her breast. He tugged the blue shirt out of her shorts and his hand went beneath the material, pushing away the flimsy lace of her bra to cup her breast.

She felt a heated lethargy flow in her veins, a hungry need to be loved. At the same time a small voice of wisdom cautioned to take care, because in a moment there would be no slowing him down. His body was insistent, its warmth enveloping her.

She pushed away. "Jake, slow down."

He gazed at her and drew a long breath, his eyes holding a look of hunger for her that was as plain as spoken words. "Samantha," he whispered while his thumb flicked over her nipple. Sensations

74

streaked like lightning. She gasped, clutching his arms, feeling the hard bulge of muscle. His hand slid to her bare thigh, past the brief bit of cloth of her shorts. His fingers shifted the lace panties away, touching her softness, to feel that she was ready for him, her body warm and moist.

Heat gushed upward, filling her, and she was lost to the pressure of his hand, clinging to him as friction became a torment and ecstasy. Tension coiled in her like a spring wound tighter and tighter. Suddenly he groaned and crushed her hard to his chest, his mouth coming down on hers with a savage need as he kissed her passionately until she felt faint and breathless and on fire.

"Jake." Samantha leaned away, and he released her. She walked away from him, her heart pounding for more, clamoring to be loved. Shaken, she hurt physically, and she knew he did, too.

He caught her arm and pulled her down on a chair and sat next to her. He held up his hands. "I won't touch you. Let's just talk."

"If we can."

Discussing Salido High's football team, Jake settled, trying to cool down. She had been ready for love, her body trembling. Eager was an understatement. She singed all his nerves. He looked at her in the darkness, at her profile, the curves of her soft, full lips. Dangerous ground. Think about something besides sex with her. She had been grand with Melody. As natural as if she had known her forever. His bed was only fifty feet away inside the house. Pick her up and carry her in there and see how long her protests would last.

He knew they wouldn't, yet he didn't want involvement, he didn't want to silence her protests by taking advantage of her physical needs.

While she talked about Bernie's team, Jake watched her and was tempted to follow his inclinations. Damned inclined to.

She stood up. "Jake, we have a long drive back, and I think I should go."

He stood, caught in indecision, something as common for him as snakebite. With a switch of her hips, in her graceful, seductive walk, she moved away from him. She disappeared inside the house, and his choices were gone.

He joined her, walking in silence through the house, feeling the urge to stop her. Emotions warred within him. He reached around her to open the door.

Samantha paused and then followed the course wisdom indicated and went out ahead of him, welcoming the cool night air, afraid to say anything to him.

At her house, he kissed her quickly and released her. She watched him walk back to his truck before she went inside. The night with him and his kisses had shaken her, awakening feelings long dormant. And she'd had so much fun with him and Melody.

"Samantha?" Phoebe came from the living room. She blinked in the hall light. "I didn't hear you come home. My goodness, you look like you got caught in a fierce wind."

"I've been on a picnic, Aunt Phoebe."

"Did he propose?"

"No, ma'am, he didn't. He said he'll never marry."

"That means diddly-squat. Bring him in sometime when you come home, and we can all watch movies. Tonight is really a good picture. It's an old Humphrey Bogart. The man is fantastic. Come watch."

"Aunt Phoebe, in three hours I have to get up to go to the restaurant."

"Honey, you work too hard. Why don't you sleep in tomorrow?"

"I can't do that. Good night." She hurried to her room. She went to the open window to sit down and look at the white full moon. Jake was driving home beneath the same moon, breezes blowing in the truck, unless he closed the windows and put on his tapes.

She remembered the hot spiral caused by his kisses and caresses. She ached for him, wanting him. Dating him had been fun at first, but now he was becoming vital to her. He was becoming her best friend. She was juggling schedules, rearranging her life to go out with him. She didn't have time or a place for an affair. And how badly she might get hurt. Stay aloof. Good advice if she had heeded it that first night when she was stuck in the pantry.

She peeled out of her clothes and slid between the sheets, feeling their coolness on her hot, dry skin. Sleep wasn't going to come. Her body's clamoring for him wouldn't be assuaged, her need for his touch and his lovemaking wouldn't stop with the dawn.

The next weekend she went to the rodeo with him, and during the following week she saw him when he stopped by the restaurant. Twice he brought Melody with him, and they all ate together.

Getting ready for Salido Sam's big opening, she had run ads in the Monroe, the Salido, and the Sangley papers. She had placed a full-page ad in the Monroe College paper. Friday, the tenth of April, was the official first night of the restaurant.

By seven the place was packed and a line was waiting outside. The karaoke was loud, voices rising in a din while waiters rushed back and forth from tables to the kitchen. The smell of barbecue sauce filled the air and ceiling fans slowly revolved. Bernie was dressed in a rented buffalo costume, and Samantha wore a denim Western miniskirt and a Western shirt. She glanced up as familiar broad shoulders filled the doorway. Eagerly she went forward to greet Jake.

"Wow, lady, do you look great." His dark eyes went over her making her aware of the skimpiness of the outfit. "Looks like opening night couldn't be better."

"Yes, and we're swamped. Thanks for coming." She had been watching for him during the past hour.

"I brought friends. We need a table for ten."

She laughed. "You're really drumming up business. It'll be about a forty-minute wait."

"If I can stand and watch you, fine."

She smiled at him as she glanced up from writ-

78

ing his name on a tablet. "You can squeeze into the bar, or you can wait outside and I'll find you, or you can wait here."

"We'll go to the bar, get drinks and then wait outside."

"I'd like to talk, but I have to go." She looked at more people squeezing in through the door. She started to walk away, and Jake caught her arm.

"Sami, this is a huge crowd. Could you use an extra pair of hands in the kitchen tonight?"

Relief overwhelmed her until she glanced at his fresh plaid sport shirt, his crisp jeans. "You're with your friends—"

"Could you use extra help? I know how to wash dishes," he offered in a crisp, no-nonsense manner.

"Oh, Jake, yes!"

"Let me tell my friends. You want a dishwasher, bus boy, or waiter?"

"Actually, I can use another cook the most."

"Done. Get going."

"You're a dream come true," she exclaimed, suddenly forgetting the crowd and the restaurant and the problems. He looked handsome, capable and calm, and she stood on tiptoe to kiss his cheek.

He winked at her. "We'll discuss that at length next time we're alone."

"Get an apron from the kitchen."

"Samantha!" She turned as Phoebe came forward. "The table is ready for the party of eight, and I can't find them."

"Try one more time, Aunt Phoebe." She felt

79

sorry for her aunt, whose hair was falling in tendrils over her eyes. Phoebe looked harassed, but Samantha needed every bit of help she could get. She saw Jake go through the swinging doors to the kitchen, and she felt a surge of gratitude to him.

Bernie stepped to the karaoke and announced the next song, and words flashed on two large screens on either side of the small stage. Customers sang, and she gazed at the crowd, realizing the people clustered in the center of the restaurant were beer drinkers—the diners were on the fringe. Brushing hair away from her eyes, she rushed to greet another group.

Half an hour later she stopped in the kitchen. Asa flipped a burger and Jake plopped patties on the grill. He wore a long white apron and he worked swiftly, glancing at her as she crossed to him. "How're supplies?"

"Fine," Asa replied, "and we're doing great with another pair of hands in here. Man can cook, thank God."

"You can have a regular job," she said dryly to him.

Jake grinned. "Anything to help."

"I got your group seated fifteen minutes ago, so I cut their wait."

"Thanks for playing favorites."

"For you, sweetie, anything," she answered in a contented purr.

He arched his brow. "You would say that when my hands are full of fries and you have fifty people waiting for you."

With a laugh she left the kitchen. She returned in an hour to lean one hip against the counter beside him. "The dinner orders are slowing to drink orders. You may be excused to join your friends if you'd like."

"Not as long as I can help you." His gaze was warm. "I can wait tables and serve beer with the best of them."

"Fine. I won't argue with you," she promised, moving away from him.

An hour later she searched for him and found him carrying in two cases of beer from the alley.

"Your friends are leaving. Jake, I really appreciate what you did." She squeezed his arm. "You're a friend in need."

"I'll speak to my friends, but you're not rid of me yet. If I hang around, I might get to take you home tonight."

"By then I'll probably fall asleep before you can close the door of the truck."

"I'll risk it," he said easily, and she knew he was doing what he wanted.

"Thanks," she answered, grateful for his help.

Bernie appeared. "This is great, Sis, but man is this hot!" He rolled his eyes and stroked his furry head and left the kitchen.

"How does he get to work in a place that sells beer? He's under twenty-one."

"Sheriff Dolby said since he was hired as the buffalo, he could perform. I don't know if the Sheriff is looking the other way, or what, but I didn't question it. Myra and Tom couldn't work here after nine. During dinner they were waiting tables."

"I saw them and talked to Myra."

"I'm sure Myra talked to you," she remarked, knowing the crush Myra had on him.

"I'd call this a success."

"The first night is a victory." Elation and satisfaction filled her. "I just have to keep them coming back."

"Well, you're doing something right."

"I think you had a hand in this. Several people said you told them about the restaurant. Thanks."

"Think nothing of it. I'll extract payment later." He gave her a teasing leer that made her smile.

"It is good, Jake. I'm so thankful. Even Mr. Yarrell is here, but then just about everyone in town is here tonight. Word must get around."

Finally it was two o'clock, and she closed the bar and sent Bernie and Asa home. The last customers left by three, and by half past three Jake caught her hand as she was putting away the last of the dishes.

"You go sit down and I'll close and lock up. What lights do you leave on?"

"One in the kitchen and one over the bar."

He nodded, looking at the restaurant with its pots of ferns and philodendrons. The white painted walls were covered with bright signs and posters of Monroe College football players and the basketball team. He walked across the room to drop a quarter in the jukebox and punch an old, slow song. Samantha sat at an empty table, and he opened two cold beers and went out to her, setting one in front of her.

"I'd lay a wager that you didn't have dinner to-night."

"You'd win," she admitted. "If I drink that, I might slide right to the floor asleep."

"I'll chance it." He drew a chair beside hers. "Turn your back to me."

As she turned around, he took a deep swallow of cold beer and set down the bottle, reaching out to knead her shoulders. "Let me show you how to relax," he coaxed quietly.

His hands were strong and warm, and in minutes she felt the tenseness go out of her shoulders. He massaged her neck, running his fingers through her hair and drawing out the strands. Each stroke left a tingling pleasantness in its wake, and she closed her eyes. "This is beyond the call of duty. Everything you did tonight was. Jake, I'm exhausted. I'm not sure if I'm making sense."

"Don't worry about it. You're coherent and you don't have to do anything. If you fall asleep, I promise to get you home."

His hands drifted down over her back, massaging muscles, moving lower. Feelings diffused and changed as his hands became lighter, the strokes more erotic. Music swirled around them in the silent room as his hands worked magic, her skin tingling.

"Turn around," he ordered softly and picked up her foot, scooting back his chair. He shoved off her shoe and massaged her stockinged foot, holding her foot on his thigh and watching her. His hands drifted up to knead the calf of her leg and then the strokes became long and light, changing as he watched her. His hands drifted to caress her thigh and she caught him.

"Jake," she said, her voice soft and breathless. She felt fully awake, attuned to his touch, wanting more. As his hand slid beneath the skimpy short skirt and he tugged down her sheer pantyhose, he watched her.

Her heart thudded with anticipation. Lifting her into his arms, he settled her on his lap and bent his head to kiss her. Samantha returned his kiss. Passion was charged with deeper feelings. Tonight she had discovered they could work well together. He was capable, considerate, sexy, and all three were an irresistible package. With every kiss, she had a stronger response, because when she gave physically, she gave emotionally. Each time together they moved closer to a brink that would change their relationship forever.

Finally she caught his hard wrists and stopped his caresses. He gazed into her eyes, moving suddenly, lifting her off his lap and leaving her, going across the room to the jukebox.

Samantha realized he was trying to cool down and control his body. She stood up, straightening her clothes and going to switch off the bar lights. Watching him walking around in the semidarkness, she wondered how deeply in love she was with him already. Before they left the café, Jake gave her one swift hug, looking into her eyes with a mixture of satisfaction and longing.

At her house, he stood with his arm across her shoulder. "Thanks for what you did tonight," she said.

"Glad to help. The first night was a great success. When do I get to take you out?"

Thinking about the crowd they had, the success that they had to repeat over and over, she looked away. "I don't know when I can leave. If I'm this tired every night, you won't want to go out with me."

"All the more reason you should take a few hours. You've earned it. Take next Sunday night off."

She looked up at his firm jaw and his mouth. A whole evening with Jake away from the restaurant.

"Good."

Their Sunday-night dates became regular for the next month, the only time she felt she could get away from the restaurant. Through April the restaurant stayed busy beyond all her dreams, and people were coming from as far away as Ardmore and Durant and Sherman. One Friday afternoon in May she took off to get her hair done, sinking down on the chair with relief as Mrs. Parson picked up her purse to leave.

"Samantha, let me congratulate you on catching Jake Colby. Your family needs a connection like that." She frowned, peering down her nose. "I've heard that the restaurant is getting real rowdy, You know Salido doesn't need disorderly college people. If you are serving beer, you should think twice, before something terrible happens. I told Phoebe she should have a frank talk with you, because I'm certain Asa won't listen. Lord knows, you come from a long line of beer drinkers."

"Yes, ma'am."

"You heed what I say. I told Wilson Yarrell to talk to you, but he's so happy with the manner in which you're repaying your bank loan, that I'm sure he wouldn't care if you sold beer on Sunday."

"Yes, ma'am."

"Goodbye, Ellie."

"Bye, Mrs. Parson. Thanks." She pocketed the quarter tip.

"The restaurant is just great," Ellie said, as soon as the door closed, "and don't you dare change anything. That's the most fun anyone can find for the next hundred miles. Vernon and I will be there tonight."

"Good."

"Aren't you excited with the success of it?"

"I'm still holding my breath. Oh, Ellie, I just pray it continues. Isn't it amazing?" she asked, excitement filling her over a phone call she'd received that afternoon. She was bursting to relate her good news to Ellie, but she wanted Jake to be the first to know about it, so she kept quiet.

"You've done a great job. I just wish some of these new people pouring into town would stop here and get their hair done." She frowned, looking at Sam in the mirror. "I sure could use more business."

"Maybe they will come."

"Not unless they move here. No one stays long enough. But some businesses are booming," she stated wistfully. "Mrs. Yardley has rented the old Washburn building across the street from you, and she's putting in a craft shop."

"I've bought the empty buildings to the north.

86

If we keep getting the crowds, we can expand and I can tear the buildings down and use the land for parking. It's too early yet to tell. The Chamber of Commerce wants me to speak next Friday morning at their breakfast. Kathleen Attaway and Wanda Mayfield are both going to open bed-and-breakfast places in their homes and the Chamber seems to think we can turn Salido into a tourist attraction. This is a picturesque town with it's Victorian homes, old offices, wide streets and tall trees. The traffic is slow."

"Why would we attract anyone other than to your restaurant?"

"Aunt Phoebe's into it, too. She's getting more handmade things in her shop. Mr. Yarrell said the Chamber thinks they can capitalize on our turn-of-the-century buildings and the early days when outlaws hid here."

"The Drayton Gang? Who would care?"

"People are interested in things like that."

"I wouldn't care about the Draytons, but maybe others do. Something else to tell you that's a lot more important — I got Vernon to look at wedding rings last Saturday."

"Congratulations, Ellie! That's real progress."

"Yes, except he would only stand on the sidewalk and look. He wouldn't go in any of the stores after the first one. We went to Ardmore and the first place we stopped was Hanforth's. Vernon stuttered so badly when he asked to look at rings, he refused to go inside any other store and talk about rings after that. Even so, I think he's weakening."

"Good luck, Ellie."

Ellie sighed and looked at herself in the mirror. "I'm not getting any younger. Vernon needs a wife. I can operate my shop three days a week from nine to five, and the rest of the time I can stay on the farm. It would work out fine. I own this house, and Nancy Beth wants to rent it and keep the shop going the other three days of the week."

"Sounds great," Samantha said as Ellie brushed out her hair.

"Your hair shines like corn silk. It's so soft. You have a date with Jake Sunday night?"

"Yes." Samantha wondered if anything in Salido was a secret. Everyone knew exactly what everyone else did, except no one knew about her afternoon phone call yet. They probably knew she had already paid back half her loan to the Salido Bank.

"That's getting to be regular. And you've been out to his ranch and met Melody. That sounds serious."

"She's an important part of his life."

"He dotes on that child. I cut her hair occasionally."

"She's adorable and he loves her." Sam stood up. "Thanks, Ellie. I'll see you tonight."

"Sure. I'll bet Jake Colby doesn't stutter when he looks at rings," Ellie murmured in a wistful voice that Samantha barely heard. She stepped outside and let the screen door bang closed. Her thoughts shifted to anticipation of Sunday night and finally sharing news about the phone call with Jake.

# Chapter Four

Sunday night Jake picked her up at half past five. As they left the house, he draped his arm across her shoulder.

"Hey, I wish that sparkle in your eyes was for me. What's up?"

She laughed as she clung to his arm. "Don't underestimate yourself!"

He looked down at her and arched his brows. "I think I just changed my plans for the evening." He studied her and shook his head. "Come on, confess. Something good has happened."

"You're right." He held open the door of the truck, and she looked up at him. "I can't wait to tell you, but I meant what I just said, too."

He ran his fingers along her bare forearm and stepped an inch closer. "How I'd like to pull you close now, but if I do, I'm sure four faces will be pressed against the windows watching me."

"More than four. Wanda Mayfield lives across

the street on the corner. She's one of Aunt Phoebe's best friends and she watches us as much as Aunt Phoebe does. I hear them compare notes."

"Maybe we should give them something to talk about tonight," he said, his eyes twinkling. He stepped the last bit of distance, swept her into his arms and leaned over her. She clung to him, feeling as if she would fall except that his strong arms held her. She opened her mouth to protest, but his lips touched hers and he kissed her soundly. Finally he swung her up and released her.

Whistles and catcalls came from the front porch, and she looked around to see Tom and Bernie making kissing motions. Dazed, she gazed at Jake and shook her head. "You've done it now. I might as well wear a scarlet letter."

"For a kiss?"

"Look at Bernie and Tom. Aunt Phoebe will go into shock. Wanda is probably on the phone, and by ten o'clock it will be all over town. Next Friday when I get my hair done, I'll get a lecture about loose morals from Elvira Parson."

"On the other hand," Jake added softly with devilment dancing in his eyes, "I hope the kiss was worth the hassle."

She looked into his dark eyes and felt bubbly inside, happy to be with him. "It was definitely worth a scarlet letter."

"For a ruined reputation, I should get to do more."

"You can work on it," she teased, flirting with

him and turning to climb into the truck before he could take her up on her statement.

He caught her wrist. "That's a challenge, lady."

"It was meant to be," she retorted, enjoying herself.

"I'm tempted to haul you out of the truck. But then what I have in mind I don't want to do with an audience."

A liquid warmth diffused through her as she was held by his dark eyes. She felt a silent promise that he was going to rise to the challenge she so recklessly had flung at him.

"Maybe I should be more cautious."

"Too late now. It's not your nature."

"You don't know me that well."

"Oh, yes, I do. You're the woman who tries to climb out tiny little windows and borrows money from banks to go out on a limb to save a business. No, you're willing to take risks."

"I'm taking one right now. We both are."

"We're doing all right, so far," he replied solemnly. "No broken hearts, no emotional upheavals."

Suddenly she felt serious, too. "Jake, let's keep it that way."

He smiled, changing like quicksilver back to teasing her. "You're way too late." He closed the truck door and went around to climb inside and drive through town. "Let the gossips speculate. We're getting out of here."

He took her to a roadside diner with a small

dance floor and a stage with a guitar player and a drummer. Seated at a thick, polished wooden table, Jake leaned back and studied her. "Now what, besides my kisses, put that glimmer in your eyes?"

"Friday, the twenty-ninth, I'm going to have an interview with Channel KZZZ from Tulsa," she announced with excitement.

"That's great!"

"They've heard about the restaurant and some other businesses in town that have changed."

"I think you've got a smash hit on your hands. And I think you're transforming the town."

"I've noticed changes." She felt surprised each time she discovered one. "Wanda Mayfield is turning her home into a bed-and-breakfast place, and it'll be charming. Her house was built in 1899. It's filled with antiques, and Wanda loves to cook and talk to people. Aunt Phoebe has made arrangements with Wanda to tell her guests that Aunt Phoebe will give a tour of Salido."

"A tour of Salido?" Jake grinned. "That should take five minutes."

"No. She's got it all worked out. They'll visit the old jail, and she's talked to Paul Warner with the Chamber of Commerce who says the city is going to clean the old jail up for her. Salido has a colorful past. She's going to tour the train station, and we have the steam engine left over from the late 1800s. She plans to take them out to the cemetery where the Draytons are buried.

And she can show them the shack where the Draytons were supposed to have hidden between train robberies."

"That's amazing." He leaned across the table to tilt her chin up. "You don't look like you'd be a catalyst for an entire town, but you have been."

Aware of his finger touching her lightly, she blushed beneath his gaze, feeling warm and pleased by his remark. "I'm happy, and I still just hold my breath over the restaurant. This week finals are over at Monroe. I don't want to think about school being out for the summer and business dropping off when students go home for vacation." Glancing around, she noticed three burly men at the bar. The black-haired one turned to stare at her. His glance raked over her and rose to look her in the eye. He winked, and she shifted her gaze to Jake, suspecting it was best Jake didn't know the guy was watching her.

"Monroe College has a summer enrollment." Jake leaned back as the waiter brought catfish and cole slaw and rice on thick platters.

"Jake," she said when they were alone. "Would you do something for me?"

"Anything you want, sweetie," he drawled in a suggestive manner, curious what she wanted.

"I'd like you to be at the restaurant when I have the interview."

"I promise. Anything else? Massage? An hour of seduction? You name it, and I'll deliver."

"Sounds inviting. I hope this offer isn't open to everyone."

"Only to you. Which one would you like? Or all?"

"I'd like—" She paused, and he felt a tight knot inside. He had been teasing and she was now, but suddenly he wished she meant what she was about to answer. "The massage sounds the safest, doesn't it? Yet an hour of seduction, Jake?" she asked in a soft voice that was as sultry as a New Orleans night. "With you? How can I resist that proposition?"

"Want to leave now?" he asked, meaning it. For one breath of a second he looked into wide eyes that met his gaze directly. Then she blinked and smiled and retreated.

"And waste a perfectly marvelous catfish?"

"I rate behind the catfish," he remarked lightly, yet feeling a peculiar ripple of disappointment. He tried to get back on neutral ground with her. "I've talked to Ed Naylor, and he's opening a deli on Main. He thinks you're bringing all sorts of business to town. And since you're such a success, how about taking off tomorrow night? You've said Sundays and Mondays are the slowest."

She tilted her head. "My new manager, Ted Gillette, is doing a great job. I think I can manage that."

"Can I push for Wednesday?"

"Let's just try Monday and see how it goes." Jake studied her, his gaze drifting down over the pale blue cotton shirt she wore. He was beginning to view the restaurant as a three-headed monster that took all her time and attention. Without any fuss or bother or any great strategy she had single-handedly turned a ghost town into a thriving little community. Still she was tied to the restaurant more than ever.

"I've taken Melody to visit her grandparents."

"Where do they live?"

"In Dallas. I flew her down there Friday. I'll go back and get her Wednesday. Her grandmother is all the things her mother wasn't. The Rangels were torn up over our divorce, and I don't think they see or hear from Diantha too often. Peg Rangel is good with Melody, and both Peg and Frank love her."

"She's lovable like her father."

He arched his brows and looked at her, realizing she was more relaxed than when he first met her. Then he could hardly coax her thoughts away from the restaurant and the problems. He was thankful for her success, hoping it would continue so she could ease up on work. "You and Asa deserve this."

"Thank you."

"I promised Melody I would call at half past seven every day, so if you'll excuse me—"

"Sure." Samantha watched him slide out of the booth and cross the room to a pay phone by the bar.

She bit into the flaky catfish, enjoying the quiet, thinking about Jake when a man slid onto the seat beside her. It was the dark-haired man from the bar.

"Hi, baby."

"I'm with someone, mister."

"He's on the telephone with another woman. I heard him. Honest Abe," he swore, holding up his hand. "My name's Zebby." He crowded against her, his brawny arm touching her. A black T-shirt stretched across his thick chest.

"Look, this is our booth. You have to leave," she announced with annoyance.

"Come dance with me," he urged, his words slurring. "I have a bet with the guys that I can get you to dance one dance."

"You just lost the bet. I suggest you leave before my date gets off the phone."

"C'mon, sugar. He's two-timing you." Zebby caught her wrist "One little dance won't hurt." He slid toward the edge of the seat and tugged on her wrist.

"Let go of me before I scream," she threatened, feeling revulsion at his touch.

"And bring your old man back on the run? There are three of us and one of him. We're bigger. And meaner. One dance."

Jake's back was turned as he talked on the phone, and she didn't want him hurt on her account. Zebby tugged on her wrist. She scooted with him, and he arched his brows in surprise, grinning and blowing beer-tinged breath on her.

As he stood up, shifting his bulk, Samantha raked her foot behind his, hitting his feet. He staggered, and she came up, pushing him. Losing his balance, he released her wrist, stumbling back, crashing into a chair to sit down hard on the floor. She slid back into the booth and glanced over her shoulder. Jake hung up the phone and crossed the room, increasing his stride, a thunderous look on his face.

"What the hell?" he asked, looking at the man and then at her.

"He's drunk and he's leaving. It's all right."

"He was bothering you."

"No, Jake," she began, her heart beating with fear for what Jake might do. There were three burly men and she didn't want him in a fight.

Jake turned as the man stood up. He doubled his fist, slamming a hard right to the man's jaw, sending him staggering across the room. The two cronies slid off their bar stools and headed toward Jake.

"There goes a good catfish," Jake mumbled, standing with his feet spread and his fists doubled as one walked up and swung. Jake ducked and the punch went wild. Jake slammed his fist into the man's stomach as the other man jumped on Jake. Both crashed into a table and went down.

In seconds Jake rolled on top and slugged the man, who now lay sprawled on the floor. As Jake got to his feet, a bouncer had Zebby by the arm, and the second man backed away from Jake.

"Fight's over," the bouncer announced, returning to get the man on the floor.

Jake rubbed his jaw when he slid back into the booth. "Are you all right?" he asked her. Before she could answer he grinned. "Dumb question—you flattened him."

"Your cheek's cut. Are you all right?"

"I'm okay." He pulled out his handkerchief to dab at his scraped cheek and his bloody knuckles.

"Jake, your hand's hurt! Why do I feel responsible?"

"Don't. You can't help it if you're a knockout."

She wrinkled her nose at him. "Some knockout after working ten hours in a restaurant today."

A man in an apron approached their table. "Sir, are you all right?"

"Sure."

"Sorry. We're getting them out of here. Dinner is on the house. I'm sorry for the trouble."

"Thanks." Jake held out his hand. "Jake Colby. This is Miss Bardwell."

"Salido Sam's?" he asked, worry leaving his blue eyes as he smiled and raked blond hair from his face. "I've heard about your barbecue sauce, Miss Bardwell. Glad to meet you." He shook Jake's hand. "I'm Quint Lowman. You've really gone to town with your restaurant," he said, turning to Samantha again. "I have to stop by soon."

"Anytime. We're open seven days a week. Let me know when you're there."

"I will. Nice to meet you folks. Come back."

"Thanks," Jake replied, looking at her and smiling. "I'm with a celebrity."

"My barbecue sauce is what's the celebrity. Hot and juicy and delicious."

"You or the sauce?"

She wrinkled her nose at him again.

He caught her hand and looked at her knuckles. Her fingers were pale and slender on his brown ones. "What did you do to the guy? It doesn't look as if you delivered a sucker punch."

"I'm used to dealing with boys after years with Tom and Bernie." She took her hand from his.

"That was no boy. I was only gone two minutes and you get into a jam."

"I didn't bring it on."

"I suspect your nice long legs brought it on."

"Not so. I was sitting here eating my catfish when the guy slid into the booth and wanted to dance."

"So you decked him. See, you're not cautious. If you were a prudent person, you'd have waited for me to come back and get rid of the guy."

"I'm accustomed to fighting my own battles."

He gazed at her and took a long drink of cold beer. He would bet everything in his wallet that she was accustomed to fighting her own conflicts. Sometimes Asa might help, but he was probably the only one who could or would. And Jake felt as if he wanted to shoulder some of that burden that she carried. Whoa, Colby. Whoa. Watch your thinking. He studied her,

99

knowing she was getting to him. She looked more delicious than dinner, and he suddenly lost his appetite. He wanted her in his arms.

After dinner they left the restaurant, speeding away.

"You're headed the wrong direction for Salido," she stated quietly.

"Come out to the ranch for a while. I'll get you home before the late movies are over."

He couldn't see her expression in the darkness, but she didn't refuse and his pulse accelerated. Wind whipped them, the spring air carrying the faint scent of fresh green hay and growing alfalfa. It was a warm night, heat lightning flashing in the thunderheads on the horizon.

He slowed behind the house that had yard lights burning. When they entered his kitchen, he crossed the room to pour her a glass of Chablis and get a beer for himself. He carried the wine to her across the kitchen. Only the light above the sink burned, giving a dim glow, highlighting her auburn curls, throwing her cheeks and eyes into shadows. Watching her, Jake sipped the cold beer while she took a drink of wine and looked at him quizzically.

"Are we going to sit down?"

He set the chilled bottle on the counter and took her wine from her hand. "I have a better idea," he said in a husky voice.

He caught her wrist so lightly, tugging gently. With a lift of her breasts as she inhaled, she came forward and there was no mistaking the ea-

gerness in her gaze as she looked at him. He
pulled her to him to kiss her, enveloping her in
his arms, feeling heat converge and muscles become taut. She was soft, tantalizing. He wanted
to make her melt with need, to find what excited
her, to make love with her until she was gasping
with ecstasy. His tongue slipped over hers, prob-
ing, kissing her thoroughly while his hand went
to her waist, finding the button for her skirt. He
twisted it free and slid down the zipper, pushing
away the cotton skirt.

In minutes he pulled away her shirt and bra
and stepped back to cup her breasts as his gaze
drifted down. Her full, pale breasts were soft
and warm, her nipples hard peaks. She wore bikinis that were only a scrap of lace, the thick
auburn curls between her legs a dark shadow beneath the bikinis. She had a body to melt the
resolutions of a saint and he wasn't that to begin
with. Caution had been tossed to the winds
when he turned for the ranch. He wanted inside
her, to feel her beneath him, to feel those long
legs holding him.

Releasing her, he yanked off his shirt. She inhaled deeply, her fingers stroking his chest, sending lightning currents zinging in his bloodstream.
He felt as if he would burst with need.

Suddenly she twisted back to look up at him.
"Jake, let's slow down. For both our sakes."

He gazed into her earnest face while his body
burned like dry grass in a summer fire. She was
the kind to want commitment, and with her

family and the grapevine in Salido, commitment would have to include wedding bells or she would be the subject of all kinds of gossip. "Dammit," he swore softly, groaning. "Let's get out of here now, because I can't sit on the patio and make polite conversation when all I want to do is make hot, passionate love with you."

She had pulled on her clothes and buttoned them. She nodded and left the kitchen fast, stepping out to the truck and reaching to open the door. He slammed shut the door and hauled her into his arms.

"You don't have to leave that damned fast. You're buttoned to your chin again, so give me a few more minutes." His voice was gruff. "Lord, I'd like to shove you down on the gravel here and take you. Or across the hood of the truck. If we spend much more time like this, I'll need a team of paramedics."

"Jake—"

He didn't care what she had to say. He kissed her hard, his hand sliding beneath her blouse to cup her breast.

The next time she broke away, he groaned. "I'm too old for this kind of thing, Samantha." He ached and he knew she did. They stood breathing hard, staring at each other.

She climbed into the truck and he slid behind the wheel, and in minutes they were headed away from the ranch house. He drove fast with the windows open and air blowing against him, knowing only one thing would cool the fires he felt. She was silent as if she didn't trust herself to speak or touch him any more than he trusted himself to.

She was within reach, only inches away. He glanced at her to find her looking at him. She looked away, turning to the window.

When would he see her again? A whole fifteen to sixteen hours sounded far too long.

"It's lightning season," she said, and he glanced at the flashes in the distance.

"Spring nights, stormy weather and a sexy woman," he replied softly.

"Jake, maybe we shouldn't go out tomorrow night. We're racing like a runaway roller coaster."

"No, we're not. We've dated since you were stuck in the window in March. That's not a runaway roller coaster. And you promised the date, and I'm holding you to it."

"You're holding me to what?" she asked, suddenly teasing him, lowering her tone to that sultry breathless sound that made him veer off onto the shoulder of the road. The truck bounced, and he whipped it back on the asphalt.

"I'm sorry, Jake." She felt instantly contrite. "I shouldn't have teased."

"Don't ever apologize for flirting, sweetie. I love it and I want to see you relaxed. And I'll show you what I'm holding you to next time we're alone," he said, lowering his voice, wanting her against him, wondering how much longer he could exercise full control and not give in to the reckless compulsion to seduce her.

"Jake, when is harvest?" she asked, and he knew she was trying to get on safer ground.

"We'll begin next week, depending on rain." She knew the answer as well as he did. "What else is safe to discuss, Samantha?"

"How about Melody's schedule?"

"She'll be gone all week and then I'll bring her back home unless she decides she wants to come before then."

There was another tense silence, and he wondered when he would be able to relax with her again? All he wanted to do was pull the truck off the road, cut the engine and take her in his arms. He tried to get his thoughts off her to a less emotional subject.

"What's your barbecue recipe, or is that a deep dark secret?"

"My finger-lickin', pot-scraping, savory sauce is a secret that not even Asa knows. Of course, he doesn't know because he doesn't care. I'm the one who makes the sauce."

Jake clutched the wheel of the truck and thought about her body that was definitely delectable. "We need another subject, Sami."

"Jake! For heaven's sake! I can tell you the story of *The Attack of the Killer Bats,* because Aunt Phoebe told me in detail over breakfast the morning after our first date."

"I think you'd better."

"It starts out with a city on some seaboard, but it was an unidentifiable city near some rolling hills with a cave. Deep in this cave are bats, and they are harmless until one time a couple of bats interfered with some farmer's crop. He sprays a chemical into the cave, and it changes the little bats into monster bats."

"This is a safe subject."

"Keep thinking about the bats."

"You think it's funny, but I ache."

"I'm sorry," she apologized, immediately sounding contrite as she placed her hand on his arm. He drew a deep breath.

"Back to the bats, love."

"Sure." She removed her hand and talked quietly until he turned into her driveway and got out to see her to the door.

"Good night, Sam. One kiss—Phoebe and I deserve that much."

"You're right." Samantha looked up at him. Her heartbeat sped up in anticipation as he moved closer.

It turned into five minutes of kisses, then she pushed against his chest. "I have to go inside now."

"Tomorrow night . . . as early as you can."

"Half past six."

"See you, sweetie." He winked at her. She went inside as Phoebe turned from the window.

"You're late getting home."

"We went to the ranch and you know what a drive it is."

"Samantha, Wanda called me tonight just in shock."

"She needn't be."

105

"Has he proposed?"

"No, he hasn't, and I'm going to bed because in about three hours I'll be back at work."

"Ellie will make a nice bridesmaid and of course, Myra."

"I'm not sure Myra could keep her hands off the groom."

"What?" Phoebe asked, her brows arching and peering at Samantha through her bifocals.

"What was the late, late movie?" Samantha asked, hoping to distract Phoebe and get her off the subject of a wedding.

"It was really wonderful—*Count Dracula's Nephew and the Beauty Queen*."

"I've never heard of it." Samantha wondered if anyone had as she climbed the stairs.

"It wasn't major stars, but it was good and scary and the nephew fell in love with the beauty queen. I'll tell you all about it at breakfast."

"Fine, Aunt Phoebe. Night." Samantha went to her room and closed the door. With her thoughts on Jake, she undressed and went to bed. Missing him, she wanted to be in his arms. She looked at the heat lightning, feeling a storm building in her.

Trying to calm, she thought about the television interview. It was fantastic and she prayed the restaurant's popularity continued and Salido grew.

They watched the playing of the interview on

the ten o'clock news at the restaurant on a television Bernie had installed over the bar. A hush came over the crowd as the interview played. Jake's fingers tightened around Samantha's and she glanced at him, thankful he was present. She felt her cheeks burn. Thank heavens for the dusky gloom so people couldn't see her blush. She leaned close to him. "I'm scared to watch. Suppose I look awful?"

He grinned and placed his arm around her shoulders, giving her a squeeze. "Physically impossible. There . . . you look gorgeous."

She didn't know about gorgeous, but it wasn't ghastly. She wasn't drooling or slumping or stuttering.

"How much has your restaurant grown?" Nate Clauson, the KZZZ interviewer asked.

"Business has been wonderful."

"Like how many customers do you have on a week night?"

She smiled at the camera. "It's been running around six to seven hundred per night."

She felt tense, thankful for Jake's reassuring arm across her shoulders. So far she was making sense. She remembered hoping she could look at the right camera and keep her wits about her enough to answer the question. Nate Clauson had put her at ease before they started taping.

"How many on a Saturday night?"

"Usually we'll have more than a thousand."

The camera panned the restaurant where Ellie and Vernon were singing on stage with the karaoke. The audience soon joined in a sing-along, and then it went back to Nate Clauson who was holding a smoked rib. "This is Salido Sam's yummy finger-lickin' barbecue and I can tell you, folks, it is as delicious as advertised. Salido, Oklahoma, a wide spot on the road, but filled with a crowd of friendly folks who like to sing and dance and eat barbecue. Y'all come!"

The spot ended, a commercial came on, and a cheer went up from the onlookers. "Free beer for the next half hour," she announced, and another shout went up.

She turned to Jake who grinned, and then Asa was there to give her a hug, and her family was between her and Jake.

"It was good, honey. You really looked good."

"Thank you, Granddad."

"Samantha, you looked beautiful. You were prettier than a lot of those movie stars I watch," Phoebe said. "Do you think you can afford to give away all that beer?"

"It's only half an hour, Aunt Phoebe, and it's good business. Where are the boys and Myra?" she asked. She spotted Jake talking to them and slid off the bar stool to go to them.

"Hey, Sis," Bernie said. "Cool."

"Yeah, cool," Tom echoed.

"It was nice," Myra added, turning back to Jake.

"Thank you," Samantha replied. "I hate to rush you, but you can't stay, because it's the drinking hour now and beer is flowing and you're minors. Sorry, but out you go. I'm glad you came down to watch."

"Night, Jake," Myra drew out her words.

"Night, Myra, Bernie, Tom," he answered, heading toward the bar.

She escorted her brothers and sister to the door and turned back to face Ellie and Vernon. Ellie gave her a hug. "Your hair looked great!"

"Thanks to you."

"It was a good interview," Vernon said. "I can't believe they taped while we were singing. I'd had too many beers."

"You both looked great."

"Congratulations, Samantha," Ed Naylor called, waving at her.

"I need to find Jake. Excuse me, Ellie, Vernon."

It was thirty more minutes before she worked her way through the throng of well-wishers to Jake who sat at the bar.

"Everything is under control. Ted is doing fine and looks as if he can competently hold down the fort. How about escaping the planet?" Jake asked, leaning close to her ear.

"That would be wonderful. Although this doesn't wear me out like it did those first weeks."

He took her hand and led her to his truck, where she leaned back against the seat. "Thank you for being there, and I'm grateful for your getting me out."

"You're welcome on both counts. You should

pack them in after this."

"Jake, it's been so good. I'm going to be able to take one kid at a time and get their teeth straightened and get braces. Bernie has an appointment in Ardmore with an orthodontist next Monday morning."

Jake squeezed her hand. "You're doing a fantastic job."

"Not me alone! Everyone has helped, including you."

"I know you didn't have dinner. We'll stop at Lowman's."

When they finally returned home, Jake went inside to sit with the family while they replayed a tape of the interview and discussed it. Finally he stood up.

"I better get home. I have a long drive."

"You better stay, Jake," Phoebe urged. *"Road to Rio* is coming on and it's a hoot."

"Jake, stay and watch," Myra pleaded. "This one is kinda funny,"

"Thanks, but morning comes early." Jake walked to the door with Samantha. They crossed the porch and went down the steps to the truck.

"I'm surprised Myra isn't still with us. She has a bad case for you."

"She'll outgrow it and then wonder why she ever thought such an old man was cute."

"I'd hate to lose you to a fourteen-year-old," she teased.

He wrapped his arms around Samantha. "That's not how my taste runs," he said softly, kissing her throat below her ear. "It runs to sexy women who are over voting age and have legs to die for, lips to dream about, and a body—"

"Jake," she whispered, turning her head. His mouth covered hers, and he tightened his arms to kiss her.

When he released her and climbed into the truck, she stepped back to watch him. She wanted more and knew he did too, yet neither of them wanted to cross that line into intimacy that would complicate both their lives. They were dancing dangerously close, going home aching, unable to sleep. She ran her fingers across her brow.

Then Jake was caught up in harvest because part of his land was covered in wheat, and she didn't see him for two weeks in June. The restaurant thrived, and she was busier than ever. When harvest was over, Jake made a date with her for Monday night the third week in June.

Three minutes after she was alone in the truck with him, heading to Lowman's, she knew that the absence had only made things more intense between them.

She watched fields flash past for a while and then turned to look at Jake, who seemed solemn. He gripped the wheel tightly with one hand as he drove fast. She looked out again, recognizing a bridge coming up over a creek and feeling a sense of shock. Where was he headed and why?

# Chapter Five

"Jake, you passed the turn to Lowman's." She shifted around to look at him. He glanced at her, his dark eyes impossible to read in the night, his cheeks in shadow, highlights showing his prominent cheekbones.

"Do you know how long since we've been alone? Melody is in Dallas again and Mrs. Latham is gone for the week. We have the ranch alone. I'll feed you, I promise. Now if you want me to be able to drive, you'll talk about the restaurant and all you've been doing."

She felt trembly, eager for his kisses, her body changing now, like petals opening in sunshine. Tactile awareness grew, her breasts feeling tight as she anticipated being alone with him. "The restaurant is doing fine, even with school out for the summer. I don't know where they're all coming from. We had an interview in the Ardmore paper, the Durant paper, the Atoka paper. It's been fantastic."

"And Bernie's braces?"

"He's glad to have them, so he's cooperative. Now he's talking about a car, but I have a mountain of debts to clear first and Bernie can get around town on his bicycle. He says he can't date on a bicycle. The boys are busy with their ball teams, and Myra is swimming this summer and gets phone calls from boys. Thank heavens they can't drive to take her out.

"It won't be long until they can. Has Asa slacked off working so hard?"

"Not much, even though Ted is doing a good job as manager between his summer classes at Monroe."

Jake took Samantha's hand, placing it on his warm thigh. "Maybe we should go back to the restaurant for a while," he suggested. She smoothed the skirt to her green sundress and looked up to catch a glance that was filled with smoldering intent.

They ate at Lowman's, Jake watching her over dinner and leaving half of his baked chicken untouched. He left to phone Melody, and Samantha remembered the brief fight with the three men a month earlier. She watched Jake walk back, his jeans low slung, his long legs moving in an easy gait, and she felt a surge of desire.

"Want to stay and dance or ride out to the ranch with me?"

She slid out of the booth to stand and face him. The wise answer would be to stay and dance until they couldn't go to the ranch.

As she debated, he took her hand. "C'mon. You know I'll take you home whenever you ask me to." He led her outside where warm summer winds blew curls around her face. Back on the highway she was quiet, because she felt the crackling tension. Jake's arm was across her shoulders, his fingers stroking her nape so lightly, yet each caress was a tingling touch that fanned flames in her.

The sun was still high in the sky as he rolled up the windows and turned on the air conditioner. She looked at the golden stubble in fields. Jake was quiet as he drove, finally talking about wheat harvest until they slowed in his drive and he turned to look at her.

"You know we should have stayed and danced."

"But you live dangerously and don't have a cautious bone in your body." He touched the tip of her nose with his finger before opening the door and stepping out.

When they entered the cool, quiet kitchen, he closed the door and leaned against it, pulling her around to face him. "We haven't been alone for far too long." Drawing her to him as he spread his legs, he cradled her between them.

In minutes his hands drifted over her back, moving to her zipper to slide it away. Samantha's heart raced and heat warmed her blood as he pushed away the sundress.

"Jake —"

"Shh," he whispered, cupping her breasts in his dark hands, his thumbs flicking across her nipples. She felt her breasts tighten, feelings streaking from each brush of his fingers, her temperature rising. She held his muscled forearms, and then let her hands drift to his waist and down over his hips to his jean-covered thighs.

"You're beautiful," he said in a husky voice, pushing away her dress. Heaven help her, she wanted him desperately, she thought, trembling with need.

She stood in her high-heeled pumps, black bikini panties and a lacy black garter belt and hose. "Step out of your shoes," he whispered, and she kicked them off.

"Jake, we always have to stop, and each time like this it gets more difficult—"

"I'll stop when you say stop, but this isn't going to complicate anything." He leaned forward to take the tip of her breast in his mouth to tease, his tongue flicking over her.

She gasped and rocked with him and he slid his hands along her thighs to unfasten her stockings. His fingers drifted up her bare legs that were as smooth as petals of a rose.

Picking her up in his arms, he strode to his bedroom, switching on one light to shed a soft glow as he set her on her feet.

"Jake, we shouldn't—"

"I know we shouldn't," he whispered, bending to kiss her throat, "but we don't do what we should all the time." He tugged at his belt buckle, freeing it, twisting the tight buttons on his fly. His heart drummed like wild horses galloping away. He wanted all of her, the fire in her, the laughter, the warmth. He wanted to arouse her every way possible.

He bent to yank off a boot and toss it down,

115

tugging away the other boot. Her eyes opened, and he could see the protest forming. He kissed her swiftly, hard. His groin was tight, his nerves raw, aware of the slightest contact with her softness. With each kiss, each heated stroke of trembling flesh, they were crossing a line and would never go back, and he didn't want to stop. His body clamored for her, but he knew there was more than just the physical satisfaction that was driving him. He tossed away caution like a man shoving a threadbare garment to the back of the closet.

Jake's low briefs no longer contained him as he stepped out of his jeans. Her lashes fluttered and her gaze raked over him, then rose to his eyes. Her eyes had darkened with desire, the irises indigo, with the pupils dilated. Her look was direct, as intense as summer heat, and his pulse jumped another notch. He felt engorged, knowing it would take so little to push him beyond a brink, yet wanting to slow for her.

He rested his hands on her pale hips. Her bikinis were brief, cut high over her slender hips. His thumbs ran lightly back and forth over her hipbones while he took his time, letting his gaze drift down with deliberation, wanting to drive her to a frenzy.

His gaze moved up over that curly thatch barely hidden by the bikinis, up over her tiny waist to the fullness above it. She was pale in the soft light, a seductive combination of curves. Her cheeks were flushed, her gaze hot as he looked at her directly.

"I want to pleasure you," he said softly, studying her, knowing he didn't want to turn back now, yet he would stop if she asked him to. And he half expected it until he looked into her eyes. Her darkened gaze held unmistakable assent. He drew a deep breath, letting his hands slide over her, trying to get control of his body so he would have time.

He wrapped his arm around her waist, gathering her softness to him, crushing her against his chest as he kissed her. His other hand slid down her back, over the flimsy bikinis, shoving them away. She was hot and moist and ready, but he intended to take as long as possible, sliding his fingers into her softness. He felt her muscles tighten in response to the friction; he found the tight pleasure bud, wanting to drive her over a brink, to take her to peak after peak.

She gasped, her body thrusting against his, her eyes closed as she responded wildly. Suddenly she looked at him, a direct stare that seared as hotly as a blue flame. She glanced down, sliding her fingers beneath his briefs to push them off, touching him.

He caught her hand and said, "I want to love you. I can't go slow if you do that." He turned her, pulling her back against him to kiss her nape. His tanned arm was dark around her waist as he stroked her breasts, feeling the taut peaks, feeling her soft bottom pressed against him. She quivered in response, her hands caressing his thighs. She was all he had fantasized and so much more. Pulsating rhythms converged in him, thickening him.

She twisted away, kneeling to kiss and stroke him until he groaned and went down beside her, pushing her on the bed, moving over her and pausing to look at her. He had dreamed of taking her, longed to, and now she was his, eager, open to him.

Samantha gazed up at Jake's virile, aroused body, his eyes midnight black now. Her heart thudded with need. She reached up as he lowered himself, touching her, making her gasp and her hips arch. Penetration was slow, an exquisite torment as he watched her until she closed her eyes, sliding her hands across his hard shoulders.

She was tight, hot, her body quivering for him as he eased slowly into her softness.

"Jake," she whispered, sliding her hands on his thighs, his firm, smooth buttocks. "Jake, please," she whispered.

"I want to drive you wild," he whispered in her ear. "Go on, honey, move," he whispered as her hips thrust with sweet torment until he thought he would burst.

Wrapping his arms under her, he took her with deliberation until finally his control was gone. "Samantha —" He groaned and thrust deep. "I can't wait, love," he whispered and turned to kiss her, his breath hot and his kisses fierce.

She arched, her soft cries muffled. She slid her arms around his neck and wrapped her legs around him.

"Samantha, now!" he gasped, moving while she matched him in an ageless dance. She felt impaled, filled, driven to ecstasy as he shuddered with release.

Spent, she gasped for breath while he held her

tightly against him. He rolled them on their sides and turned to look at her, stroking damp curls from her temple.

"Samantha, how I've wanted you! Oh, love, I need you in my life."

His words played over her like a caress, making her warm with joy. He held her tightly, showering light kisses on her throat and temple and cheek. She touched his shoulder. "Jake."

He kissed her fingers, looking at her. "You're important in my life." She thrilled to his words, knowing that he was vital to her.

They were quiet, holding each other while their heartbeats calmed, until Jake rose up over her.

"I can't blame the guy for coming on to you at the restaurant that night. Sexy woman."

"Said the kettle to the skillet. You're rather sexy yourself. Or hot as a nuclear blast would be a better way to say it."

"Maybe it's what we do together," he replied solemnly. Jake felt stunned, in love, wanting to hold her in his arms and never let go, wanting to touch her continually. He let his hand drift down over the full curve of her hip, along her silken thigh, and he felt a trembling eagerness start again in him. He looked into her eyes, and she gazed back with the directness that he liked.

Samantha studied the angles and flat planes of his masculine features, drawing her fingers across the roughness of faint stubble of a new beard starting, marveling in the differences between their bodies. How much had they just complicated each other's life? Yet she wouldn't have said no to him tonight. It was good to have a sexy man love her and pleasure her and hold her, to share the intimate moments of spent passion.

"Sweetie, you're a ten."

"And you're mentally off and need glasses. See these?" She pointed to the freckles on her nose. Leaning forward, he kissed the tip of her nose lightly and then turned his head to kiss her fingers, taking her second finger in his mouth and drawing away slowly, turning to look at her, his sexy intentions obvious in his kiss and his eyes.

With only a look he changed the air to steam and charged her system with swift hot impulses. He made her feel a need that played over her skin and then centered low within her. She ran her hand along one of his bare thighs, sliding her hand between them, feeling him hard and hot, touching the crisp hairs nestled at the base of his manhood. His eyes narrowed slightly as she tilted up her face and parted her lips.

He leaned down to kiss her, pushing her back on the bed, and she clung to him, astounded at the urgency she felt.

"Jake, I have to go home," she said later. "They won't notice the hour until dawn. If one ray of sunshine hits the earth and I'm not there, Aunt Phoebe will call you first and then Sheriff Needham and then the national guard."

Jake sighed, caressing her hip and thigh, wanting her in his arms for the next week. He had the ranch house to himself, and he didn't want to take her home. Yet he knew she was right. "I don't want to, but I will."

"Jake." She touched his arm lightly, and the tone of her voice made something inside turn a somersault. "Tonight was special."

He leaned forward to kiss her in answer, and a long time later she pushed away. "I have to go home." She moved away, crossing the room to the shower. He gazed at her, wanting to pull her back down, feeling his body respond to her walking away from him. Nude, creamy-fleshed and long-legged, her smooth silken skin taut over a saucy bottom, she left the room and left him panting, hard and hot. When had he felt this way about a woman? This insatiable need and mind-gone concentration on every little thing about her?

He had been wildly infatuated and in love with Diantha, blind to her selfishness. He had wanted her with all the heat and ardor of a twenty-three year-old man who lived and worked in isolation. Now he was not young and infatuated. He was thirty-three, cynical, satisfied with his life, dating often enough to satisfy physical needs. Until Salido Sam and her mouth-watering barbecue and her lip-smacking sexy body and her bone-melting lovemaking.

Get a grip, Colby. All he wanted to grasp was her hot, lush body. But then it was more than that. He wanted her company, her fun. And he couldn't forget the moments she had spent with Melody. He stood up and moved around the room, gathering up his things. He drifted past the bathroom and heard the shower. He went to another room to bathe quickly under cold water. He yanked on clean briefs and jeans and a knit shirt

121

and pulled on boots to go look for her. She sat on a kitchen stool sipping her wine, staring into space, her gaze swinging to meet his as he entered the room.

Her blue eyes made contact, and he felt ensnared; his heartbeat altered, speeding up like a train leaving the station.

He moved to her, stopping when her knees pressed against his hips. The contact was a flashpoint, and he reached out to circle her waist. "I don't want to take you home."

She wriggled away and stood up. "You have to. It's a long trip to town." She turned to leave the room ahead of him.

"One minute, Samantha." He caught her, turning her swiftly and yanking her to him to kiss her, not wanting to give her up yet.

When she pushed away, her breath came in gasps while he tried for a modicum of self-control. "Jake, we're going home before the roosters crow."

"How I want you," he said. And he did want her, more than he would have ever dreamed possible. It sobered him and frightened him, because it was a threat to his peaceful life. He held open the door and followed her out, carefully avoiding touching her, knowing the slightest contact would be volatile.

When he stopped in her driveway, he climbed out to walk her to the door and kiss her goodnight, holding her tightly.

"I want to scoop you up and carry you back with me. This is the hardest damned thing, to tell you goodbye. Go out with me tonight."

"Yes," she answered with a look that made him feel as if he had won a prize.

When she looked into his dark eyes, she nodded.

"Fine, I'll even wait until half past six. Sami, it was wonderful tonight." With a light brush of his lips on hers, he was gone, and she went inside. Aunt Phoebe came hurrying from the living room.

"Samantha, do you know how late it is?"

"Is the last movie over?" she asked, heading toward the staircase.

"No. They go on all night, but you've —"

"What's on now?"

"Oh, it's a Marx brothers picture and really quite good. It's vintage movie night. I'll tell you the story sometime."

By then Samantha was halfway up the stairs and Phoebe went back to the living room. Samantha changed to a cotton nightgown and stretched on her bed to look through the window at the fading stars. Her body tingled from Jake's lovemaking, and she closed her eyes, lost in memories that made her sigh with longing.

"Hello, complications," she muttered aloud, then decided she didn't have to worry yet. Right now so little had changed. Yet so much had . . . because now they were lovers.

Every night that week, she went out with him. On Saturday night at the ranch as he held her in his arms, he turned a curl in his fingers.

"I should buy a house in town so we wouldn't have to drive all the way out here to get to be alone."

"With all the gossips we wouldn't have any privacy in Salido."

"That's why I haven't bought one, but I want you to myself."

"Sounds good to me." She smiled and rolled on her side to face him. His chest was broad, muscled and a marvel to her.

Jake stared at her, knowing Melody would be back next week, Mrs. Latham would be around, and he couldn't have nights alone with Samantha. And now that she was in his life, he didn't want her out of it. He turned a silky curl in his fingers and stroked her smooth shoulder, letting his finger follow the full curve of her breast. He cupped her softness in his hand, watching her as her eyes changed and she licked her lips and slipped her arm behind his head to draw his mouth down to her.

"Come here, Jake," she whispered and reached toward him, her lips swollen, ripe for kisses.

"I'm not going to let you go," he said gruffly, and she looked up at him, frowning briefly. He rubbed his lips across hers. "Don't frown, Sami. I've found you and I want you to be part of my life."

"I am part of it," she said softly in reply, her tongue flicking over his lips, and he forgot the conversation, leaning over and pushing her to the bed.

Later, after he had taken her home, he thought about her during the drive back. He was losing time from running the ranch, and he was neglecting his business. He hadn't talked to his accountant or his broker for a month, and he needed to get together with both of them, yet he didn't want to leave Salido and Samantha. He couldn't go ten minutes without thinking about her or missing her. Thank God she got along with Melody. What was he going to do about Samantha?

In August he wasn't much closer to a decision. But the last time he'd flown Melody to Dallas and finished with business appointments there, he had stopped in Cartier's and looked at engagement rings. Afterward he had been in a quandary all the way home. He wasn't ready to marry again, yet each separation from Samantha was taking a bigger toll.

Could he cope with Asa and Myra and Phoebe and Bernie and Tom? Would they expect to live on the ranch with Samantha or could they maintain the house in town without her? Myra needed her because she was only fourteen. Actually, they all needed her and Melody did, too. Maybe it was time Melody visited the Bardwells and got to know them, and then he could see how well they got along together.

He drew a deep breath, his thoughts shifting back to Samantha in his big bed, red tresses spilling behind her head, her pink and white and golden body his completely.

He would invite the Bardwells to the ranch next Sunday. Let them spend the day there and let Melody get to know them. Even though it was late, he picked up the telephone and called Samantha on her private line.

She answered quickly before the first ring was over.

"I want Melody to meet your family. Bring them

all out to dinner Sunday. Come about noon and plan to spend the day."

"My goodness, a masochist!"

"They'll be grand," he said, thinking of the Bardwells and smiling, feeling that Melody would like them. How could anyone dislike them? "We might as well get our families together. I don't think we're going to stop seeing each other." He thought about the sparkling diamond rings he had looked at.

"My whole family? Wouldn't you like a few at a time?"

"No. Let's do the whole thing, Asa, Phoebe, Bernie, Tom, Myra. I'll even rent a movie for the evening for Phoebe."

"No, don't rent a movie! Yes, we'll be there. I can answer for all of them. But you're crazy."

"Plumb nutty over a wild, wonderful woman. I miss you and hate being home without you."

"It's mutual, Jake. Tonight was wonderful."

He felt his body tightening, changing in response to hearing her voice. Erotic images flashed in his mind, and he wanted her with him.

They continued to talk until her words slurred and he clutched the phone close. "We'll end this. 'Night, sweetie."

"Good night, Jake," she whispered and hung up, thinking a real test was looming. What would they do if the families didn't get along? If Melody didn't like them, would Jake stop seeing her?

# Chapter Six

Sunday afternoon at half past twelve, Jake watched them pile out of the fourteen-year-old Ford station wagon Asa owned. "Here they come," he said, taking Melody's hand. "Let's go meet Sami's family."

Within ten minutes Myra and Melody and Tom were climbing Melody's tree house in the backyard. Bernie rode horseback, Asa studied Jake's fishing lures, while Phoebe and Mrs. Latham compared notes on their favorite daytime soaps.

Wearing a T-shirt and navy shorts, Samantha sat close to Jake, listening to them talk about fishing.

Jake cooked burgers on the gas grill, and they ate at a redwood table on the patio. As she sipped iced tea, she glanced at the end of the table to look into Jake's dark eyes, and the crowd seemed to vanish. Awareness funneled down to only Jake. The world changed to their own private place, as solitary as a deserted island. Jake winked at her, and she winked in return.

After dinner everyone except Phoebe and Mrs. Latham piled into Jake's Bronco. He took them on a tour of the ranch and stopped to let all who wanted to wade in the creek.

"Next time you come out, you'll have to bring your fishing gear. The Armuchee River runs at the south end of the property, and the fishing is good because there are a few deep holes."

"You have a nice place," Asa commented, looking around him.

It was late afternoon when they returned to the ranch house and Jake put cold cuts on the kitchen counter, telling everyone to help themselves. He had rented a Disney movie they could all watch after they ate. While the movie played, Asa fell asleep. Bernie and Tom went back out to the stable to ride.

In the kitchen Samantha put things away, bending over to place lettuce in the refrigerator. Arms circled her waist from behind. For just a moment she was pressed against a male body until Jake turned her to face him. "Stop working right now."

"This isn't work."

"Yes, it is." His gaze went over her features. "Look at our families. They get along fabulously. Melody is Myra's shadow. Of course, Myra may get tired of a four-year-old."

"Myra's good with kids. In spite of the sappy crush."

"You think it's sappy for someone to have a crush on me?" he asked with arched brows.

"When you put it that way, no. A hunk who's definitely impossible to resist—Except that she's only fourteen years old."

"I told you, it's the old-lady sister I'm interested in. The one with the come-hither looks and the fizz-your-blood kisses."

"I fizz your blood?"

"Do you ever, darlin'! I'd like to have a quick fizz right now if I could figure somewhere—" He took her hand. "Come here," he commanded, hurrying across the utility room to the large walk-in pantry.

"Jake, the whole family is here. Both families! Jake!"

He tugged her inside, closed the door to lean against it and wrapped her in his arms. "They'll have to push me over to get in."

"You can't—"

"Wanna bet?" he asked in a husky voice, bending his head to kiss her. And then she was lost, forgetting they weren't alone, forgetting her arguments, sliding her arms around his neck.

Finally she moved away from him. "You'll embarrass me. We have to go back."

"*I'll* embarrass *you?*" he asked. His eyes smoldered with hot desire and with something extra that she hadn't seen before: an indefinable look that made her feel wrapped in warmth. He looked contented, and she realized that barriers he'd had were vanishing. He was more open with her, hungry for her, sharing his life with her.

"I'm glad the families get along. Or does that statement scare you stiff?" she asked.

"I was thinking the same thing. I'm glad, too. It leaves us more options. And no, it doesn't frighten me. I wouldn't have gotten them together if I hadn't hoped they would get along."

"Let's not rush things."

"Still Miss Cool." He looked at her as they entered the kitchen, and his brows arched. "You value your independence, don't you?"

"I suppose. I hadn't thought of it that way. I just got so accustomed to it, Jake."

"I know you did." His features softened as he wrapped his arm around her shoulders and squeezed her affectionately. "Go out with me tomorrow night. It's Monday," he reminded her.

"Yes, I will. Shall we join the family now?"

"Sure," he answered, holding her close against him until they left the kitchen.

At ten o'clock, with Melody on the verge of falling asleep in Jake's arms, they walked to the station wagon. As soon as they were settled and Samantha turned the wagon around and headed down the ranch road, Phoebe leaned forward. "It's a shame the ranch is so far from Salido. You could have a wedding reception out here, and it would be beautiful."

"Did Jake propose?" Myra asked, leaning forward, too. The boys talked quietly in the back seat while Asa dozed next to Samantha.

"No, he hasn't, and I don't think he will. He's told me he doesn't want to marry again."

"Stuff and green pickles!" Phoebe snapped in disbelief. "I would wager—except I don't do things like that—he will propose within the month. This month."

"He sure is friends with you," Myra observed. "Maybe he's waiting until Melody is older. In six years she'll be ten and I'll be twenty."

"And he'll be thirty-nine."

"That's not old."

"No, it's definitely not."

"I know he'll propose, Samantha," Phoebe declared. "Men are so predictable—look at your grandfather, I could have told you that Asa would sleep all the way home."

"Aunt Phoebe, he does that every night," Myra said.

"I just know Jake had us out here today to see how Melody likes us and vice versa, and wasn't she a polite, precious child? My word, the man has done a good job with her. She's adorable and he dotes on her. Of course, he shouldn't spoil her, and a man alone with his daughter would tend to do that. Particularly one as nice as Jake Colby."

Why had he had them all out? Did he have a good time, too, or was it just her family enjoying themselves as usual? Wherever they were, her family did have fun, and maybe that was an asset. Life might come easier in the pinches.

In minutes everyone settled and grew quiet, and by the time they reached home, Samantha was the only one awake. When she reached her room, her phone was ringing, and she yanked up the receiver to hear Jake's voice.

At six o'clock the next night, as soon as they turned out of the driveway, she glanced at him. "You're not going your usual direction. We're not eating at Lowman's?"

"Not tonight. I thought I'd surprise you with a change."

"It's a beautiful night and a change is welcome. It was a very good weekend."

"It was, indeed. I'm glad business was good, and Melody is asking about you and your family, so that's nice, too."

"Yes, it is, Jake." She relaxed, turning in the seat to look at him. In minutes she felt her curiosity grow. "Where are we going?" she asked as he turned down the asphalt ribbon to a hangar that was the town's runway and tiny airport.

"I have my plane ready and we're going to eat dinner in Dallas tonight." He turned to look at her as he parked the truck. "I wish we could stay in a hotel there all night."

Her pulse jumped with eagerness. She hadn't been away from Salido in several years, and suddenly the evening seemed enveloped in a special excitement. He led her toward his blue and white twin-engine Cessna.

After they were seated in the plane and he received clearance, she watched as the ground rushed past and they lifted. Jake handled the Cessna with ease. They leveled off, and she looked down at Main Street and the restaurant. Riding without conversation, because it was too difficult because of the roar of the plane, she studied the terrain and recognized her house. Soon they flew beyond Salido over newly plowed fields and green meadows. After a time she looked at the wide, muddy Red River winding across the flat land dividing Oklahoma from Texas.

Love Field and Dallas seemed congested to them, an hour later, after being so accustomed to the small town of Salido. Jake rented a car, and the sun was still high above the horizon when they turned onto Mockingbird Lane. They drove to a sprawling rock building nestled in pines with peacocks strolling the grounds. Inside Papa Luigi's the maître d' led them past tables covered in white linen. Through wide windows, lights shone outside on a meandering creek and tall pines. In a corner of the front room a man played a piano. When they were seated and had ordered, she gazed at Jake across the candlelight.

"This is fun," she said softly, and he reached across the table to take her hand, his finger trailing over her knuckles.

"I thought you might like it."

"I got a strange phone call today."

"Obscene?" he asked gruffly.

"Don't get huffy and ready to kill for me. No, it was business. A man wanted to discuss buying

133

the restaurant. I told him it wasn't for sale, but he said to hear him out before I made that decision."

"You don't have anything to lose."

"That's what I figured. He fishes at Lake Lewiston, and in years past he has stopped at the restaurant to eat. He ate there a couple of weeks ago. He saw the interview on television and read about me in the Tulsa paper. So I have an appointment with him Wednesday morning. He's coming by the restaurant at ten o'clock."

"It won't hurt to listen. Who is the guy?"

"He's Eldon Kyriakos."

Jake looked up and lowered his glass of wine. "Kyriakos?"

"You know who that is?"

"Yes," he replied, looking at her intently. "I can't imagine him interested in Salido, Oklahoma. If you lived in a town bigger than Salido, you might know who he is. He's an entrepreneur and damned successful. He's got a hotel chain that's the main source of the Kyriakos empire. He has extensive real estate holdings and a nationwide company, Kyriakos Enterprises."

"I can't figure why he would want to see me. I'd think he would send one of his staff. He surely doesn't get involved in the nitty-gritty of his deals."

"He does. That's one of the things that makes him unique. I remember reading about him. He's a shark, Samantha. Get your accountant to go with you to the meeting. Your lawyer, too."

"At Salido Sam's? I'd feel ridiculous doing that! I don't need a lawyer and an accountant."

"You're dealing with one of the shrewdest men in business today." Jake was surprised by her news. "If I met with him, I'd have my lawyer and my accountant present."

"Well, you have more property of value than I do. I have one tiny little restaurant and the old shops beside it. I wonder why he's interested in the restaurant?"

"I think he's taken some thriving businesses before and franchised them out. That may be what he wants to do."

"A chain of Salido Sam's? That's absurd."

"No, it's not," Jake argued, realizing she still wasn't fully aware of her own success. "You have a going concern. He can afford to open more restaurants like yours."

"If I sold the restaurant, I don't know what any of us would do," she commented, looking at the splashing fountain in the center of the room.

Jake wanted to groan, because she was a babe going to face a business shark. She had no idea of the potential of the restaurant. "If you got enough for selling the restaurant, you could do whatever work you want. You could go with the advertising firm you dreamed about. Asa could retire. Phoebe could keep on with her little shop."

"That's staggering! I don't want to think about it, because then I'll start worrying."

Jake forgot Kyriakos as he let his gaze drift

135

down over her bare shoulders and her sundress with its tiny blue straps. Her skin was creamy smooth and he felt a reaction low in his groin just from looking at her. She couldn't be wearing anything under the top of the sundress, and the idea made him draw a deep breath. He leaned forward. "I know a place where we can dance."

She nodded, and within the hour she was in his arms, gazing out floor-to-ceiling glass panels at the glittering lights of Dallas. They were in a club on one of the top floors of a hotel. The music was low and slow, the beat vibrating while Jake held her.

Jake was warm, his body twisting with sexy moves against hers as she looked up. He watched her, the longing he felt obvious in his black eyes. When they left the dance floor, they went to the elevator. She didn't pay attention as they entered and he pushed a button and pulled her close. The elevator doors slid open, and instead of emerging in the downstairs lobby, they stepped into another hallway. Jake pulled out a key.

"Where are we going?"

"For just a few more hours, we're staying here. I took a suite for tonight." He swung open the door, holding her arm as she entered with him. His pulse beat wildly. "For a little while now, I'll have you to myself." He watched passion darken her eyes. Drawing her to him, he brushed her lips with his, the petal softness of hers stirring him. His lips pressed hers and he kissed her, pulling her tight against his chest.

It was nearly four in the morning when he took her home, and as he turned into her drive, he didn't want to leave her. He cut the motor and looked at her, running his fingers along her arm. "I want to take you home with me."

"I'll go inside and miss you."

He touched the cellular phone. "I'll call you on the way home." He walked her to the door, where he waved to Phoebe who was standing at the living room window. She waved back and scurried away. " 'Night, love."

"Dallas was so much fun, Jake."

"I'll call you. How long will you have to answer Phoebe's questions?"

"Not long. Commercials are probably on. As soon as they're over, she'll go back to the television."

"When does she sleep?"

"She takes little naps all through the day. She sleeps sitting up in her shop and at home. I think if you added the nap time, she's getting as much sleep as anyone else." She shrugged. "My family."

"They're adorable. I'll call in ten minutes on my cellular phone."

They talked all the time he drove home. At the ranch he looked in on Melody, brushing her cheek with a kiss. He undressed and climbed into bed to lie awake while he stared into the dark. He wanted Samantha more all the time.

She was fun, good with Melody, all the things Diantha had never been. Samantha was down to earth, independent, practical, yet there was the other side to her, the sensual woman who could melt him with her kisses. Marry her. The thought made his pulse race with eagerness. Marry Samantha. Have all the Bardwells for a family. Have her in his bed each night. The thought took his breath away.

Marriage would complicate his life, but the thought of being with Samantha all the time, whenever he came home, was what he wanted. He wanted her with him as often as possible. She could hire someone to run the restaurant. Maybe Kyriakos would buy it, and the whole problem would be solved. The restaurant could be worked out easily.

Think it over, Colby. Don't rush into anything. Mr. Shrewd had rushed into marriage before, and it had been disastrous. He shifted, staring out the sliding doors at the sky. He needed to be up early. He had a silo to repair, an errand to run in town. He wondered if sleep came any easier for Samantha. What would Kyriakos's offer be?

Wednesday morning, the second of September, Samantha dressed in a tailored blue cotton dress. Not expecting much to come of the meeting, and mildly nervous about discussing business with a man like Kyriakos, she fastened her hair behind her head. She went to work earlier than usual.

Promptly at eleven o'clock a dark-haired man in an elegant navy pin-stripe suit entered the restaurant, and she knew at once that it was Eldon Kyriakos.

He was several inches over six feet, as commanding as Jake in a more formal way. He was thick through the shoulders, and his dark hair was combed neatly away from his deeply tanned face. His black eyes were alert, and he came toward her with a hint of a smile on his face.

"Mr. Kyriakos?" she asked as he approached. She extended her hand. "I'm Samantha Bardwell."

"I'm happy to meet you." He glanced around the restaurant. "You've done a remarkable job. I read your interviews."

"Thank you. So far the response has been wonderful." She motioned to a corner table. "I don't have an office. At this hour there aren't any customers, so if you'd like to sit here, we can talk."

As he sat down facing her over a round table, he smiled. "So far? You're still not ready to claim full success?"

"I don't want this to be a brief fad."

"I would say you're beyond the fad stage. From what I understand the whole town has changed."

She felt her cheeks grow warm. "There has been a spurt of interest in Salido."

"Is the barbecue recipe an old family tradition?"

"No. I concocted that several years ago. The formula is in my head, and no one else knows it."

"Your family works with you as I understand."

"My grandfather is here every day, and the others come in when they can."

"I've been through Salido and, as I told you, I've eaten here before. I fish at Lake Lewiston. It's a beautiful lake—not a tourist mecca—and I like to get away from crowds."

She smiled. "You should be able to do that around here. My grandfather fishes at Lake Lewiston."

"You and your grandfather own this entire block. Is that right?"

"Yes. Granddad bought the buildings to the south and the lots behind them about eight years ago, when the town began to dry up and prices dropped. He thought people would come back. Since the restaurant has been so successful, I bought the two buildings to the north and the lots adjoining them on First Street, because I need more parking space. I can't afford to have the buildings torn down yet, but at least I own the land."

He settled back and crossed his legs. "That's part of what I'm interested in. I've been looking for another restaurant franchise, and my staff pointed your place out to me."

"I'm really not interested in selling this place unless it's something impossible to turn down," she added with another smile. His dark eyes were warm as he watched her and she felt at ease with him, her nervous anticipation vanishing. "Want to look at the restaurant and meet Granddad?"

"I'd like that. So you came straight back here after college."

She looked up in surprise as he moved beside her. "You already know that?"

"Yes. I look into things before I get involved in them. Tell me about the restaurant."

"We redecorated and bought a karaoke and had the small stage built. We sell the T-shirts there." She pointed to the counter by the front door. "I advertise in area papers and occasionally in the Oklahoma City paper."

"Who designed the T-shirt?"

"I did, and I did the drawing with help from my fourteen-year-old sister."

"So the T-shirt design belongs to you?"

"Yes. Here's the kitchen," she said, pushing through the swinging doors as Kyriakos followed. "Granddad."

Asa turned, an apron over his coveralls. He wiped his hands on a towel and crossed the kitchen. "Granddad, this is Mr. Kyriakos. This is Asa Bardwell, my grandfather."

"How do you do?" Asa said, shaking hands with Kyriakos. He pushed his glasses higher on his nose and peered up at the tall man. "I hear you like to fish at Lake Lewiston. I remember you caught a record-size bass there in '85."

141

"Yes. I'm surprised you would recall my prize," Kyriakos remarked, sounding pleased. Samantha was surprised because Asa hadn't said anything to her about the feat.

"Most of the time it's locals who get the big ones. In '85 and in '81 and in '77 it was a foreigner to these parts. We're trying to get a Red Man bass tournament here since the town is growing again. That would bring the big prize money."

Kyriakos smiled, looking genuinely pleased as he folded his arms across his chest. "There are about twenty-two Red Man divisions now. If you get a tournament, it would pump a great deal of money into town."

"We're hoping. Have you fished any this trip?"

"I intend to today and tomorrow."

"How do you like our place? Samantha's done a good job."

"Yes, she certainly has."

"Salido was about to dry up and blow away when Samantha thought all this up." He lowered his voice. "Frankly, I didn't think it would work when she told me what she wanted to do, but I was wrong. Get someone to show you Main Street. Across from us there are three new places that have opened."

"I intend to look around. Do you serve breakfast?" he asked, and she glanced at him, suspecting he already knew the answer as well as how much she had grossed and netted the past few months.

142

"Sure do," Asa answered. "We open at six in the morning for the early risers. This is a farm community."

"Here's a menu." Samantha handed him the single laminated sheet. "We have a simple menu as you can see. And it's home-style cooking for breakfast—flapjacks, eggs, the usual. Lunch and dinner are predominantly barbecue—either ribs or chicken. We have hamburgers, too. Now beer is the big item along with barbecued ribs."

"You've upgraded the equipment." He looked at the new mixer and the new dishwasher.

Samantha gave Kyriakos a tour of the kitchen and answered his questions. When they were back in the dining area, she handed him a T-shirt. "Have a shirt, compliments of Salido Sam's."

"Thank you," he said, looking down at the picture on it.

"Granddad is cooking some special ribs for you."

"So I'll get to taste the finger-lickin', pot-scraping savory barbecue sauce?"

"Yes, in minutes."

"Do you have any future plans for the restaurant?"

"Not yet. If we continue to draw large crowds, I'd like to enlarge the parking."

They sat down at the table, and a waiter came from the kitchen. Samantha watched Reggie casually balance a tray with two glasses of water.

His blond hair fell over his eyes, and he shook it away as he reached the table.

"Mr. Kyriakos, this is Reggie, who waits tables. Reggie, this is Mr. Kyriakos."

"How do you do," Reggie said, setting two glasses of ice water on the table. "Ribs will be ready in about twenty minutes."

"Miss Bardwell, you have a thriving business here with good food and good service," Kyriakos stated as Reggie left. "What I'm offering is to buy the restaurant and the recipe." He opened a briefcase. "I'd like to buy the buildings on this block. Salido is close to Lake Lewiston, and I think this region can be developed into a resort."

"I thought you liked to fish at Lake Lewiston because it isn't a tourist spot." Surprised he wanted the whole block, she thought what a boon it would be to the town. A few might not want new people and business, but most people she knew would welcome it.

"I do, but I also like to make money. I see potential here. I want to develop the town into a turn-of-the-century tourist attraction — you've already got the ball rolling in the right direction. The main thing is the franchise on Salido Sam's. I've been looking for something like this. The barbecue sauce is delicious."

"Thank you." She felt amazed he was so interested in the restaurant.

He nodded. "There's one more thing. After talking to you today, I'd like to hire you to open the new franchises. We'll research the best places

144

and get the building and the restaurant ready. My staff will hire and train the manager, but I'd like you there to oversee the opening."

Watching him pull papers from his briefcase, she was astounded by his proposal. She remembered Jake urging her to have an accountant, and now she wished she had heeded his advice. The job offer was something she hadn't thought of in her wildest imaginings. She realized his people had already been in and checked on everything and had probably talked to her without her knowing who they were.

Placing papers on the table, Kyriakos scooted closer so he could discuss the buildings, the market value, the salary he was proposing. Samantha looked at the figures and her mind reeled. She locked her fingers together in her lap. For a moment she thought how wonderful it would be to always know she had enough to cover each month's expenses, to know exactly what she could spend and how much she could save. It was heady to think she would be able to plan for expenses.

The restaurant was becoming more productive by the week, and the buildings they owned along Main Street had already jumped in worth. It was obvious that they would become more valuable with time, but what Eldon Kyriakos was offering her was a sum beyond all her projections. And the salary was spectacular. Her head swam when she thought of Bernie's dental bills, the dental work that both Tom and Myra needed, the glasses that Asa needed and had an appointment to get, their fourteen-year-old car that was held together with wires and prayer. She would be on a salary with a real paycheck coming in every month. She would know how much money she was going to make every month, and she could plan on things.

The figures seemed to leap up and dazzle her. How could he pay her that much? She wanted to grab the pen from his hand and sign the papers right then, but she remembered Jake telling her to take an accountant and a lawyer with her to the appointment. The money Kyriakos was offering her, plus the job offer, was incredibly generous.

"Mr. Kyriakos, this seems an astronomical amount. More than all this is worth!" Amusement flickered in his eyes as he gazed back.

"I want my employees to be happy. A lot of the success of the franchise would rest on your shoulders in getting the restaurants started and in consultation. I've checked into real estate values here, looked into the restaurant. You own the whole block on Main Street, and the restaurant is thriving, and the franchise is worth a great deal, as well as the barbecue sauce recipe. I think if you look into it, you're getting fair value, not a gift." He withdrew a folder and scooped the papers into it.

"You take all this to your accountant or someone you'd like to consult, look it over, and we'll get back together."

"How soon?"

Again she saw the look of amusement in his dark eyes. "As soon as you like. I'll stay and fish until you contact me."

She tried to think. All her impulses were to grab the papers and sign them quickly and hand him the deed to the restaurant, the recipe and the keys. The salary whirled in her mind and the things she could do she had put off so long. Myra needed her eyes checked, Bernie and Tom could quit their part-time jobs during school so they could play ball and get more hours of study done. Asa could retire. The salary plus an investment of the lump sum from the sale would be enough to take care of the whole family. When she thought of Asa finally able to retire, she felt a tight knot in her throat, and she looked down at her lap and squeezed her hands together. "Excuse me a minute." She pushed the folder off onto the chair and hurried to the kitchen.

She wiped her eyes and tried to get control of her emotions. "Granddad, how near ready are the ribs?"

"Five more minutes." He tilted his head to squint at her. "Are you all right?"

She nodded, not trusting herself to speak. Hurrying to the phone that was behind the brooms, she picked it up and dialed the ranch, praying that Jake was there although it was unlikely at this time of day. She wiped her eyes again and felt as if a mountain had moved off her shoulders. The papers aren't signed. She shouldn't start thinking about Asa's retirement until she had the contract finalized and in her hand.

"Colbys'," came Mrs. Latham's voice.

"Is Jake there, Mrs. Latham? This is Samantha."

"As a matter of fact, he's just leaving again. Let me get him." There was a clatter and silence, and Samantha drew a deep breath.

"Hi," came his warm voice that seemed to send his strength along with it. "How'd the meeting go?"

Emotions gripped her again, and she didn't want to cry, yet tears brimmed. "Jake—"

"Samantha? Are you all right?"

"Jake, he made an offer."

"Honey, what's wrong?" he asked, and the worry in his voice added to her turmoil.

"He gave me the papers to let someone look at them. I suppose I'll take the offer to Mr. Yarrell, and I'd like your opinion. Jake, it's so good I can't believe my good fortune."

"Then why do you sound like disaster's struck?"

"Because I can't believe it and I'm so relieved." She wiped her eyes.

"I'm coming to town. I'll pick you up at the restaurant and take you to the bank. That's good news, Sami."

"Jake, this means Granddad can retire."

"Now I know why you sound like you do,"

Jake said, some of the concern leaving his voice.

"I'd better get back. I left Mr. Kyriakos at the table and Granddad said our ribs are almost cooked."

Jake laughed, and the sound helped her get control. "I'm on my way unless I'll get there too soon. If you're still with him—"

"No, we're going to eat lunch and then we're through. Please come."

"Right now. Get someone to take your place tonight and tomorrow night. We celebrate with the family tomorrow night and just us tonight."

"Yes, sir! Oh, Jake, I can't believe it."

"You deserve it, Samantha." His voice was filled with warmth.

"As much as I hate to, I need to go. 'Bye, Jake."

She knew she shouldn't tell Asa now, or all hope of his cooking during lunch would be over. And he wouldn't want her to consult anyone. He would be ready to take the deal, too. He wasn't in the kitchen, and as she pushed through the swinging doors, he was sitting with Eldon Kyriakos. She knew the two fishermen were probably talking about Lake Lewiston. Steaming platters of ribs were on the table.

Motioning to Eldon Kyriakos to sit back down, she pulled a chair from another table. "Share some of this with me, Granddad," she urged, noticing he had placed the folder of papers on the floor beside the chair.

"I'll take a rib," he said, scooting around.

149

"After lunch, I'm taking Mr. Kyriakos home if you can hold down the fort here. I want to show him my latest lure. It's perfect and it's a new one. I've been telling him about my favorite spot on the lake. He has his and I have mine, and we're trying to decide which one is best."

She barely heard beyond taking Mr. Kyriakos home. She looked at the elegant man sitting across from her and thought about their house. Phoebe would be at the shop, Tom and Bernie at work, Myra was baby-sitting with Jenny Lou Crane's twins, so no one would be home. The house was cluttered, dishes were in the sink from breakfast because everyone left early in a hurry to get to work. The kids were enrolling in school today. There was no one to clean until they all got home later.

She shrugged away worry. They didn't have the life-style of Mr. Kyriakos, so there was no need stewing over Granddad inviting him home.

She was too excited to eat, passing Asa another rib and in minutes shoving the whole plate in front of him while he discussed bass and bluegill with Eldon Kyriakos.

She glanced at the man who might change all their lives. He laughed with Asa, yet Samantha had the feeling that he wasn't completely relaxed. His eyes were impassive, his answers and statements polite as if he were accustomed to keeping up a guard.

And finally they were through and Kyriakos stood.

"Can you get along without me?" Asa asked. "I'll be right back."

"Yes, Granddad." She gave his hand a squeeze. "Thank you," she said, offering her hand to Eldon Kyriakos. "What time would you like to meet tomorrow?"

"How about three tomorrow afternoon?"

"Fine."

"I'll be here at three then."

The door opened and she turned to see Jake stride into the restaurant.

# Chapter Seven

Samantha's heart missed a beat, and for just a moment she forgot the offer, forgot Kyriakos. Jake was dressed in a charcoal suit and dark tie, and he looked as imposing as Eldon Kyriakos. As his gaze met hers, she felt a surge of reassurance. He crossed the room to them.

"Mr. Kyriakos, this is my friend Jake Colby. Jake, I'd like you to meet Eldon Kyriakos."

"Glad to meet you," Jake said, shaking Kyriakos's hand.

"We're going to the house so I can show him my lures," Asa said, shaking hands with Jake. "Want to come along?"

"I'd like to, but I have an appointment. Thanks, Asa." He turned to Kyriakos. "I hope you like our town and restaurant."

"I can honestly say that was the best rib dinner I've ever had."

"Good. I agree with you about the ribs and sauce. You should have good fishing, too. It was nice to meet you."

"Nice to meet you," Kyriakos said. "Goodbye, Samantha. The rib dinner was all it's advertised to be."

"Thank you. Tomorrow at three."

She watched him leave with Asa and she turned to look up at Jake. He took her arm and went through the kitchen and out the back door to the alley where he turned to look at her.

"Jake, you won't believe what he's offered."

Jake looked at the sparkle in her eyes and felt a surge of happiness for her. He pulled her close, catching a scent of her rose perfume. "I'm glad, Samantha. You and Asa deserve this." He ran his hands on her arms lightly, knowing she was bursting with excitement.

She pulled back to look up at him. "He's offered me a job, too. I'll manage this one and help him open new restaurants that he wants to franchise."

"You'll work for Kyriakos?" Jake felt a swift shock. "He's been studying this place."

"He'd tasted the ribs and sauce before today because he's eaten at the restaurant when he's fished at Lake Lewiston. Jake, I can do all the things for Bernie and Tom and Myra now," she said, her voice sounding filled with joy. "And Granddad can retire."

"You do a few things for Samantha, love." He wondered if she ever thought of herself.

"Jake, this does do everything for me! It's so wonderful" Her arms tightened around him, and she pressed her face against his chest and he re-

153

alized she was crying. His arms tightened and he held her close, letting her cry, thankful for Kyriakos's deal because it would take so much responsibility off her shoulders. Jake stroked her head until she wiped her eyes and looked up.

"Sorry."

"Don't be ridiculous. I'm so glad, honey. It's marvelous."

"I want to go over everything with you and I thought I would take Kyriakos's plan to Wilson Yarrell for his opinion."

"Good idea."

"I can't imagine not accepting this. It sounds unbelievably generous."

"I know he's getting his money's worth, because he's a shrewd bargainer. It just so happens you're ready to sell what he wants to buy. And he didn't appear on a whim. He's had his people check all this out."

"I haven't told Granddad or anyone except you, and I don't want to until it's decided. You know my family will be hysterical. And it will be all over town within three seconds after Aunt Phoebe knows. Or Myra."

"Fine," he said, feeling amused. She was right about Phoebe.

"Jake, I can't believe I'll have a regular salary like other people." Her voice was earnest, and he felt a clutch in his heart because he knew how hard she'd had to work and all the responsibility she shouldered for the Bardwells.

"You deserve this, sweetie."

"I'm okay now. No more tears."

He smiled and touched her cheek. "I'm taking you out to celebrate tonight. Did you make arrangements to have someone take your place at the restaurant?"

"Not yet."

"Do that now if you have to drag someone in off the street to run the place for you. Then you can go see Wilson."

"Yes, sir!" she answered, laughing. Jake leaned forward and brushed her lips lightly. He held the door as they returned to the kitchen.

"Have you had lunch?" she asked him.

"Unfortunately, yes."

"I'll cut you a slice of pie. You can eat while I make my phone calls to get an employee to take my place while I'm gone. I need to check with Wilson Yarrell and ask how soon I can see him. So, do you want blueberry or apple?"

"Apple pie."

While he ate a slice of golden pie and drank a cup of steaming black coffee, she made phone calls. She talked to the cook, then she walked across the room to him. "Mr. Yarrell said to come over now and he could see me."

"I figured he would," Jake said dryly. "The pie was delicious."

"Granddad made the pies this morning. He's getting really good at it."

"I think he and Kyriakos found a mutual interest with their fishing."

"You know Granddad and fishing and his

lures and tackle. I can't imagine Eldon Kyriakos at our house, but then you survived it, so I suppose he will."

Jake smiled and gave her a squeeze. They stepped outside, Samantha clutching the folder of papers tightly in her hand. "Want to come with me now or do you want to look at this later?"

"Let's step into the copy shop and make some copies and I'll go over to Ryan Cain's office and read. You come to his law office when you're done."

In minutes they parted and she crossed the street. He watched her walk toward the bank, his gaze drifting down over the sexy sway of her hips, the tight pull of blue cotton across her derriere, and he was thankful for the offer she had received. He knew without looking at the papers what Wilson Yarrell would tell her. Never again should she have difficulty getting a loan at the bank.

Jake went to the law office and as he entered the small front office, Tammie Jean Risney looked up.

"Good afternoon," she said, smiling, pushing blond curls from her face. "You came at the wrong time. He's in Ardmore today on a case."

"I didn't come to see him. I came to sit down in a quiet corner and read."

"Aw, gee. I thought you were going to say you came to see me," she teased him. They had gone to school together, and he was friends with Fred, her husband, who was Salido High's football coach.

"Darlin', I could ask you to run away with me, but I know Fred would beat me to a pulp. I'd be a little wizened speck needing two nurses to help me around the ranch."

"You might be right," she said, laughing. She waved her hand. "You can even have his honor's office all to yourself."

"You're a doll."

"I hear you and Samantha are dating, and I think that's nice for both of you. I don't know how you wrestled her away from the restaurant, but then I don't know how she wrangled you off the ranch. She's really done something with the restaurant, hasn't she?"

"It's great."

"Fred and I went last Saturday night and we had the best time. I'll tell her when she comes in. And Fred would run off with her if she'd promise to cook those ribs for him every week."

"He'll have to fight me on that one."

Shedding his coat, Jake went into Ryan's office and settled on the leather chair behind the desk, sitting down to open the folder. He read swiftly, scanning the figures, astonished to see that Kyriakos wanted all the buildings owned by the Bardwells. It was a spectacular offer, and Jake was surprised at the amount, because he thought it was far more speculative than he would have guessed Kyriakos would be. He slowed to read specifics about Samantha's job which was not part of the contracts, but the figures were down.

An hour later he heard the front door and Samantha's greeting to Tammie Jean. He closed the folder and picked up his coat.

"Here I am, keeping quiet before Tammie Jean gives me Ryan's phone calls to handle."

"I want to hear him sing with the karaoke this weekend," Tammie Jean said to Samantha.

"You'll have to talk him into it. I wouldn't begin to try."

"If we have snow Saturday, I'll sing. Thanks for the use of the office and tell Ryan I stopped by."

"You bet. If it snows you have to keep your promise. I remember when you sang at the senior breakfast."

He grinned and held the door for Samantha. "And I remember when you and Fred got caught skinny-dipping—"

"Jake Colby, you swore you wouldn't tell!"

He laughed and closed the door, turning to take Samantha's arm. "Now can I take you home, and you get ready to go out with me to celebrate? Or we can go like you are now, because you look gorgeous."

"Thanks, but take me home." She glanced at her watch.

"You won't be any good at the restaurant, because I know you're in shock, so don't think about going back to work."

"You might be right."

As soon as they were in his Bronco, she turned to him. "Mr. Yarrell looked everything over and said he thought it was a grand offer."

"I do, too. It's a good offer. I'm surprised he has that much faith in Salido, because what he plans goes beyond just the restaurant."

"He thinks Salido and Lake Lewiston can be a good tourist attraction."

"Oh, Lord."

"He wants to build a lodge at Lake Lewiston." Jake nodded. "That's a beauty of a lake, and it is damned good fishing. I've wondered why someone hasn't come in and done that sooner. I can see why he has such a keen interest in buying part of the town." Jake turned into the driveway of her house. Samantha climbed out, and he draped his arm across her shoulder.

"Anybody home?" she called, and received only silence. Her gaze drifted over the stack of magazines on the stairs, the shirt draped on the banister, a shoe against a corner. "Look at this. Granddad brought Eldon Kyriakos here."

"It won't matter," Jake said, pulling her around, his hands on her waist. He felt a hungry need for her. "It's been too long," he said, his voice lowering. He bent his head to kiss her, his mouth firm on hers, and Samantha wrapped her arms around his neck and stood on tiptoe.

When Jake trailed kisses to her throat, he tugged her belt free and unbuttoned her cotton dress, his fingers lingering on her warm flesh.

"Jake, I never know who will come home or

when they'll come." She caught his hand.

"You're changing clothes. I'll help you get started," he said, pushing open the top of her dress to slide his hand beneath it.

For a moment she yielded to his caresses as he cupped her full softness, kneading and stroking her breast. She caught his hand. "Aunt Phoebe could appear any minute now. Make yourself at home, and I'll hurry."

"Take your time. Want me to come help?"

Samantha looked into dark eyes that were heated with desire and felt another flutter in her pulse. "No, you can't come help, but it isn't because I don't want you to. Go get a beer if you want."

He nodded, but didn't move and she headed toward the stairs. She reached out and knocked the top off the newel post. She knelt to pick it up, glancing at him. "Now I can finally get this fixed."

"If you'd told me, I would have fixed it." He crossed to her as she jammed it back. He removed it.

"Where's Asa keep a hammer?"

"In the kitchen drawer near the door." She went upstairs and at the landing looked down to see Jake still standing at the foot of the stairs.

"I like the view."

"Pervert."

He grinned as she went around the turn and up the rest of the stairs. She yanked off the dress and studied her clothes, her mind con-

160

ZEBRA HOME SUBSCRIPTION SERVICES, INC.
LUCKY IN LOVE
120 BRIGHTON ROAD
P.O. BOX 5214
CLIFTON, NEW JERSEY 07015-5214

This is your
best chance
to get
"LUCKY IN
LOVE".
Fill in the
coupon
and mail this
postcard
today.
(See inside for
FREE
OFFER.)

# FREE BOOK CERTIFICATE

## LUCKY IN LOVE

P.O. Box 5214    120 Brighton Road    Clifton, New Jersey 07015-5214

Zebra Home Subscription Services, Inc.

**YES,** I want my luck to change. Send me my gift of 4 Free LUCKY IN LOVE Romances. Then each month send me the four newest LUCKY IN LOVE novels for my Free 10-day preview. If I decide to keep them, I'll pay the low preferred Home Subscriber's price of just $3.00 each; a total of $12.00. This is a savings of $2.00 off the publisher's cover price. Otherwise, I will return them for full credit. There is no shipping and handling charge. There is no minimum purchase amount and I may cancel this arrangement at any time. Whatever I decide to do, the Free books are mine to keep.

NAME

STREET ADDRESS                                    APT.

CITY                          STATE              ZIP CODE

(      )
TELEPHONE NUMBER                   SIGNATURE (if under 18, parent or
                                             guardian must sign.)

LILBOB

Change Your Luck Today. Fill-out And Mail The FREE BOOK Certificate. We'll Send You Your Free Gift As Soon As We Receive It!

stantly jumping back to the offer. She crossed to the phone and sat down on the sagging mattress and called the restaurant. She recognized Asa's voice when he answered.

"Granddad? I'm at home and I'm going out with Jake. Ted said he could be there tonight to manage things. He'll be in at five. Jake wanted to take me out. Mr. Kyriakos made us a nice offer and tomorrow morning I'll go over it with you."

"You want to sell the place?" Asa asked, sounding surprised.

"I'll still work there managing it, and I imagine you can, too, if you want. It's a nice offer, Granddad. I showed it to Wilson Yarrell and Jake has looked at the papers. If you want, I can come back down to the restaurant and show them to you now, or I can leave them under your pillow."

"Leave them under my pillow. Jake thinks the sale would be good?"

"Yes, sir, he does. So does Mr. Yarrell. So do I and I think you will, too."

"I trust your judgment, honey. You got us this far."

"Granddad, I'm not telling the family until we've discussed it. I think it's best not to tell them until we're sure we have a deal."

"It's that good, huh?" he asked, his voice sounding curious.

"Yes, sir. Jake wants to take me out. He said I won't be able to work, anyway, for thinking about the offer and he's right," she said, hearing hammering downstairs.

"Maybe I'll come home early. Don't tell me now, though, because I need to do some cooking. You sound real happy, honey."

"I am."

"I didn't give it much thought, because I didn't think you'd be interested. You go out with Jake, and we'll talk in the morning. Have a good time. I love you."

"I love you, too," she said, feeling her throat constrict again as she thought about what the sale would do for Asa. Wiping her eyes, she replaced the receiver and went to the closet to look at what she could wear. Jake had seen everything she owned. She pulled out a green sundress and went to the bathroom to shower.

Forty minutes later she went downstairs to look for Jake, and an hour later they flew toward Houston to celebrate.

Over dinner Jake looked at the sparkle in her eyes and he realized how keyed up she was. Her cheeks were flushed, and she smiled continually. He felt a deep-running happiness for her, and he was even more sure about what he wanted in the future.

Now wasn't the night to discuss their relationship, because her thoughts were on Kyriakos's deal, but Jake thought about marriage often. As he looked at her, he felt a hot twist of longing. It was desire and love. This change in jobs should make it easier for her to accept a proposal, because her family would be well taken care of by the proceeds from the sale.

"Tell me what Kyriakos said." Jake watched her as he sipped his white Chardonnay.

"I'll work in Salido most of the time. When he's ready to open a new place, I'll go wherever it is for the opening. Then I'll return to work in Salido. Jake, it sounds grand. Of course, the most marvelous thing to me is the regular salary. Until the past few months, the restaurant has fluctuated so badly. Some months I couldn't take home a salary." Suddenly her gaze changed, and she reached across the table to take his hand.

The casual touch made his pulse jump. He squeezed her cool, slender fingers.

"I've talked all evening, and you're nice to sit and listen to all this."

"I want to hear it and I'm glad you've told me your plans. That's why I'm here. If I had just sold the ranch, you'd discuss it with me." He raised her hand to brush her knuckles with his lips. Her skin was soft, faint calluses on her palm from work in the kitchen at the restaurant.

"Let's go dancing and you keep talking and I'll keep listening and looking. I'm happy for you, honey."

She looked down, biting her lip, and he knew whenever she thought about her family and particularly Asa, she became emotional. "I haven't told Granddad the details yet. I left the papers for him to look at tonight, and he said we'd talk in the morning."

"I imagine he'll sleep undisturbed by the offer, because Asa takes life as it comes, and his first love is fishing."

"After this he can spend all the time he wants at Lake Lewiston."

Jake motioned to the waiter and they left. Their hotel suite overlooked the twinkling lights of town, but she barely noticed, because as soon as he closed the door, Jake pulled her into his arms to kiss her.

With clothing strewn from the door to the bed, he made love until finally he was poised above her. "I love you, Samantha," he said hoarsely.

She drew a deep breath, pulling him down. "I love you," she whispered in return.

Need swamped him, his pulse roaring in his ears, his heart pounding. He felt as if he would burst if he didn't take her then. He lowered himself, rocked by her softness, trying to keep control to give her as much pleasure as possible until he was pushed over a brink.

Later as she lay in his arms, he held up her hand, playing with her fingers. She wriggled away and leaned over him.

"Jake, I'm so happy!"

"So am I, love."

"I can't wait to see what Granddad has to say."

"Speaking of family—I better take you home now."

"Want to be rid of me?"

164

He rolled her over, turning to look at her and pull her to him. "What do you think?" His hands stroked her breasts and she inhaled swiftly, catching his hands.

"I was teasing. I do have to go home." She slid away and gathered her things, leaving him as she went into the bathroom. He stared into space, trying to think where to take her out when he proposed. He strapped on his watch and looked at the time. He needed to get her home.

They flew to Salido and drove down dark, deserted Main Street toward her house. As Jake turned the corner onto Oak, she could see the blaze of lights.

"Jake, look! Do you think something has happened?"

# Chapter Eight

"Yes, I do," he said dryly. She should have guessed. "Asa couldn't wait to tell the family."

She clutched her heart and sighed. "If that's all—" She straightened in the seat. "I was scared something dreadful had happened to one of them."

Jake turned into the driveway and came around to take her arm.

"Come in with me—"

The front door burst open and Bernie stuck his head outside.

"She's home!" he shouted, and Samantha walked faster.

"Bernie! Lower your voice. You'll wake all the neighbors." Her pulse raced, because her family knew and Asa knew. She couldn't wait to see him.

A light came on in an upstairs bedroom across the street and Samantha saw the curtain jiggle.

"Jake, this deal may be all over Salido before I see Mr. Kyriakos again."

166

"It shouldn't change his offer if they put up banners."

"You're sure?"

"I'm positive, Samantha. He knows what he wants."

"I'd like you to stay for a little while, but I'll warn you, this will be bedlam."

His answer was lost as the door burst open again and Myra, Tom and Bernie came rushing out. Phoebe followed them.

"Granddad told us about Mr. Kyriakos," Bernie said. "He's buying the restaurant, and we'll be rich!"

"We're going to be a lot better off than we have been," she replied. "Now let's get inside before we wake all the neighbors."

"Is this true, Samantha?" Phoebe asked

"It's true, Aunt Phoebe, but let's talk in the house."

They entered the hall and Asa was waiting. "Evenin', Jake," he said, shaking hands with Jake. His blue eyes sparkled as he looked at Samantha and shrugged. "I let the cat out of the bag." Asa held out his arms, and she felt a twist to her heart.

Samantha walked over to hug him. She looked up at him. "Do you like his offer?"

"It's a dream come true, honey. For all of us." Tears filled his eyes, and she felt another wrench.

"I want ballet lessons," Myra said, turning on her toes.

"Listen, all of you," Samantha ordered, in

control of her emotions. "I haven't accepted the offer yet. He could change his mind—"

The groans drowned her out, and she waved her hands. "Cool it until I see him tomorrow and it becomes official. Now can you do that?" she asked, looking at each one and finally at Jake who smiled and winked.

"When the deal is finalized, I'll call home. Jake wants to take us all out to celebrate tomorrow night."

"Whooie!" Bernie shouted, jumping in the air. Myra and Tom let out whoops.

"Until then," Samantha admonished, "not a word to anyone."

"You're going to work for this Mr. Kyriakos?" Phoebe asked.

"Yes, I am. I'll have a wonderful, regular salary and we can all count on a certain amount coming in each month." She glanced at Asa. "Granddad can retire if he wants. You too, Aunt Phoebe."

"Oh, dear, no. I love my little shop. I might get my hair fixed by Ellie though. That would be nice. And I've been wanting to send off for some material to make a dress to wear when I take people on tour. You know, Samantha, I think there'll be more people here, visiting Salido."

"I'm sure there will be."

"Granddad said we could open a bottle of wine and celebrate," Bernie wheedled. "He said we had to wait for you and Jake."

"I don't think we should celebrate until—"

"Samantha, this is just a little celebration," Asa prompted. "They've been waiting hours."

She glanced at Jake. "All right. Let's open the wine."

Bernie led the way to the kitchen, and Jake took the corkscrew to open the bottle and pour. Myra and Bernie passed out the drinks.

"To the sale." Jake lifted his glass to touch Samantha's and then Asa's and Myra's before he took a sip. He looked in Samantha's eyes and saw her satisfaction and joy.

"Can we get a new car?" Myra asked. "Something cool like a Corvette."

"No!" Bernie interrupted. "A pickup like Jake's. That's what we need."

"We couldn't all get into a pickup," Myra stated.

Samantha wound her way past the family and took Jake's arm to go to the front porch and sit on the swing.

"You're a good sport to stay through all this." Relaxing, she swung gently back and forth while a soothing breeze blew over them.

"You're going to have your hands full at home."

"It'll calm down. It all sounds so big to them now, and I don't want to dampen their enthusiasm about it tonight. When they find out the money will go into the bank for their college educations and it'll go for straightening teeth and getting glasses and repairs around here, they'll settle down."

"I'm sure they will. They're too close kin to you, love. Asa looks as if he's in more shock than you."

"I guess he felt more responsibility for us than I realized." She placed her head on Jake's shoulder as he rocked gently. "I don't think I'll sleep tonight."

"You're not going to have to worry about it much longer. It's four in the morning now."

"No!"

"If we were still in Houston, I might get you to sleep," he said softly, looking down at her and kissing her temple.

"Why do I doubt that we would sleep?"

He laughed and turned her chin up to him to kiss her lightly. "It was fun."

"Yes. I'm going to be nervous today, waiting for three o'clock to come."

"It will roll around, and the deal will be done."

"Can you be there?" She wanted his calm presence.

"You want me?"

"Very much. Bring Melody into town with you and she can stay here with Myra." She touched his thick curls. "Jake, I can't wait for three o'clock."

"It'll get here, love. I promise you."

She finally kissed him goodbye and watched him drive away. Asa told her to stay home during the morning, so she slept five hours and spent the morning doing chores at home. At one o'clock she took a leisurely time to dress in a straight green cotton sheath and green pumps. She washed and dried and fluffed out her hair, letting it curl loosely over her shoulders, looking at herself. What changes would the sale bring into her life? So far she felt keyed up and excited. She fastened gold hoop earrings in her ears and a thin gold chain around her neck, glancing again at the time. Her nervousness mounted as the hour neared to meet Kyriakos.

It seemed like days instead of only hours, but finally she faced Eldon Kyriakos across the same table at the restaurant. They made their agreements, signed the contracts, and then the preliminaries of the sale were over. She shook hands with him, and he turned to shake hands with Asa and then Jake.

"We'd be happy to have you stay and celebrate with us," Jake invited. "I'm taking everyone out."

"I'd like to, but I have an appointment in Tulsa. When I leave here, I fly to Tulsa, and at seven this evening my staff has set up a press conference. The media is interested in what I plan to do here and at Lake Lewiston." He turned to her. "Thank you, Samantha, Asa. Here's to a rosy future," he said, holding his glass of water while they had a brief toast.

As soon as Kyriakos left them, she kissed Asa's cheek and turned when Jake gave her a squeeze.

"Congratulations, honey."

"I'll call and tell everyone we're coming home," Asa said.

"We'll get a lot of attention the next few days," she said to Jake.

"You mean you'll get a lot of attention. If it gets too bad, I'll take you away or you can come hide at the ranch."

"Thanks. Here comes Wilson Yarrell." Surprised, she looked toward the door.

"You're going to find all sorts of new friends," Jake remarked dryly.

The banker smiled broadly as he approached them. "Samantha, I had to come over and congratulate you. Hi, Jake." Wilson Yarrell shook hands with Jake and turned to take Samantha's hand. "This is just wonderful for you and Asa and your family and our town. It's a red letter day for us."

"Thank you, Mr. Yarrell."

"Wilson, Samantha. I've known you all your life. No need for formalities."

For one minute she remembered her arguments with him over the few thousand for the loan to fix up the restaurant. She smiled and picked up the folder. "I'll stop by the bank in a little while."

"Good. Anything you want, you just come see me."

"Thank you."

"Where's Asa? I want to congratulate him."

"He's in the kitchen calling the family. Jake's

172

taking us out tonight to celebrate."

"Good for you. Have fun all of you. I'll just step into the kitchen and speak to Asa. See you both later."

"My goodness, he's gotten friendly. When I went into this business, I had to argue for thirty minutes to get my loan."

"You'll see a lot of changes." Jake looked down at her and she smiled, feeling excitement bubble in her, wondering if all the Bardwells' problems were over.

At five o'clock Jake herded them into his Bronco, and they fit into a plane he'd chartered with a pilot to fly the family to Dallas. They ate dinner high in a restaurant overlooking Dallas, and while everyone was talking, Jake reached over to give her hand a squeeze. She returned it, wanting to be alone with him.

Melody sat between Phoebe and Myra, who both fussed over her, and she seemed to enjoy herself. When they were back in the plane, she scooted closer to Jake. "Can I stay at Samantha's tonight? I'll sleep in Myra's room. She asked me."

"We'd love to have her. Let her sleep over, Jake," Samantha urged. "School starts next Monday, and things will change then, but this week our schedule is easy."

He glanced at Melody and nodded. "It's fine. I'll pick you up in the morning."

173

"I'm not baby-sitting tomorrow. I can be home with her," Myra said.

"I'll be there most of the time, but I'm going to Ellie's and get my hair done," Phoebe said.

"I'll come around eleven to pick her up." Jake glanced at Samantha. "And take you to lunch."

"All right, but pretty soon I have to stop taking so much time off and settle back to work. It'll be a while before the closing on the real estate transaction."

"When do you start to work for him?"

"We have a closing date set for September eighteenth. I'll start to work the first of October."

That night when they were finally home and everyone settled and Jake had kissed Melody good night, Samantha sat on the porch with him. When he said it was time to start home, she squeezed his hand.

"Thanks for the dinner for all of us, for chartering the plane and flying us to Dallas."

"Next time we'll try for a day at Six Flags."

"You can't keep taking this whole family on these jaunts."

"I enjoy your family," he said walking around to the driver's side of the Bronco and opening the door. "I wish you'd go home with me."

"I can't."

He tilted her chin up and kissed her lightly. "When do I get you to myself? Sunday night?"

"Fine. I wonder how long it will take for me to realize this has really happened?"

"I don't think it'll take long. You'll be constantly reminded by the changes."

"I suppose. I'm going to have to figure out allowances for Bernie and Tom and Myra, although Asa will want to do theirs."

"You're more their mother than their sister."

She shrugged and glanced at the house. "I've had to be. Granddad and I just pool all the resources to make ends meet. I don't mind. Two lots are still in his name, so some of the money goes directly to him. The rest of the real estate he had deeded over to me so it would be in my name if anything happened to him. That way the money goes to me, but I still feel like the proceeds from the real estate are Granddad's." She reached out to place her hand against Jake's chest and look up at him. She didn't really want to think about real estate and business. She wanted to be with Jake. "I'll be glad when Sunday night gets here."

"So will I, love." He kissed her cheek and climbed inside to drive away.

At the restaurant the next day Samantha looked up as the door opened mid-morning. It was the lull between breakfast and lunch and few customers came to the restaurant. When the door was open, sunlight splashed over a woman with the reddest hair Samantha had ever seen. It was a shining nimbus of scarlet flames around her head.

"Samantha, I think we should order another three dozen buns," Asa said behind her, coming out of the kitchen. "We're—"

"Granddad—" Words failed her.

"Good morning," he said politely to the woman, glancing at her over his glasses. Samantha stared in shock as she recognized the woman with the fiery hair.

"Aunt Phoebe?"

"Good God!" Asa exclaimed, pushing his bifocals up. "Holy elves!" he exclaimed again. "You've been in the paint bucket—"

Samantha nudged him. "You had your hair dyed?" she asked, staring at the brilliant red hair and her orange-brown brows and lashes.

"Do you like it?" Phoebe smiled, turning her head.

"You look like Little Orphan Annie turned a grandmother," Asa said. "My God, Phoebe, the fire department will hose you down. They'll think you're on fire."

"Oh, Dad, don't be ridiculous!" She patted her hair. "I just love it and I think I look years younger and will have more mystique now."

"Mystique!" Asa exclaimed. "You stand out like a two-headed pink mule."

"That's quite a change, Aunt Phoebe. Ellie did your hair?"

"Yes, she did. She said to tell you that she's sorry, but she has to cancel your time today."

Samantha felt a swift rush of disappointment because she had looked forward to sharing her good news with Ellie. It was the first time in

176

years Ellie had canceled, and Samantha wondered what had happened.

"I think I look so much like Nell Payne—remember the actress? You're too young, Samantha, but Dad, you remember her and her gorgeous red hair."

"Phoebe," he snapped, "that woman—"

"Granddad, may I see you just a moment?" Samantha asked quickly. "Aunt Phoebe, sit down and I'll get someone to bring you a cherry coke. We'll be right back." She steered Asa toward the kitchen, and the minute they stepped inside he looked up at her, pushing his glasses higher on his nose.

"Reggie, my aunt is out there," Samantha said. "Would you take her a cherry coke please."

"Sure," he replied, reaching for a glass. "For Mrs. Ruffin?"

"It's the woman whose hair looks on fire," Asa explained.

"Granddad—" Samantha glanced at Reggie. "Yes, it's Aunt Phoebe."

"You think Reggie would recognize her? I didn't know my own daughter at first," Asa said as Reggie left the kitchen.

"You have an appointment with the eye doctor in three hours. Granddad, listen. It won't do any good to fuss about her hair, because it's dyed. It has to grow out now."

"Can't they dye it some other color, like a normal brown?"

"Do you think Aunt Phoebe would look good

with brown? And it would be red-brown. She is so happy with it—what's it going to hurt?"

He studied Samantha and rubbed his chin and finally shrugged. "I guess you're right. Why not? I'm not taking her fishing with me, though. She'd scare them away."

"You don't have to take her fishing. Most of the time she's in her shop or in front of a television."

"Or giving visitors tours of the town."

"It'll add a little spice to the tour."

He smiled. "Okay, I won't say another word. How you'll get Tom and Bernie and Myra—"

"Oh, my gosh. I better go out the back way and catch them before they see her," she said, feeling panicked. "Granddad, Jake is picking up Melody and then coming to get me. If he gets here while I'm gone, send him to the house."

"Yep. I wonder if it glows in the dark?"

"Of course not! Granddad, you know how sensitive Aunt Phoebe is. She'll be crushed if the kids laugh at her or if anyone is unkind about her appearance."

"I won't say another thing to her about it."

Reggie returned, chuckling, but the moment he saw them, he ducked his head and hurried across the kitchen and went out the back door.

"Kid's about to bust his sides laughing," Asa said. "What do you think Bernie and Tom will do? That was just Reggie, who isn't related to her and his brain runs on two watts."

"I'm on my way home," Samantha stated

178

grimly, yanking off her apron and hurrying out the back door. Reggie was chuckling, puffing on a cigarette which he hid from Samantha instantly.

"I'll be back soon, Reggie." She didn't care to talk about the family to Reggie. She rushed down Main, the sun hot on her shoulders as she spoke to everyone she passed.

Cars drove by on the wide cobbled street, and while she hurried along, she heard a low whistle.

"Hey, pretty lady, how about a ride?" came a male voice.

She laughed and turned around to see Jake pull to the curb. She climbed in beside him. "You'll stir up rumors if people heard you and didn't see whom I accepted a ride from."

"Everyone in Salido knows my truck," he said, stroking her knee. "What's the rush?"

"Oh, Jake. The changes have started: Aunt Phoebe got a new hairdo. It's fire-engine red and it's all fluffed out. She thinks it's wonderful. I took Granddad aside and got him calmed down, but I was hurrying home to get to the kids before they see her. They're going to explode."

Jake chuckled. "Phoebe enjoys life. She's putting some zing in those tours of hers. I heard someone in Monroe say they didn't know someone in your family was married to one of the Draytons."

"What?" Shocked, Samantha stared at him.

He grinned. "Phoebe's just putting a little life in her tour. You know she takes visitors out to the cemetery to show them the Draytons' graves."

"We're not related to the Draytons! For heaven's sake—"

"Let her enjoy herself, honey. What's it hurt?"

"That's what I said to Granddad about her hair. My word. She's telling people we're related to outlaws."

"They've been dead for generations. It adds some color."

"So does her hair. I don't know if I can control Bernie on this one."

"Want me to talk to him?"

"You think you can convince him?"

"I think so," Jake answered easily.

"Buster, you've got a deal," she said in a sultry voice, drawing her fingers along his thigh, feeling the hard muscles. "You get Bernie to lay off teasing her, and Tom and Myra will follow his lead. You do that," she stated in a breathy voice, leaning closer to him, "and I'll try to think of something to do to please you."

"Samantha, I may hit a tree if you don't behave." Jake gripped the steering wheel. "And we're coming back to this conversation when I'm not driving."

She smiled at his profile and finally he glanced at her. "I won't be able to get out of the truck."

"You'll calm. Thanks, Jake. Now pray they're home."

They were all on the porch, and as Jake and Samantha approached, Melody ran out to meet them. She wore blue shorts and a blue shirt and her hair was in pigtails. He caught her up to hug her. "How's my girl?"

"Fine. Myra braided my hair. See?"

"It's cute. Honey, you and Samantha and Myra stay here a minute. I want to talk to the boys." He swung her down on the porch and she ran to Myra.

"Bernie, you and Tom come with me. I need to see you guys."

Bernie looked worried and Tom mystified as both went down the porch steps. Myra raised her eyebrows. "What's up?" she whispered to Samantha. "What have they done?"

"Let's go inside and you and I can talk. I want to comb my hair, so let's go up to my room."

Myra's eyes became round and she took Melody's hand. In her bedroom, Samantha brushed her hair as Myra sat on the rocker and gave a kaleidoscope to Melody.

"Myra, there's something I want you to promise me you'll do."

"What's that?"

"Be good to Aunt Phoebe."

"Why wouldn't I be?"

Samantha took a deep breath. "She's dyed her hair bright red."

"Is that all? Sure. What's the big deal? Is that why Jake is talking to the guys?"

"It's glow-in-the-dark red and all frizzed out. Granddad didn't recognize her at first."

"No kidding?" Myra's brows arched. "Cool!"

"Reggie had to run out into the alley to get over his laughter."

"Aunt Phoebe? Gee, when will she be home?"

"Anytime now. Will you not tease her?"

"No! Wow. That may be kinda neat and punk, you know. Maybe we could put a green streak—"

"Myra! Don't you dare put a green or yellow or any other color streak in her hair. Promise me!"

"Aw, Samantha, why not? Gee, red. If she had a green streak in it and maybe purple, and we combed it straight up in the air—wow!"

Samantha marched closer and leaned forward. "Don't even think about it."

Myra blinked. "All right, all right. But Aunt Phoebe's fun. I mean she watches all the movies and she might like some black leather boots—"

"Myra, so help me . . ."

"Okay, I won't suggest it. Now if she does it on her own, don't blame me."

"I'm going down to find Jake. Melody, let's find your daddy."

Melody took her hand and they went downstairs where Jake and the boys were tossing a baseball in the front yard. Bernie grinned and looked at her as they came outside.

"We promised Jake we'd be good."

"Thank you. I don't want Aunt Phoebe hurt. It's done and she has to live with it."

"We're going, guys," Jake said, taking Melody's hand. All three got into the pickup, and

Jake buckled Melody in beside him.

From the truck Samantha waved to her brothers and Myra. "Thank you," she said to Jake.

"You're welcome. I think they're rather intrigued with the whole idea."

"Myra thinks it's grand. Wanted to dye a green streak and get her black leather boots."

He chuckled. "See, lots of worry about nothing. Just relax—" He broke off to give a low whistle. "Wow. The media will love her."

Samantha looked down the street and spotted the flaming halo of red caught in full glory in midday sunlight as Phoebe walked home.

"Wanda Mayfield may have to go to the emergency for shock."

Jake hit the horn a couple of times. Melody rose up as far as the buckle would allow and waved, and Phoebe returned the greeting.

Samantha stared at Phoebe's hair and wondered if some of the changes would make Phoebe's hair pale in comparison.

"Jake, this is the first day, and already we've had one drastic change in the family. And what I'd like to do—"

"What's that?" he asked, turning to park in front of the restaurant.

They went inside and sat at a corner booth. "What is it you'd like to do?" he asked after he had ordered ribs and a child's plate for Melody, and Samantha had ordered a salad.

"I need some clothes for my new job. I've made nearly everything I own and Myra's clothes too, and they're all worn. I want to go to Ardmore and shop for a few things. Just so I'll have a couple of dresses to work in when I'm away from here. I don't own a suit."

"How about taking off next weekend? I'll pick you up Friday and you can shop in Dallas. We'll take Melody to her grandparents—" He paused to look at her seated beside him. "Would you like to see Granny and Gramps?"

"Yes, sir. Today?"

"No, in a few days. You could meet them, Samantha. We'll come back Sunday, and that would give you all day Saturday to shop."

"Sounds great, Jake." She saw the flare of passion in his dark eyes. They would spend the nights in each other's arms. She glanced out the front window. "I hope today doesn't hold another surprise."

Hours later she remembered her words to Jake. When she walked in the house and closed the door, Tom tried to bite back laughter.

"Samantha?" Myra called from upstairs. Tom ran out giggling, and Samantha's suspicions stirred.

"Yes?"

"I've got a surprise. Close your eyes."

# Chapter Nine

"You didn't dye your hair?" she snapped.

"No, but I want to talk to you about that. Close your eyes. Lori Marie cut my hair, and it's real cute."

Samantha wanted to groan, but she had allowed Myra to choose her own hairstyles for two years now. "My eyes are closed," she said and listened to footsteps.

"Ta-da!" Myra exclaimed and Samantha opened her eyes to see Myra in raggedy cutoffs and a tank top and a new haircut.

"Oh, no. Myra—"

"I think it's great!"

Samantha stared at hair that was an inch long on one side, gradually tapering to shoulder length on the other side of Myra's face. "Myra, that's crazy. You look as if you stepped out of the middle of a haircut."

"It's uniquely me. Now, please, please, please let me bleach it blond."

The no was on the tip of Samantha's tongue,

but she stared at the long-short style and decided to let Myra get some things out of her system. "Yes, if you'll let Ellie or someone who knows what she is doing dye it for you. No more home cuts by your friends."

Myra ran down the steps and lunged to hug Samantha. "You're a neat big sister!"

Samantha laughed, looking at the black earrings dangling in Myra's ears. "Why not? It'll take some of the attention from Aunt Phoebe."

The back door slammed and Bernie came striding into the hallway. He was in faded, torn cutoffs and a T-shirt and worn sneakers, his long brown hair curling on his shoulders. "Hi. Samantha, may I see you a moment?"

She prayed it wouldn't be any worse than the hairdos, because she knew from his tone of voice that Bernie wanted something.

"Gol, what happened to you?" he asked Myra, touching her short hair. She jerked her head away.

"Lori Marie cut my hair. I think it's neat."

"Weird. But okay." He looked at Samantha and she turned toward the dining room. Myra tagged along, and he glared at her.

"Beat it, kid."

"Aw, Bernie."

"And don't listen at the door."

They entered the dining room and closed the door and he knelt to look through the keyhole. "Sis, I want to ask you if I can do something."

Bernie made most of his decisions, because he would be out of school in one more year and on his own, so she wondered what was coming that he felt he needed her permission. It had to be big.

"Sis, you know the money from my job that I was saving to go to college?"

"Yes."

"Well, I figure from what you say, that we'll have money for college. So what I'm wondering is, can I get some wheels with that money."

Bernie and Tom had been good to ride their bikes when their friends drove cars. She nodded. "I think that's fine if you get some kind of nice used car that you can afford and keep in shape."

"Geez, Sis, that's great. Will you smooth it over with Granddad? You know, that's really great! I hoped you'd feel that way, because I'm test-driving right now."

"Test-driving? Bernie, you can't go out and get something brand new."

"It's had one owner and it's a dilly. I can get it for all but one hundred dollars of my savings, but then it'll be mine free and clear and I'll have transportation to school next year and in college."

"That's wonderful. Let's go look at it."

He held the door and she felt a ripple of suspicion. He was still too polite and the deal sounded too good.

"Geez, Sis, you are great," he exclaimed, giving her a hug. "The greatest. Oh, by the way. It's not a car."

She stopped and looked at him. "Not a car?" She peered through the front window. "Bernie—"

"Come on!" he exclaimed and ran outside, jumping off the porch steps.

She went out and stared at the big, black Harley Davidson sitting in the front yard like a hulking monster. Panic seized her. "Bernie, no!"

"You said I could. I'd rather have this than some old rolling junk heap."

"I didn't know—"

"This is great and I'll wear a helmet and I won't speed."

"Wow, Bernie," Myra said, running her fingers along the handlebars. "Give me a ride."

"Bernie, I need to see you alone," Samantha said emphatically.

"Aw, geez, Samantha. Come on, you said I could get transportation."

She turned and went inside, and in seconds he joined her and closed the door.

"No."

"Samantha, I want this. If you say no, Granddad will refuse and I won't get to keep it. I promise I'll wear a helmet."

"Bernie, bikes are so dangerous."

"Look, in a month I'm eighteen. In a year I'll graduate and I'll buy one then, anyway. How much will I ride this around Salido?"

She thought it over, knowing that he would be

able to make his own decisions soon and he had worked hard to save the money. She studied him, seeing a faint stubble of beard on his chin, looking at the firm muscles in his arms, knowing he was growing up. And he had been so cooperative through the tough times. His blue eyes were wide, expectant. "All right, if you'll follow some rules."

"Okay," he replied, suddenly smiling, his crooked teeth and new braces showing.

"You can't let Myra ride on it at all. Even though Tom will be seventeen this year, I don't want him taking it. I don't care if you teach him to ride it, because I know you will, anyway, but don't let him have it."

"Okay. Thanks. That's great, Sis." He grinned. "Want to go for a spin?"

"No! Bernie, please be careful. I don't approve and I'll worry about you."

"I'll be careful," he promised and winked at her. He left the room, his long brown hair swaying with his steps, the one earring glinting dully. Bernie was growing up. Their lives were changing; Jake was all important in her life now. With the restaurant's success some of her friends were changing, particularly Ellie.

She thought about Ellie canceling their appointment. She had only done that twice in all the years since Samantha had returned from college. And Ellie hadn't called about the deal with Kyriakos. Usually if there was any big news, Ellie was on the phone as soon as she was finished work.

Samantha's thoughts shifted back to Jake and the next weekend, when they were going to Dallas.

On Saturday in Dallas Jake gave her the car he had rented when they'd arrived at Love Field. They would stay overnight at the Fairmont. He had errands downtown in walking distance of the hotel, and he said he would see her back at the Fairmont at four, giving her the day to shop.

At four o'clock he looked up when she unlocked the door to the suite and entered. He let out a low whistle and came up out of the chair, his senses reeling. She wore a purple dress of some soft, clinging material that sent his temperature climbing like a tropical heat wave as he watched her hold open the door. "I have boxes . . ." she said, blushing, and he knew she had never gone on a shopping spree before in her life as the bellboy wheeled in a cart. Jake pulled out his wallet to tip him and watched her walk into the room. The door closed with a click, and they were alone.

"Come here, Samantha," Jake told her softly, watching her cross the room to him. He framed her face in his hands. "You look gorgeous."

She looked up at him, her eyes changing to blue flames. "I bought this dress with you in mind. I'm glad you like it, Jake."

"What I like most about it," he whispered, kissing her throat and caressing her nape, finding the zipper and tugging it slowly down, "is taking it off you."

It fell around her feet, and if she cared that her best and newest dress lay in a heap on the floor, she didn't seem to notice. As he leaned back to look at her, he forgot it. She wore scraps of hot-pink lace, a bra and panties that he could stuff into his wallet without causing a bulge.

He flicked the clasp and pushed away the bra to caress her. "You are the most gorgeous woman," he said, suddenly wrapping his arms around her, wanting her badly. Jake kissed her hard, crushing her to him, winding his fingers in her long, silky hair, feeling the heat of her mouth, her soft body in his arms.

He forgot the gift that he had intended to give to her when she came home. Over an hour later she lay stretched against his naked body, both of them warm from lovemaking. As he trailed his fingers along her shoulder, he remembered the necklace.

"I went shopping, too." He slid off the bed and returned. Samantha watched him walk with as much ease as if he were fully dressed. Her pulse skittered as she looked at the flex of powerful muscles, his flat stomach and broad, powerful chest, his narrow hips and maleness. She didn't notice that he had a package in his hands until he placed it on her legs. She stroked his thigh and sat up to open a box wrapped in bright green foil and tied with a silk bow. She tore away the paper swiftly, to find a long velvet box.

She looked up at him. "Jake?" She opened the lid. Her breath caught as she looked at a sparkling diamond pendant. Jake took it to fasten it around her slender neck, and it was cold against her flesh, glittering in the afternoon light.

"Thank you, Jake. It's gorgeous." She felt overwhelmed with the gift, because she had never received anything like it.

Her gaze swept over his strong shoulders and she pushed him down. "Jake," she said softly. "Be still." She shifted to kiss him lightly across his jaw and down his throat to his shoulder, over his chest. She shifted, her tongue trailing fire along his belly and lower, moving down, her fingers stroking him as she kissed his thighs, and he shifted his legs, winding his fingers in her hair.

Suddenly he came up to roll her down and move over her, kissing her hard, his hand stroking her as he plundered her mouth. He spread her legs wide, moving between them to plunge into her, his control shattered by her moist warmth, by her hips thrusting to meet him.

Later as they lay wrapped in each other's arms, her hair spread across his shoulder, she held up the pendant. "Jake, this is beautiful."

"So are you. And we should have twenty-four more undisturbed hours we can spend in bed."

"You won't be able to get up."

"Want to bet what I can get up?"

She laughed as he watched her, and then he bent his head and she wound her arms around his neck. She felt warm, loved, joyous with Jake and her new job. She stroked his shoulders, thinking about the new responsibilities, the solid bank balance.

"Jake, I feel so lucky."

He kissed her throat and gazed into her eyes. "So do I, love. Thank heaven for small pantry windows."

# Chapter Ten

Late Sunday they returned to Salido, and Monday afternoon at closing time Samantha went to Ellie's shop. As she entered, Ellie looked up.

Running her fingers over her tight, black curls, Ellie frowned. Watching her, Samantha felt a ripple of shock.

Ellie's eyes narrowed and she stared at Samantha. "I thought you might stop by."

"Ellie, what's wrong? Has something happened?"

"You don't know?" she asked crossly, brushing black curls away from her face again.

"No. That's why I'm here," she answered, bewildered by Ellie's obvious anger.

"How can you keep from knowing? Our arrangement's over. You don't own the restaurant any longer, so you can't keep your part of the bargain."

"Now I can afford to pay you when you do my hair."

"I've already filled your time," she announced coolly, turning away.

"Ellie! What's wrong?" Samantha crossed the room to her.

With towels in her hands, Ellie turned around. "You and I don't have anything in common, Samantha. You're rich—you have a fancy job."

"I work at the restaurant the same as I always have, for heaven's sake!" she exclaimed, stung by the words. "Ellie, that's absurd. My bank balance has changed—I haven't. It's only been a few days."

Ellie moved away from her to a hamper where she tossed the towels inside and slammed the lid. She picked up a brush and threw it down on the table and turned to yank the plugs of the hand dryers and hot combs from outlets. Her movements were jerky, filled with tight anger. "No, it's not absurd. You date Jake Colby, one of the wealthiest men in this part of the country. You sold the restaurant for a fortune. You have a fancy job. We don't have anything in common."

"We have all the years of friendship." Samantha felt hurt and filled with dismay. "I thought you'd be happy . . ."

"Happy? If it were the other way around, would you stay friends with me?"

"Yes, I would," she replied solemnly, feeling in her heart that she could answer in the affirmative.

195

"Oh, come off it. No, you wouldn't. How could you be at ease?"

"Ellie, that's just absurd."

"It's not. Our lives have taken separate paths."

"You're still friends with Aunt Phoebe and she's wealthier now. This will be her good fortune, too."

"No. She didn't make the sale or change the town or the restaurant. You must feel like Miss Miracle Woman. Phoebe doesn't date a wealthy rancher. She still runs her shop and has her tours."

"I work at Salido Sam's and live in the same house, and when I started dating Jake, you thought it was great."

"That's before you fell into the money pit." She glanced at her watch. "I have a date with Vernon, so if you don't mind—"

"Ellie, our friendship that we've had since first grade is over?" Samantha asked in stunned disbelief. She looked around the small shop where they'd had so many laughs and had shared all their problems and where Ellie had always given her a sympathetic ear.

"I think so." Ellie stared at her, her cheeks red, her lips closed in a thin line.

"Ellie, please stay friends," Samantha implored, hurting and feeling a tight constriction in her chest. "Besides Jake and my family, you're my best friend. You'll toss that aside without

196

giving me a chance to see if I change?"

"You will. You haven't yet, but you're going to. You can't keep from it."

"Ellie, look at my granddad and Aunt Phoebe and the kids. Do you think we'll all be different?"

"No, I don't," she retorted belligerently. "No, I doubt if Asa will. Or Phoebe. But the kids will, and you will. Already Bernie has a motorcycle."

"He bought that with the money he's earned working at the gas station, and you know it!"

"This is just useless. You'll change, and then you won't care, so go on, Samantha. Go on with your marvelous life."

"Ellie, please," Samantha pleaded softly, feeling almost sick from the rift. Ellie turned her back, straightening cords and putting away the combs. She looked over her shoulder.

"You and Jake may be old news soon, too. Even if he is successful, he's a country boy."

"What do you think I am? I was born and raised here."

"Goodbye, Samantha."

She stared at Ellie in amazement and hurt. Then she turned and left the shop and hurried down the street. Still aching with shock, she entered the house. Phoebe was in the front hall.

"Hi, Samantha." She squinted her eyes and peered up at Samantha. "Honey, what's wrong?"

"Aunt Phoebe, I just saw Ellie. She's angry

with me over selling the restaurant. She's furious about my new job."

"Oh, honey," Phoebe sympathized in a soft voice. Phoebe hugged her, and for a moment Samantha patted her frail shoulders.

"Ellie's mad and probably jealous."

"You knew she was mad at me?"

"Yes. She fixed my hair, and she's so enraged there's nothing you can do about it. Maybe in a little time, if she sees you haven't changed, she'll get over her anger. Besides, honey, she may be jealous of what you acquired."

"I know I was lucky, but I worked hard."

"You didn't do anything to cause her anger, so you can't do much to change it."

"It's so hard to believe. I just made the deal. I haven't changed in a few days' time."

"She was furious from the day you were made the offer, because Ellie has it in her head that you'll change and be one of those glamorous women like a movie star."

"I won't. That's impossible."

"I know that, honey, and she should, too, but she doesn't want to face the fact. And I don't think her business has grown the way several in town have. I'm sorry, because you were good friends, and I know it pains you."

"I didn't do anything except try to make a good business deal that helps the whole family."

"That's what's important, Samantha. Maybe

it's times like these when you find out who your true friends are."

"I would have sworn Ellie was one. She sure stuck with me in the bad times." Samantha gazed into Phoebe's sympathetic eyes before turning away. She went upstairs, closing the door to her room and sinking down. The phone rang, and she picked it up to hear Jake's voice.

"Hi. You're home early."

"I just walked in a few minutes ago."

"What's the matter?"

"What makes you think anything is wrong?" she asked, rubbing her forehead.

"C'mon. I can tell that tone of voice. What's happened?"

"It's Ellie. She's so angry, Jake. She says I'll change, and we can't be friends now that I've sold the restaurant."

There was a moment of silence. "I'm sorry. I'm coming to town. Go out with me."

"I won't be good company. I'll probably be better off working."

"I won't be."

She smiled. "Liar."

"C'mon. Get someone to take your place and we're going out. Put on your jeans and get ready. I'll make you forget your troubles or my name isn't Jacob Liddel Colby."

"Liddel?"

"Whoops. Now you know my darkest secret."

199

"I think Liddel is nice," she said, thankful for his support and glad he was perceptive.

"But the name is Jake and it's staying Jake."

"Yes, sir."

"Rescue squad on the way. Get into your jeans. How I wish I could."

She laughed and listened to the receiver click and felt better, until she stared into space a minute and remembered Ellie's anger. A knock came, and Phoebe opened the door.

"Are you all right?"

"Yes. I'm going out with Jake."

"You're okay?" Phoebe asked, looking worried.

"I feel like someone died."

"A friendship did. You go out with Jake. He'll cheer you up. That's good." She smiled and closed the door.

Samantha called the restaurant and hurried to shower, wondering if Ellie would speak when they passed on the street.

The next week passed in a flurry. After the official closing, and signing the contracts for the real estate sale and the sale of the restaurant, Jake flew them all to Dallas for another celebration. The following two weeks Samantha took off work. She studied and made investments, got ready for the new job and took a few days to go

200

to Houston with Jake. She and Asa and Bernie looked at cars, test-driving several. They purchased a black Bronco like Jake's.

And then she settled back into a routine that was the same and yet wasn't the same. The worry was gone. The restaurant's popularity grew—Monroe's fall semester was in full swing. The salary check was regular and her hours were better. Asa continued to cook at lunchtime and seemed to enjoy his freedom.

The first new opening came the second of November in Chicago. When she told Jake she would be gone for three weeks, his eyes narrowed, but he merely asked about her duties and where the restaurant would be located. When the time came to go, he flew her to Oklahoma City to catch a plane to Chicago.

As they stood in the waiting area at Will Rogers Airport, he rubbed his finger along her wrist. "I have your number where you'll be at night, and I know where to call you during the day. Samantha, are you sure you want to go alone?"

"For this first job, yes, I am, Jake. Let me find out what I'm doing and how I do it. Later we can both go, but right now, I might not have any time to see you."

"Okay, maybe you'll finally get more use out of the M.B.A. you earned. I guess I'm concerned because not only will I miss you, but you said that you've never been to Chicago. You told

201

me you've never spent much time in any city that size."

"I'll be all right." She felt pleased by his concern.

"If you decide you want me there, give me a call and I'll come."

"To the rescue."

"I don't know why I'm worrying," he said, rubbing the back of his neck and giving her a lopsided grin. He placed his hand on her shoulder. "Call me tonight."

"I will. Don't worry about me. I'll be fine."

"I know you will. Lord, I'm going to miss you."

A voice called out a number, and she waved her boarding pass at him. "I think I'm supposed to go." She gazed up into his dark eyes and felt a pang. It would be the longest she had gone without seeing him since they met. "Jake—"

He pulled her to him to kiss her. Her hands were pressed between them against his chest, and she wiggled them away. He shifted and wrapped his arms around her and held her tightly.

When he released her, she felt breathless, wanting to stay home and at the same time wanting to accept his offer of going to Chicago with her. She knew he would, without hesitation, yet she felt she had to do this alone. She took a deep breath. "Time passes fast."

"Not when you're the one waiting," he said

quietly. "Get going, Sami."

She hurried toward the plane and glanced back at him. He stood with his feet spread apart, his hands hooked in his belt and a solemn expression on his face that made her feel as if she were being torn in two.

"Jake," she whispered. She turned and hurried toward the plane, finding her first-class seat that had been paid for by Kyriakos Enterprises.

As they taxied away from the airport, she stared at the terminal building and wondered if Jake watched her plane. Chicago. Her palms became sweaty at the thought of being all alone in a city that size.

She read during the flight, her nerves jumping in anticipation of the day. They circled O'Hare for twenty minutes before they were cleared to land, and the airport was jammed with people. The walk to the baggage claim area was long; the wait for her luggage was twenty additional minutes. As she made the long ride into town, she looked at traffic and buildings, feeling dazzled by it all.

At the hotel, she checked into the room reserved for her by the company, unpacked and sat down to call Jake, leaving a message with Mrs. Latham that she was in Chicago.

After changing clothes and eating a light lunch, Samantha took a cab to the restaurant, marveling along the way at the size and congestion of the city, the tall buildings, the crush of people. Awed, she stared at the one-story brick building sprawled on a landscaped lot. Glass and red brick and bright new signs were a far cry from the simple restaurant in a turn-of-the-century building in Salido, Oklahoma.

Her palms were sweaty and she felt chilled and frightened as she paid the driver. Pausing, she continued to stare at the fancy new building, and she felt out of her depth. This wasn't at all like the restaurant at home, and the people weren't going to be the same.

She felt a sense of panic, wanting to turn around and head back to the hotel and to Oklahoma. Squaring her shoulders, she strode toward the double glass doors.

She entered a lobby with pillars of used brick, green ferns in clay pots every few feet, and seating areas enclosed with shining brass rails. A tall cardboard Salido Sam and buffalo stood grinning at her beside the entrance to the bar. She had an impression of polished floors and mirrors and sparkling glassware in the bar.

"May I help you," a blond man in rimless glasses asked. He wore a white apron, and he dried his hands on a towel.

"I'm Samantha Bardwell. Is Mr. Jacoby in?"

"Miss Bardwell! Paul Dirksen. I'm a bartender. He's over this way. I'll get him."

He was gone and back in a minute with a

stocky, dark-haired man with light brown eyes. He flashed a smile that revealed white teeth beneath a hawklike nose. "Miss Bardwell, I'm Tony Jacoby," he greeted warmly.

She shook hands with him. "It's Samantha."

"Let me show you around, and then you have to taste our sauce. Mr. Kyriakos said we're not to open our doors to the public until you say our sauce is one hundred percent right."

"I'm sure it will be."

He grinned at her. "That's nice. Wait until you taste it. Here's the bar and we have everything. A full bar and a bartender with experience. You can see all the dining area here in front, our dance floor, the stage and karaoke."

She looked at the polished tables, orange paper napkins, small stage and dance floor.

"Let me show you our kitchen." He led her through two wide swinging doors into a kitchen of gleaming stainless steel that made her feel as if she had climbed inside a commercial refrigerator. High overhead fans revolved slowly.

"My goodness," she exclaimed in awe, thinking of their battered old pans, the ancient grill, the faulty exhaust. She didn't know what half the appliances in the room were, and she felt a pang of regret when she thought what Asa had had to work with all these years. "This is magnificent."

"Our kitchen?" he asked, laughing.

"You should see ours!" She blinked, wondering when she had become so emotional.

He looked at her warmly. "This is going to be good. I have a feeling. What's your sign?"

"My sign?"

"You know . . . when were you born?"

"July twenty-eighth."

"Ah, you're a Leo! Perfect, the same as mine. I knew this was going to be good. This month my horoscope says there will be cause for celebrating at the office and that this is an excellent time for starting a new job. I can feel in my bones everything is right." He leaned close to her. "Do you feel it, Samantha?"

"Yes," she answered, laughing, feeling relieved to meet him and find he wasn't formidable.

"Good! And look what I have for you," he said, reaching into his pocket. He handed her what looked like a wilted blade of grass until he began to straighten it out in her hand.

"I went out last Sunday and got these for everyone in the restaurant. It took three hours and two fields."

"A four-leaf clover?" She glanced up at him. "I thought good luck came only to the finder."

"No! Most definitely to the possessor. Now come meet everyone and then the real test — we'll taste the sauce."

Relaxing, she followed him through the restaurant to meet five employees. Then Tony led her back to the kitchen to a gleaming pot with bubbling sauce and an automatic stirrer.

He ladled out a soup spoon filled with red sauce, poured it into a small bowl and brought a teaspoon. "Now comes the moment of truth."

Suddenly four employees were standing around watching her. Tony closed his eyes and pulled out another wilted four-leaf clover to hold in his palm. She felt her pulse beat swiftly again and her nerves go back into action. She took the spoon and dipped into the hot sauce, waiting a moment to let it cool and then tasting it. She looked at pale brown eyes and she smiled.

"It's delicious, and it's perfect. It's just like Sa-lido Sam's finger-lickin', pot-scrapin', savory barbecue sauce from Oklahoma."

A cheer went up, and white hats sailed in the air, and then everyone went back to work.

"Come with me." Tony led her to the bar where he pulled out a cold bottle of champagne. He looked at her and lowered the bottle. "No, this is premature. We'll celebrate after the opening night. Ah, Samantha. My horoscope said this would go smoothly. I've opened many new restaurants. Usually everything is screwed up from the first nail in the building to the menu on my last day at the place, but this—" he waved his hand "—is a dream. Don't take it as typical. You'll have an opening like this one, once in a blue moon."

She laughed, feeling pleased. "I was so scared.

Now I'm not. But I don't know Chicago, and while I'm here, I'd like to get a few things."

"We'll see to that. For the next three days we'll get ready for the opening, and then if all goes well and the screw-ups are minimal, I'll show you Chicago and where to shop."

"And I'd like to get my hair done." She shrugged, looking at the gold chain around his neck, the diamond on his finger and his flat gold watch.

"I know just the place. Until then, we roll up our sleeves and go to work. Come to my office and you can put your purse away and tell me about your restaurant."

She entered a spacious office and stood looking at the oil painting behind the desk, the ferns, the bar in the corner, the teak desk. Her gaze went back to him, and he looked amused and curious. His dark brows arched. "Something is wrong? This is better than your office?"

"I don't have an office."

He blinked and looked at her. "You don't have an office?" he repeated, sounding shocked. "A cubbyhole?"

She shook her head and perused his again, astounded at the elegance of it. "No. I don't have a safe . . ."

"Where do you keep the money?"

"In the cash register, and then I walk down to the night depository when we close."

"Mama mia! You walk to the night depository? Samantha, do not ever go on foot to the night depository in Chicago with receipts from the restaurant. Never."

"I didn't plan to," she assured him, looking at a ceiling fan turning slowly overhead.

"Where do you conduct business?"

"Anywhere, but I never have to. Or didn't until Mr. Kyriakos arrived on the scene. Mr. Kyriakos and I made the deal at one of the tables in the restaurant."

A slow grin broke across Tony's face, and he shook his head. "You and Eldon Kyriakos sat at a table in your restaurant and made the deal to buy a whole block of Main Street in Salido, Oklahoma?"

"That's right. And then, Tony, he went home with my grandfather to look at fishing lures."

"Oh, my God. I knew you were provincial, but saints and angels, this is another age and another planet." He sat in a chair and stared at her with his mouth hanging open. "A restaurant chain bought at a table in a little restaurant on Main Street in a town of only a few thousand?"

"Not even a few thousand. Although now we're growing."

"Sweet saints in heaven."

She smiled and shrugged. "You'll have to come see us sometime. We were going to look at something, Tony."

He blinked. "Oh, yeah. Over here."

And from that moment on until nine o'clock that night, she was busy at the restaurant. There were kinks, but Tony called them nothing, and by the time she was alone in her hotel room and had showered and climbed into bed to call Jake, she was exhausted.

" 'Lo," came his voice, and she felt something twist inside. She clutched the phone, overcome by longing for his easygoing strength. Jake was fun, reliable, exciting and she felt empty without him.

"Hello?"

"Jake?"

"Honey, are you all right?"

"Yes. I'm exhausted, and I'm just so glad to talk to you and hear your voice."

"You're sure you're all right?"

"I'm positive, if you'll just talk to me. How was your day?"

"We lost a steer. A fence was down and I repaired that. Mrs. Latham gave me your message that you had arrived safely. So how's Chicago?"

"Jake, you wouldn't believe this restaurant. It's so fancy. I can't think of it as a Salido Sam's. I've never seen such equipment."

"And how's the new manager?"

"Tony? He's adorable."

"I feel like getting on the next plane and coming up and punching him out. How adorable?"

She laughed, relaxing. "Not that kind of adorable. I was so scared of what he would be like and that he'd realize how little I know—"

"Sami." Jake's tone was suddenly solemn. "You know more than he does about Salido Sam's."

"I suppose. He made me feel that way, too, and he said this is a perfect opening. He told me he has done these time and again and everything is going right, on this one. He's done everything to make me feel better about it and to share the work load. We're both Leos and his horoscope indicated this would be a good month for a new business."

"I feel better about you working with him now," Jake commented dryly.

"He spent Sunday afternoon hunting four-leaf clovers for all the employees and me."

"Tell him to find one for me, and maybe I won't have to mend any fences."

"I'm exhausted, and I'm glad he told me it's going well, because a lot of things seemed snarled up today. Ingredients haven't arrived that have been ordered . . . The menus were printed wrong and have to go back to the printer's. It doesn't look so perfect to me, but he thinks it is."

"How's Chicago?"

"All I've seen of it is what I pass in a cab. It seems enormous and busy, and I'm glad I'm not driving my own car."

"I miss you," he murmured in a husky voice. "Just knowing you're in town and I can get in to see you anytime makes you seem close. We never have been apart three weeks."

"I know, but then I'll be back home for a long time until the next Salido Sam's opens."

"I'm already counting the minutes. I ride in that fund-raising rodeo in Monroe Saturday night. This is a special deal and not part of the usual rodeo circuit. I wish you were going to be there. Bernie and Tom are coming."

"Please call me that night when you get home. I'll be worrying about whether you got stomped by a bull or thrown over the fence."

"I'll call, but I'll be all right. No one is holding a gun to my head to get me to ride."

"How can it be fun?"

"Fun isn't the right description of bull-riding. It's a challenge. And so is this separation. I want you in my arms."

She wriggled down in bed and listened to his husky voice until she was too groggy to talk coherently. She glanced at the clock. "Jake, it's after three and I have to go to work at nine. Nine seems incredibly late, but I'm beginning to fade."

"Good night, love."

" 'Night, Jake. I miss you." She replaced the receiver and was asleep in minutes.

Four days later Tony came into the kitchen at eleven o'clock. "Samantha, come with me," he said, interrupting her while she discussed recipes with Gene Silvestri.

Samantha shook her hair away from her face and left the kitchen.

"We'll stop in the office and get your purse, because we're leaving the restaurant."

"Oh?" she asked in surprise, studying him with curiosity. "Where are we going?"

He smiled as he held the door to his office. He opened the desk to hand her purse to her. "I will show you places to shop, and you have a four o'clock appointment to get your hair done. This is something you wanted to do while you're here, and I intend to help you."

"Tony—"

He waved his hand and interrupted her. "Since your arrival you've given all your time to this restaurant. Now we'll take some time for you. I will pick you up at six o'clock."

"Oh, Tony, that's wonderful, but I don't know if I should take time away from the restaurant."

"We'll manage. If we can't, we're in sad shape, because soon you'll go back to Oklahoma," he stated, heading for the door. She went outside to his car with him, and he turned out of the restaurant lot.

She watched traffic speed past. Tony drove fast, weaving in and out of cars, and she wondered if she would ever become accustomed to a city like Chicago.

He wheeled over to the curb and she climbed out. With a broad smile he came around to take her arm and steer her to a fancy shop. It was hushed inside.

"Tony, I need a department store."

"No. You're in Chicago. Get some special things. Some frou-frou and chic dresses that you don't get in Salido."

"Good morning," came from a woman who smiled as she came into the room.

"Good morning. This is Miss Bardwell from out of state. She's here to shop." He turned to Samantha. "You tell her what you'd like to see."

"First have a seat, and I'll bring coffee. I'm Marla Winslow."

Over cups of steaming coffee, Samantha looked at the dresses that were presented to her and selected four to try on. Tony was a patient audience, giving her his comments. She bought two dresses, and when they stepped outside, he put the boxes in his car and took her arm to move down the street. "Now a department store."

"I want to get something for my aunt and my little sister and a little four-year-old. And I have to get something for four men."

"Four?" he asked, raising his dark brows.

"My grandfather, my two brothers and a friend."

"Ah, the friend. The father of the four-year-old?"

"Yes," she answered as he opened the door to a busy department store.

They ate lunch at an outdoor café, and by three she felt she was through shopping. "Tony, I have everything I need."

"Then we go for the frou-frou." He took her to another department store. "Now, I'll meet you here in forty-five minutes. Go buy something frivolous and slinky."

She laughed and left him, doing what he suggested and finding him five minutes before they had agreed to meet.

"A woman who is on time from shopping? Impossible."

"Here I am."

"Now to the beauty salon." He told her the beautician's name and said he would pick her up at half past five.

Samantha sat in the chair, watching her hairdo change, wondering how Jake would like it. At a quarter after five as she left the shop, she looked again in the mirror at the pageboy that came just above her shoulders. Her hair was shorter, more sophisticated, and her reflection startled her, because her appearance was different.

"Magnificent! Ooh-la-la. You look marvelous!" Tony exclaimed when she met him. "Very nice. Now back to the spareribs. I can't get the slaw recipe exactly right. It still doesn't taste like it should."

They discussed slaw, and she forgot about the mound of boxes until he took her back to the hotel. As he stopped at the curb, he turned to her. "Want some advice?"

"Sure, Tony."

"Rent a car. The company pays the expense, and you'll learn this town."

"I don't think I'll be back to Chicago."

"You might not, but you'll get accustomed to the city, and you won't feel so lost."

"Thanks." She smiled at him, and when she had her boxes unpacked, she called the concierge to make arrangements for a rental car and a map of Chicago. Before she left for the restaurant the next morning, she called Tony.

"I took your advice. I've rented a car and I'm leaving here now, and if I don't show up soon, send a scout to look for me."

He laughed. "Drop bread crumbs and you can find your way home tonight. I'll see you soon."

Terrified of the traffic, yet glad to have a car to get around, she arrived at the restaurant without difficulty. Two nights later they had a practice dinner for invited guests. It was chaos and left several things to be straightened out. Then it was time for the official opening. Dressed in the denim skirt and chambray shirt she had worn in Salido, she felt a nervous tremor. It was one thing to draw a college crowd in southeastern Oklahoma. Quite another to pull a crowd in Chicago.

At five Eldon Kyriakos appeared. Looking dark, handsome and urbane, he made her think of Jake, and she felt a surge of longing for home. Kyriakos walked over to her and took her hand. "Samantha, you'll help draw a crowd. Tony says you're all set, and it's going smoothly so far."

"This is only my second opening, and the one in Salido was really not that special because the café never was closed. This is a marvelous restaurant."

"I think we'll do well. I have a first-class manager in Tony."

"Yes. The barbecue sauce was just right the day I arrived."

"Good. Have fun tonight. The ads on television look good."

"We're already getting a crowd, and the T-shirts are selling fast."

In another hour they were jammed with a crowd, and by one in the morning, Tony was wringing his hands. "We've got to get more beer, because we don't close for another hour and we're running out."

He picked up the phone and punched num-

217

bers. Trying to help any way she could, Samantha worked swiftly to open more longnecks and hand them to a waitress. Before the evening was over, she was carrying a tray and waiting tables, and she was amazed by the size of the crowd. The place was packed, people singing together, the noise level high.

Finally at three a.m. they closed, and Samantha leaned against the wall. "I'd say that was a success, Tony."

She had fastened her hair behind her head with a rubber band during the evening. As she kicked off her high-heeled pumps, she heard a pop and looked over to see Tony opening bottles of champagne.

"We celebrate!" he announced while the help gathered around and Tony began pouring the bubbly liquid. His tie was off, his shirt unbuttoned halfway to his waist. His sleeves were rolled up and locks of black hair fell over his eyes. His girlfriend, Maria Fornaciari, had come, and she handed a glass of champagne to Samantha.

"Our first toast is to ourselves! We did a damn good job tonight!" Tony said, holding a glass high while everyone cheered. Samantha sipped and looked into Tony's brown eyes, and he smiled.

"And the next toast is to the person who made this possible, who made the sauce, and who made everyone's job easier tonight . . . Samantha Bardwell!"

Another cheer went up, and people raised their glasses to her and drank as Maria and Tony began pouring refills.

"I'd like to make a toast to all of you," Samantha announced. "And especially to Tony Jacoby who helped me get through my first official opening."

By the time she finished her glass, she was aware of being exhausted, and she told them goodbye and drove back to the hotel. When she unlocked her door and stepped inside, she paused in surprise. On the desk was a bouquet of red roses.

She dropped everything and hurried to retrieve the card to read, "Congratulations. Love, Jake."

She kicked off her shoes and stretched out on the bed to call him. Glancing at her watch, she felt a swift rush of longing when she heard his greeting.

"Did I wake you?"

"No. I've been reading and waiting for your call. How'd it go?"

"The roses are gorgeous. Thank you. It went great. Hectic and busy and we ran out of things, but got more in time. We had a fantastic crowd. Jake, I can't wait to get home."

"I wish you were here right now," he stated gruffly.

"I thought the time would go quickly, but it hasn't. I'm doing better about driving in traffic. It doesn't make me as nervous."

"Don't get where you enjoy it and don't want to come home."

"No danger! How's Melody? I wish I could have talked to her," she said, realizing how much a part of her life Melody had become.

"She wants to know where you are and what you're doing. I took her by the restaurant to see Asa. I talked to him again this morning, and the family is fine. Melody picked out another tune on the piano, so I guess she plays by ear."

"That's great. Inherited talent?"

"Hardly," he answered dryly. "You haven't heard me sing with the karaoke."

"I've meant to ask you about that. You should be a good singer."

"How do you figure that?"

"Your sexy voice, darlin'," she answered in a throaty tone.

"If I could just reach through this phone—"

"I'll be home soon. What's happened in Salido?"

"Someone's announced the plans from Kyriakos Enterprises to build the lodge at Lake Lewiston, and it's getting a mixed reaction. Most people in town are glad, because it'll mean more business, but a few people are protesting."

"Asa loves the idea. He's bought a new boat

and he can get away from the crowds and the restaurant. Anything else going on?"

"Crawley's cow got out last night and wandered into town and got into some sacks of feed in front of Hoot Vinson's feed store. Gene said Hoot shouldn't have left the feed out like that, and Hoot said Gene should keep his cow at home."

She listened, relaxing, missing Jake so badly it hurt. She wiggled her toes, which stung from standing long hours in high heels.

They talked until five in the morning, and she fell asleep in her clothes, waking at seven.

The days were busy, the time interminable, and finally at half past seven in the evening on November twenty-second, she stepped into the hallway at Will Rogers Airport in Oklahoma City. She searched the crowd for Jake and met his dark gaze, her breath catching. It took control to keep from throwing down everything and breaking into a run.

## Chapter Eleven

Jake watched Samantha step into the hallway and he felt something twist inside. His pulse raced and he moved through the crowd toward her and then he stopped to watch her walk toward him. He felt hot, as if a ball of fire had mushroomed and caught him.

She looked sophisticated, gorgeous, sexy. She wore a long deep-blue top and short matching skirt. The effect was dazzling with her legs showing from inches above her knees down to her high-heeled pumps. Her hair was different, swinging slightly with each step. The makeup was subtle, but highlighted her fine cheekbones and emphasized her sensual, full lips.

Desire was intense, but along with it was an undercurrent of surprise at how she had changed. Was it only skin-deep? She looked more assured, more sophisticated. He felt stunned by the transformation, and then she was inches away and all he could do was reach for her and haul her to him.

He kissed her hungrily, his mouth savage with

need, and she clung to him and returned his kisses as hotly.

"Let's get your things and go where we can be alone," he urged in a husky voice, taking her arm and holding her close against him while he shouldered her bag.

In forty minutes he closed the door to a hotel suite and pulled her to him. "You look gorgeous and perfect, and I'm going to undo all of your flawless appearance." He wound his fingers in her soft, silky hair while he gazed into her eyes.

"I missed you so badly." She trailed her fingers over his shoulders and tugged at his silver belt buckle. "Jake, it seems forever," she whispered. Her heart thudded and her hands shook. She had missed him so badly, and now she wanted to touch him and kiss him and feel his arms around her.

Clothes were tossed aside and he held her tightly, kissing her, stroking her smooth flesh. With his pulse roaring, Jake bent over her, wanting to kiss every inch of her. Finally he couldn't wait, losing restraint and picking her up in his arms.

He lowered her to the bed and moved between her legs to possess her, finally gaining control of himself so he could slowly. He watched her as she held him tightly, her white teeth biting her full lower lip, her eyes half closed as she moaned with pleasure.

They moved together, urgency building. She

ran her hands along his smooth back. "Jake, I need you," she gasped.

They climaxed, clinging to each other, and Samantha felt a gush of pleasure as she locked her arms around him. And then they shifted and turned, Jake raising himself up to look down at her.

"Thank heaven you're home. I hope he doesn't open another restaurant for years."

She laughed, burying her head against his furred chest. Letting her hands drift over him, she relished the hard lines of his body, the crisp hairs across his chest and on his legs. "It'll be New Orleans in three months."

He groaned. "As soon as February? Lord, Samantha."

"Shh. Don't think about it now. I'm home and I'm in your arms, in case you've forgotten."

"Hardly," he said dryly, stroking her back. "Melody wants to see you, too, and Bernie and Asa and Myra volunteered to go pick her up tomorrow. She'll be at your house when we get there."

"Good! I brought her a teddy bear."

"Your family thinks you get in tomorrow, but now I wish you had told them you'd be in next week. I feel like a starving man faced with a soft, yummy cream pie."

"Cream pie?"

"Yes, and I want to eat every bite," he murmured, nuzzling her neck.

224

At midnight Jake ordered room service to send up two dinners of chicken breasts, a bottle of Chablis and a jug of coffee. He yanked on his jeans and closed the bedroom door when he heard the knock.

Samantha slid out of bed and went to the bathroom to shower. When she came out, wrapped in a thick, blue terry towel, Jake handed her a glass of wine. "Dinner is waiting."

"I'm starving." She leaned forward to kiss him, tasting wine on his breath, and in minutes the towel and jeans were gone and dinner forgotten.

An hour later they sat in the rumpled bed and ate cold chicken and drank wine. Her hair was a tangle around her head, in damp curls again, and she looked the way she always had.

As he sipped chilled white wine, he studied her. "So how do you like the job now?"

She wiped her mouth and fingers and pulled the sheet up under her arms. "I love it, Jake. I like the responsibility, and while I miss you and miss being here, I liked the excitement of someplace new."

He wanted to ignore the disappointment he felt, knowing it wasn't right to hope she hated it. He loved his work and knew how terrible it would be to have a job he didn't like, yet as he watched her sip the white wine, he wondered what a difference this would make in their lives.

They left the hotel the next night at eight. Jake flew them to Salido and drove her home.

She wore a blue chambray shirt and jeans and he kept his hand on her shoulder or her knee all the way from the hangar to her house.

"Tomorrow night I'll pick you up at five."

She nodded. "I feel as if I've been away from home forever. Come inside with me. Everyone will want to see you, too, and Melody is already here. It's still early."

"You can stop giving me reasons. I'm coming with you."

She climbed out of the truck as Bernie jumped off the porch and Phoebe, Myra and Melody hurried down the steps. Samantha looked at Bernie. "My word, you've grown since I left!"

"I might have."

"Help Jake with the packages. I brought something for everyone." She turned to pick up Melody. "Hi! I'm glad you're here. I brought you a surprise, and I'll show you when we go into the house."

"I missed you," Melody said, touching Samantha's chin. She gave the child a squeeze and set her down to watch her go to Jake.

Samantha looked at Myra. Her gaze ran over Myra's bleached hair that had been cut short all over her head, dangling earrings, heavy makeup, a tank top and a skin-tight skirt that barely reached her thighs.

"Myra?" Samantha blinked. "You look different."

"Hi, Samantha. Glad you're home." She turned to catch up with Bernie and Jake and Melody. Samantha and Phoebe followed. Asa waited on the porch. "I'm so glad to be home."

"How did it go?" he asked.

"Fine. I'll tell you all about it. Where's Tom?"

Asa and Phoebe looked at each other. Phoebe shrugged and scooted into the house.

"Granddad, where's Tom?"

"He's got some new friends over in Monroe, and he's been over there a lot lately."

"Tom? How'd he get to Monroe?"

"Sometimes he takes the station wagon. Sometimes he has a friend here who'll come get him."

"What's he doing in Monroe? And how did he meet anyone from Monroe High?"

"They're not from the high school. These are college boys, who've been to the restaurant."

She felt a stab of worry. Tom was almost seventeen and had always followed Bernie around or run around with his Salido friends, who were his own age. When they went inside, she passed out packages, and in minutes the room was filled with tissue paper and boxes.

Jake stayed until two in the morning, when Phoebe was settled watching *The Ectoplasm Versus the Mud Monster.*

With Melody staying the night, Jake and Samantha walked to his truck. As she kissed him goodbye, he drew a deep breath. "I'd like to haul you into the bushes."

"If you did, someone would talk to us."

"I can't wait until tomorrow."

She kissed him again, drawing her lips over his, feeling the sensuous friction, her heart pounding with love for him. She caught him tightly around the waist. "I love you, Jake."

He groaned. "Now I really want to haul you into the bushes. I'll call in a few minutes."

She nodded and stepped back, her body still tingling from nearly twenty-four hours of lovemaking. She watched him get into his truck and drive away. Twenty minutes later he called her on his cellular phone.

They talked two hours. After she hung up, Samantha fell asleep to wake at half past six, when people were stirring in the house She pulled on her jeans and a T-shirt and went to find Myra, who had her hair in hot curlers and was standing in the bathroom. Leaning over the sink, Myra was putting on makeup.

"Myra, you're wearing too much makeup."

"This is what the girls are doing."

"Even so, you take off some of that junk so you look normal."

"Samantha, I'll look like a freak if I don't."

"You look scary with so much on. And no more tight, short skirts for school. I'm surprised they didn't send you home."

Myra's face flushed, and she puckered her lips to put on lip gloss.

"Did you get in trouble at school for wearing

a short skirt?"

"Nothing much. They just said it was short. Old Miz Gloppy."

"Mrs. Galopianne isn't that old. You wear something normal and lay off the makeup."

"Yes, Samantha," she said with sarcasm.

Worrying about the changes in Myra, Samantha went downstairs. She had long ago assumed the role of second mother to them, and all three siblings knew if they didn't win Samantha's approval, Asa would enforce what she said. Now it was growing more difficult than it ever was when they'd been buried under financial burdens. The kids were getting older, and they had more money to spend. They also had more leisure time, since they didn't have to hold part-time jobs. She wondered if the extra time and money was turning into a problem.

As she sat at the kitchen table, Tom came in. He looked half asleep as he staggered to the refrigerator and opened it, removing a bottle of milk and tilting it up to drink.

"Ah-ah, no, no," Samantha stated. "Drink from a glass."

"Hi, Samantha. Welcome home," he greeted her hoarsely.

"Where were you?"

"Out."

She looked at his bloodshot blue eyes, his pale freckled skin. She stood up and walked over to him. "Where were you?"

"With my friends," he answered, blowing stale breath on her.

"Tom, you've been drinking beer!" she snapped, shocked. "Where did you get beer? You're underage."

"A friend got it for me, and it was just a little. And I'm over sixteen years old."

"You can barely stand. You have to be twenty-one to buy beer. I'll bet your head hurts."

"Yes, it does."

"I have the keys to the wagon, and you're not to take it. You stop the beer drinking, because you'll only get into trouble. And don't drink and drive."

"Gol, you sound like some kind of public service announcement."

She blinked, amazed and worried about him. "You go back to being sober."

He steadied himself by gripping the side of the refrigerator. "Yeah, sure, Sis."

Myra came in dressed in a tight jeans skirt that came to her knees. It was a few degrees better than the short skirt of the previous day, so Samantha remained quiet, wondering what else had happened in her absence. "Aunt Phoebe is helping Melody dress, and then they'll be down to eat."

When the others were gone, Asa leaned back in his chair. Samantha poured them both another cup of steaming coffee. He studied her through his new rimless glasses.

"Honey, I've been thinking about it, and since I only cook at lunchtime, I've been fishing more and I like it. You know I don't have to work now. I think I'd like to retire."

She smiled at him. "I think you've more than earned it. Retire today. I'll call the restaurant."

He chuckled. "I really wouldn't mind doing that. It's a gorgeous fall day and anytime now we'll have cold weather. I'd like to just head on out to the lake. My friend, Bart, and I will take the boat. Would you call the café, honey? I wouldn't mind never setting foot in the place again."

She laughed and reached for the phone. "Sure."

"Samantha, do you feel that way? You could quit and get an entirely different kind of job. Something in advertising like you thought you wanted when you went to college."

"I like this job. I loved the opening in Chicago. It's exciting, and next time I'll get to see New Orleans."

"Okay. Thanks for calling." He left the room, and she heard him whistling a tune.

She phoned the restaurant and ran her fingers across her head. Some things were wonderful and others weren't so great. Myra looked twenty years old, and Tom was running around with boys three years older than he was. Bernie was on a Harley Davidson now, and she had lost her best friend.

Look on the bright side. No debts. No constant worries. College would be paid for, and they now drove a new car and could get another if needed. She had an exciting, challenging job. She would be with Jake tonight, and both families and his in-laws were having Thanksgiving dinner at his ranch.

That night she ate dinner with Jake and Melody at the ranch. After dinner she read stories to Melody, and finally Jake carried her to her room to bed and returned to pour two glasses of wine and sit down with Samantha.

"She likes you, pretty lady."

"Thank you. She's really sweet, Jake."

"How was it, getting back in the groove in Salido?"

"Nice. Except things have changed. Asa retired. As of this afternoon. I talked to him this morning, and he said he would prefer never to set foot in the place again. I got someone to replace him, and he went fishing with a friend."

"Good for him. Asa's how old?"

"He's eighty-one now."

"It's time he retired and enjoyed himself. He loves to fish, and he has the new boat. First thing you know he'll be a guide out on Lake Lewiston."

"That's one of the good things."

"What are the bad things?" Jake asked, scooting closer on the sofa. "Turn around." He began to knead her shoulders while she talked.

"Myra looks like she's twenty. You saw her the other night. Skirts that barely cover her fanny, boys calling—and they're older boys who drive— makeup an inch thick on her face. Tom is running around with guys three years older than he is. Bernie is out on the Harley Davidson at night. Aunt Phoebe got contacts."

Jake laughed. "Phoebe's something else. First thing you know, she'll bring home a boyfriend."

"I passed Ellie today, and she wouldn't speak."

"I'm sorry, Samantha."

"You don't sound surprised."

He shrugged. "Salido is a small town. When anything happens, it's like dropping a rock in a bucket of water. The ripples touch all sides of the bucket."

"You knew that then. Mrs. Potter didn't speak to me today. Why would she be aloof?"

"Some people aren't happy about all the new people coming to Salido. Whit Potter's business depends on his wheat crop, not who comes or goes in town, and she doesn't like her little town to change."

"I didn't know people felt that way."

"They don't all feel that way. Anyone who has a business here is delighted about the new-comers."

She twisted around to look at him. "Jake, they've moved the date up for the New Orleans opening."

His dark eyes narrowed, and she saw the flash

of anger that cut through her like a knife. "Please come to New Orleans with me."

"What dates?"

"I go the first week of January."

"I can get away part of the time. Can you get away any of the time that you're there?"

"I should be able to some, but it won't be a whole lot."

"I'll bring some books," he retorted lightly, but his dark eyes held hers with a look she couldn't fathom.

Leaving Melody in Dallas with her grandparents, Jake took five days to go to New Orleans in January. He had visited the city before for weekends and ball games. After two days he was restless. Samantha worked until nine at night, and then they would go out to eat, and he would show her parts of the city. He loved the sparkle in her eyes. During moments with her he forgot his boredom, because he could see she was enchanted with the city. And then in their quiet suite, the hours of love made up for all the hours alone. He tried to curb his patience, because he knew she loved her job and was good at what she was doing. Her drive and intelligence were part of what had drawn him to her in the first place.

He ate at the restaurant two nights, sitting in a corner. Occasionally she would join him for a few minutes at a time.

Finally they flew home together, and life returned to normal. When he was back in Salido, his thoughts turned to marriage.

He had a date with her Saturday night, and they were going to the movie in Monroe. When they got to the lineup for tickets, Ellie and Vernon were in front of them.

Ellie glanced at them, her gaze running over Samantha's jeans and fringed suede coat and she nodded. "Hello." She turned her back and Vernon looked around.

"Hi, Samantha, Jake." He shook hands with Jake while he looked at Samantha.

"How are you, Ellie?" Samantha asked.

"I'm going inside, Vernon," Ellie said and hurried away.

Samantha started to follow, but Jake caught her wrist and she stayed with him. "How could she dislike me so much when we've grown up the best of friends?" she asked, after he bought two tickets.

"People change. You moved into a different world, and maybe she feels left out," he said quietly and she looked up at him.

"Do you dislike my job, Jake?"

"I'm glad you like it," he answered carefully, "but I'd be lying if I said I like you to leave town."

"I don't want to be separated, either," she reassured him, feeling relieved by his answer.

The next time Samantha saw Ellie was the sec-

235

ond week in February, when she stopped in the grocery to get some things on her way home from the restaurant. Samantha wore a new, green wool dress and her hair hung in a pageboy. As she hurried down an aisle, she came face-to-face with Ellie, whose gaze went over her.

"You've changed your hair," Ellie stated bluntly. "Who did the styling?"

"Someone in a shop in Chicago."

"I figured you'd change to someplace fancy."

"You're the one who wouldn't take me, Ellie."

"You're clothes are different, too. I knew you wouldn't stay the same. And you'll lose Jake. Just see if you don't. A lot of people wish you'd never opened Salido Sam's. Do you know how much this town has changed? Now people are moving here and building houses, because of the fishing at Lake Lewiston. They didn't even know Lake Lewiston or Salido existed before."

Samantha hurt, and she thought she had gotten over allowing Ellie to hurt her badly. She wanted to argue that other people liked having the town grow. She knew there was no point in discussing it, because she couldn't change Ellie's mind. She noticed the ring on Ellie's finger.

"You're engaged."

"I figured Phoebe told you. The wedding will be next month."

"Congratulations," Samantha said stiffly, knowing that a year ago she would have been maid of honor. "Goodbye, Ellie." She turned

236

away, hurrying to the cash register to pay for her purchases and go home.

As she drove, she thought about what Ellie had said about Jake. She was wrong there. Things were fine between them, they had both been busy with families during the holidays, but along with a Christmas gift of diamond stud earrings, Jake had asked her to take a week with him at the end of February and go to the Caribbean.

She had accepted, turning to kiss him. "It'll be tricky explaining to my family. Asa may come after you with a shotgun, although I don't know what they think we do when we go to Dallas for a weekend. I'll warn you now, Asa and Phoebe are a little old-fashioned."

"I'll take my chances on them and on the shotgun wedding," Jake had said, nuzzling her throat. "A whole week with no families, no worries, nothing but fun."

She had laughed and twisted to kiss him, and all talk about the trip vanished.

Before the trip it wasn't Asa or Phoebe as she had expected that she had trouble with. It was Tom. She sat across from him in the room he shared with Bernie.

"Mr. Baker said you've been cutting school regularly. Tom, your grades have always been good. What are you doing?"

"Nothing. Just having a little fun. Blake and Drew don't have afternoon classes. It's no big deal. I'll catch up."

"It is a big deal. I'm leaving town, so I won't lay down rules and go, but when I get back, I want you to stay in Salido during the weekdays."

"Aw, Samantha, that's stupid."

"Your grades are what's stupid. Tom you have a D in geometry. You've never had a D in your life."

"Don't make a federal case out of it. I'll bring the grade up." He squinted at her. "If I get my grades up, can I go to Monroe during the week?"

"I'll think about it. You must bring your grades up either way. In the long run, you're the one who's going to be hurt by low grades."

"Gol, pick on someone else. Hell —"

"Watch your language."

"Okay," he said, flushing. "Did you know Myra is dating Gip Johnson from Monroe College."

"Myra dating a college boy?"

"Yeah. That's worse than a D in geometry. She'll be mad I snitched, but he's kinda wild, and I don't much want my sister going out with a dude like that."

"How long has that been going on? He doesn't come to the house."

"No, she meets him down at the drugstore. You won't let her ride Bernie's bike, but she rides Gip's."

"Great heavens," Samantha exclaimed, her worries compounding. She didn't want Tom going to Monroe and letting grades slip and drinking beer any more than she wanted Myra out with a college boy and riding a bike. "Thanks for telling me. You go to class."

"Okay, okay."

She left the room, and that afternoon she waited for Myra to get in from school. Myra tossed her books on a chair and headed toward the kitchen.

"Hi, Samantha."

"Myra, come here. I want to talk to you."

When she closed the door to the living room, she turned around. "I've heard in town that you're dating Gip Johnson, a freshman at Monroe."

Myra's lip thrust out and she blinked. "Where did you hear that?"

"At the restaurant." Samantha refused to reveal that Tom was the source. "You're to stop dating him right now."

"You can't do that!"

"Yes, I can. If you date anyone, they'll come to the house and meet the family. Or are you that ashamed of him? Or is he that ashamed of you?"

"No! I'm not ashamed of him," she said, blushing and glaring at Samantha. "That's not fair."

"Then why haven't you brought him home for us to meet?"

Myra blinked. "You can't make me stop dating

him. I'll run away—"

"When you do, remember, the money doesn't go with you. If you run away, you're on your own for the rest of your schooling. For your groceries and a roof over your head."

Myra's eyes filled with tears. "I'm not going to run away, but please don't make me quit dating him. He's cool . . ."

"I don't care if he's cold as ice, you can't go out with him. You can't date someone you won't bring home to let the family meet. Until you're older, you can't date someone in college. Period. Understand?"

Myra burst into tears, and Samantha left the room, closing the door quietly behind her. That night she talked to Asa and Phoebe about Tom and Myra, and both agreed to keep tabs on the two while Samantha was gone.

And then finally she was on board the plane with Jake for the flight from Dallas. As they flew over the blue waters of the Caribbean Sea, she let go of the problems.

Jake had leased a villa between Cozumel and Tulum in a small resort, Akumal. When he paid the cab driver, Jake picked up the luggage and unlocked the door to a sprawling white stucco house overlooking the white sandy beach. He dropped the suitcases and turned to take her in his arms. "This is ours, and we'll be alone with no phone and no interruptions. I'll have you all to myself."

Her heart beat with eagerness as she gazed up into his dark eyes and he pulled her closer to kiss her.

The first day Jake taught her to sail the Sunfish, showing her what to do. She watched the ripple of his muscles, his skin dark from the sun, his curls tangled by the wind, and she felt exhilarated, as high as if she had been drinking wine all day long.

His body was powerful and lean. He wore only a narrow black swimsuit that revealed all his muscles, his maleness. He glanced at her and slid over the side. "Let's cool off and get back in."

"Won't the boat drift away?"

"We won't be that long," he said, and she followed him into the water, feeling its coolness close over her. He sliced through the surf with strong strokes and surfaced. She followed as she shook water away from his face.

"Jake, look at the boat!" she exclaimed, horrified by the distance already separating them.

He grinned. "Beat you there."

"Never!"

She plunged after him, but in seconds he pulled ahead with long, steady strokes that closed the distance between him and the small boat. He climbed over the side, and when she caught up he reached down to scoop her in. The boat rocked wildly. He sat and held her close and let it steady. She laughed and he kissed her, the tang of saltwater on his lips.

The fifth day they snorkeled. Jake stopped watching the colorful blue and yellow angelfish, the sea fans and rainbow parrotfish in the crystal waters. Instead he studied Samantha swimming ahead of him. The week had been paradise, and it wasn't because of the tropical setting. She had relaxed, shed the responsibilities of home and her job. The veneer of sophistication that she'd been developing vanished, and she was full of fun.

He thought about their nights. Last night they'd gone to an outdoor dance floor built over the sea. They had danced to steel drums and a fast beat, until they were both sweating. And later in his arms she'd been passionate and eager and inventive. His pulse changed while he remembered, and his body responded to the steamy recall.

With the constant swimming, she'd let her hair go back to its natural auburn curls that he loved. Now her hair was wet and sleek, streaming back from her head as she swam. He watched her slender legs kick through the water and thought about her blue eyes that darkened in passion. He felt a flush of heat in his groin and suddenly he wanted her, all her eagerness and her softness.

He took a deep breath, tossed aside his breathing tube, and reached out to catch her ankle, yanking her back to him. She twisted to look at him, frowning and meeting his gaze.

He saw the change come over her as he reached out to take her breathing tube and they both shot to the surface where he pulled off the goggles.

"Hey! You're throwing away some perfectly good equipment."

"Swim for shore, or I'll drag you in by the hair."

Her brows arched as she looked at him. "You have an arrogant side, Colby. To hell with you."

She twisted to swim away from him, diving below the surface of the water and vanishing as swiftly as a porpoise.

Seeing the challenge in her blue eyes, he went after her. Catching her, he yanked her up to the surface, both of them splashing noisily as she fought him. He held her with one arm and peeled away her turquoise swimsuit with the other. Then he kicked off the tiny scrap of black that was his swimsuit.

"Jake!"

"You've been giving orders for so long, you don't know how to take any," he said, pulling her under with him. He blew out his breath as his mouth closed over one of her nipples and he flicked the bud with his tongue, feeling it harden. She struggled, kicking and pushing, and he thrust them both to the surface again.

"Jake, stop that. My suit is floating away." Samantha felt angry, impatient with his cavalier

243

treatment, until she looked up into his eyes that burned like rampaging fires. Her breath caught, and she felt his hands slide between her legs. "Jake," she protested, but all force was going from her voice. "Jake, not out here. Suppose a boat comes along . . ."

"They don't know who the hell we are. It won't come out in the Salido News," he said gruffly.

She felt his fingers probe her softness, seeking the secret places that could make her melt to his will.

"You're taking advantage of me," she whispered, suddenly closing her eyes as his fingers stroked her. She clung to his shoulders. "Jake—"

"What? Say it, Samantha. Go ahead, say it."

She clamped her jaws closed, still fighting him in the smallest way possible while her body responded to his caresses, and she was lost, her hips moving wildly while her fingers bit into his shoulders. "Jake!"

"Say you want this," he ordered.

"Jake!" she gasped, her body moving to his touch, reacting wildly. He was taking her to a brink that made her forget everything—boats or where they were or their argument. Suddenly he removed his hand, releasing her.

Her eyes flew open. She ached, now wanting him desperately. He stared at her with a hard, possessive look on his face. His eyes were intent, his lips slightly parted, and his chest expanded as he inhaled.

She felt a tug of wills that was primal, and then she didn't care. She wanted him to love her, to finish what he'd started. "Jake, please," she whispered.

He yanked her to him, kissing her hard as she felt his hot, strong body in the cool water. He released her. "We're swimming in. I want more than we can do here. Head for shore."

This time she didn't argue, but swam with him. When he stood, he caught her up in his arms. Splashing noisily, he waded out the rest of the way with her, striding through thigh deep water as if he were on dry land.

She slid her arms around his neck, trailing her fingers over his broad chest, up the strong column of his neck. Drops of water were crystals on his dark lashes, and his eyes devoured her. Her heart pounded as he set her on her feet and kissed her, his hands sliding over her. In minutes he picked her up, holding her waist as he kissed her throat. "Put your legs around me," he commanded, lowering her on his rigid flesh, moving slowly.

"Please, Jake, I want you . . ." she whispered urgently, on fire, feeling the hot, velvet tip of his manhood.

"I want to demolish that cool reserve of yours."

She gasped and clung to him as his slow, partial penetration drove her wild with need. "Jake, please," she whispered, kissing his throat, her mouth covering his.

"We'll take time, Samantha," he whispered, his voice a rasp, while his heart felt as if it would pound out of his chest. She moaned with passion, her body silky and soft and ready, her passion driving him to a brink faster than he had intended.

And then he thrust deep, his control gone, barely aware of her soft cries, her hands digging into his shoulders.

Samantha felt caught and carried on a current until release burst. She clung to him, her breathing and heartbeat returning to normal. He shifted her, pulling her into his arms to sit down on a chaise with her.

"Jake, that was decadent."

"The hell it was. It was grand."

"We've lost our breathing gear and goggles and swim suits."

"We both have other suits, and I'll find the other stuff."

"Oh, sure. You have the whole ocean to look."

He chuckled. "We weren't that far out, and the water is as clear as the air. Wait a minute." He shifted her to the chaise and stood up to cross to a patio chair. He picked up his shorts and rummaged in a pocket. Returning, he moved with ease as if unaware of his nudity, and her gaze went over the angles and planes and whipcord strength of his body. Her mouth went dry as if she hadn't just caressed and kissed him, and she ached to touch him again. Her gaze drifted between his legs, the dark mat of hair and his maleness, and she felt heat spread in her lower body.

"You are something to behold, Jake Colby."

"You're absurd," he stated softly, kissing her, sitting down and pulling her onto his lap again. "Here, love." He thrust a small box into her hand.

She looked at it and saw it was a jeweler's velvet box. And small enough for a ring. She snapped it open and a four-carat diamond flashed brilliantly in the tropical sunshine.

"Jake!" she gasped, staring at it and feeling stunned. She looked into his black eyes that held an unmistakable need and she felt emotions surge.

"I love you, Samantha, and want to marry you."

# Chapter Twelve

"Oh, Jake," she exclaimed, feeling a rush of joy. As she stared at the ring, she thought about Salido and the families and the ranch and her job. Emotions spun and collided like meteors crashing to earth as possibilities and problems loomed. She looked up at him. "Our families—"

Something flickered in his eyes. Had he expected her to throw aside all other considerations and instantly accept his proposal? Surely not, when they both had relatives to consider. They faced each other, and she wondered if a barrier had come up between them.

"They get along great," he stated quietly. "We can work that out. I can have a home in town some of the time."

"You'd do that?" she asked in amazement.

"Yes, I'd do that. When Melody is school age, I'll have to have a town home."

"I'd want to work," she said, and a closed look came to his features, the impassive gaze that he could turn to the world so easily. And this time there was no question in her mind that a barrier had risen between them.

"I know you like your job, but I'd like you to give up opening new places and being gone weeks at a time. I want my wife home, Samantha. I had one marriage where my wife didn't want to stay in Oklahoma."

"It's only a few weeks at a time," she argued softly, feeling the rift coming as she looked at his implacable expression. He was so easygoing, yet the few times he had felt strongly about something or become angry, he could be hard and tough and unyielding.

He stared at her as she turned the box in her hand and the diamond glittered in the sunlight. "It's beautiful."

"But you're not placing it on your finger."

"Jake, it isn't just you and me." She met his gaze again. "There's Melody and all my family, Asa, Phoebe, Myra, Tom and Bernie."

"Asa and you got enough out of the sale to take care of them without you working. The families get along fine. Melody is crazy about Myra and Phoebe and Asa, and they seem to like her."

"They do," she replied, looking at the ring, feeling assaulted by joy and anxiety. "Jake, I love this job. This is why I got an M.B.A. I like the responsibility." She met his dark gaze. "I'd like to have the experience of several years before I quit, so if I need a job again, I'd be qualified."

As they stared at each other, tension grew, and she hurt. It was the first time they had really disagreed, because from the night they'd met there had been a mutual enjoyment, a deep, compelling attraction. They were compatible, the sexual moments were magic. She needed his strength, his companionship, yet her job was vital. A muscle worked in his jaw, and his eyes were midnight dark, cold and hard and forbidding.

"Samantha, I love you and want you for my wife. I don't want another career woman for Melody to miss and never know. I don't want an empty bed while you open restaurants in Seattle and Baltimore and Miami. I want you at my side. Maybe that's damned old-fashioned, but I got burned badly the first time, and so did Melody."

"I make a big salary and I'm saving part of it to send the kids to college. They have funds set up from the sale, and Asa is providing for them, too. But part of my salary goes to my family and—"

"I'll take care of them. I can send all the kids to college, and I know you have funds set up. It isn't the family, Samantha," he observed softly. "You love your work."

She looked at the glittering ring and wondered if she was throwing away happiness with both hands. Yet the thought of giving up her new job and all the excitement and challenge of it was enough to give her pause. She reached out to stroke his dark hand, brushing the sprinkling of fine hairs across his wrist.

"Look at this." She waved her hand at the whitewashed villa with bright yellow poinciana flowering trees. She glanced at flaming bougainvillea, the red tile roof and graceful palms on a white sand beach that ran down to crystal-blue water. "Jake, here nothing is real. It's a tropical paradise where time stops, responsibility is gone, families don't make demands. Can we wait until we get home, where things are normal, and talk this over then?"

He looked fierce and intent as he stared at her. With deliberation he slipped his hand behind her neck and drew her toward him. His eyes seemed to pull her down into darkness that tugged at her heart and soul. "I don't want to lose you to a damned restaurant," he said gruffly, brushing her lips with his.

Jake hurt, because he saw what she wanted, and he suspected once they were back in Salido, she would feel even more strongly about it. He wasn't going to give up without trying to win her, because he loved her. She was a shimmering flame, stirring desire, bringing laughter and love back into his life.

He loved her slowly, taking his time until she pushed him down on the towel and moved over him, her tongue and hands drifting across him, driving him beyond control. He groaned and shifted above her, nudging apart her legs to take her.

Later as he held her, Jake felt something sharp poke his thigh and he reached down to pick up the box with the ring. He snapped it shut and tossed it onto another chaise.

"Jake—"

251

He turned to kiss her so she couldn't talk about the ring. He wanted her and couldn't imagine life without her, yet he wasn't going into a marriage like his first. He didn't want a dedicated career woman who put her job and money over love and family.

They swam again, and he fished out their goggles and breathing tubes, but the swimsuits were gone. They waded out and picked up towels to go inside. He scooped up the ring, wondering what would happen when they returned home.

That night when Samantha lay in his arms, she could see the stars twinkling in an inky sky that blended with the dark water. Occasionally a boat would pass with running lights shining brightly. Jake's breathing was deep and even, and she ran her hands over the thick mat of hair on his chest. She felt torn in two, because she loved him deeply. Yet she didn't want to give up her salary and independence.

She slid out of bed and walked outside, standing on the patio and gazing over the cool white sand at the dark water. With a faint clatter, palm fronds shifted gently with the breeze that blew off the sea. Moonlight gleamed on the water, and she felt as if she were caught in two opposing currents. She loved Jake and all he was offering, but she wanted her career.

She tried to close her thoughts to the dilemma. They had agreed to wait until they were home and back in routines, so she would not let worries intrude on their idyll. She went back to bed, sliding close to Jake to hold him.

And all too soon they were home, turning into her driveway in Salido. "Jake, the week has been wonderful."

"I think so too, love," he said lightly. "I'll get your things."

He carried suitcases, and all the family piled out to meet them. When they told Jake goodbye, Samantha walked out on the porch with him.

"Tomorrow night I'll pick you up at six, and we'll have dinner with Melody."

"Fine," she answered, knowing he wanted to spend some time with Melody after being gone a week.

"I'll call you later," he promised, walking backwards across the lawn. As he climbed into the truck and left, she went inside to pass out gifts she had brought back.

Later in bed she stared at the sky, unable to sleep. There were the same stars that had been over them at Akumal when she had been locked in Jake's arms. She missed him dreadfully, and she knew that soon she was going to have to make a choice between her career and Jake.

They spent the next three evenings with Melody, and then Wednesday night Melody and Jake ate dinner at the Bardwells' and they stayed until ten when Jake said he had to take Melody home.

Samantha walked to the Bronco with him while he carried Melody, who dozed with her head on his shoulder.

"Jake, next week is when I go to San Francisco.

You said you'd see if you could come."

"I just missed a week of work, and I don't know if I can get away. We've got our winter wheat crop in, but I'm buying some cattle and I have things I've put off. I'll see what I can juggle around."

" 'Night." She brushed his cheek with a kiss. "Melody is asleep."

"See you tomorrow night."

She watched him buckle Melody in and drive away.

To her relief he flew to San Francisco two days before the restaurant opening.


Jake entered the restaurant the night before the official opening. He was one of the guests for the by-invitation-only evening to get out all the kinks, and from what Samantha had said last night, this restaurant had plenty. Equipment had been faulty and had had to be replaced. Supplies hadn't arrived. Three employees quit before the restaurant even opened.

He stepped inside into chaos and noise. The place was packed with waiters and waitresses rushing through the large room. Someone sang with the karaoke, belting out a song, while three couples gyrated on the tiny dance floor. The smell of grilled meat and hickory smoke filled the air, making him realize he was hungry. He scanned the crowd and then saw her talking to a waiter. She turned and came toward him, and he felt his insides tighten as he inhaled deeply.

She wore a red leather jacket, a white tank top of clinging material and a red leather miniskirt that revealed her long legs to perfection. The high-heeled red pumps added another three inches. Her smooth pageboy-styled auburn hair swung slightly as she walked, and he felt a pang, remembering that first night when he'd found her stuck in the pantry. Her blue eyes had been cool, yet with changing emotions so evident in them. He remembered the dust on her jeans and shirt, her hair falling free, the curls tangled around her face. While the woman coming toward him was breathtakingly beautiful, it was when she was in jeans or shorts or wearing nothing that he liked her best.

He watched the sexy sway of her hips that was the same; but so much else was different. She was strikingly beautiful now, sophisticated, much more poised. He glanced at the crowd and saw men watching her. The responsibility of her job had changed her. He had known she would change, but he hadn't wanted to admit it or face it. She thrived on the responsibility, and with every assignment, he felt her slipping away from him. He wanted to take her hand, lead her out of the restaurant and take her where he could be alone with her. He ached to run his hand through the perfect hairdo, to take off the sexy, classy clothes, to find the warm, down-to-earth woman that was beneath them. He jammed his fist in his jeans as she approached.

"Jake, I wondered—"

"Samantha," a waiter called, rushing up to her,

his eyes big as he tugged nervously at his collar. "They're into it in the kitchen. You better come. It's Dom and Remi in a fight and both are threatening to quit."

"I'll be right there," she told him coolly, turning to Jake and brushing his cheek with a kiss. "Thanks for coming. Everything is topsy-turvey. I have to run to the kitchen, but I'll get someone to seat you."

"I'm all right."

She flashed him a smile. "It's the manager and the cook in a fight. I can't lose my cook. I'll see you when I get things settled." She left and paused to talk to a waitress, who glanced at him, picked up a menu and flatware and came over to him.

"Mr. Colby? If you'll come this way. Sorry you had to wait."

"Thanks," he answered, following her to a booth. Often, during the next couple of hours, he saw Samantha across the room, moving through the crowd, talking to waiters and waitresses. But she never got back to his table. Finally when they played a ballad and everyone sang along, he left, stepping out into the cool night air, looking down the sloping hill at lights on the Bay. He turned to walk, stretching out his legs in a long stride as he headed to the hotel, feeling the need to walk or jog, to do something physical. He felt tense. He didn't want to settle for half a life with her, waiting while she went to openings.

At three in the morning Samantha entered the hotel room. Jake stood by the window, his hip canted as he turned to face her. Moonlight splashed over his bare chest, his dark shorts and bare long legs.

"Jake, I'm sorry. Everything seemed to go wrong tonight."

He crossed the room to pour two glasses of wine and hand her one. "Turn around," he ordered as she kicked off her shoes. He began to knead her shoulders, feeling the tense muscles in her neck and back.

She sighed. "You're a marvel. You should be yelling and throwing things at me."

"Since when do I yell and throw things?"

She laughed softly as her head rolled forward. "You don't, but you would be excused for it tonight."

"Did you keep the cook from quitting?"

"Yes, I did." She stopped to take a drink of wine. "But the manager quit. I have to hire a new manager."

He paused to frown and stare at the back of her head. "Will that keep you here longer?"

"Only a few days," she said. She took another drink, set down her glass and turned to wrap her arms around him. "I'm sorry. This was a bad night. I'll hire a manager faster than you can spit, and we'll go home."

"I have to go home day after tomorrow no matter what," he told her solemnly, struggling to keep from crushing her in his arms and kissing her until he lost all his worries and hurt.

Samantha stood on tiptoe and wound her arm

more tightly around his neck. She dreaded having to tell him that next fall she was to go to England. Kyriakos wanted to open a London Salido Sam's and she was to be gone a full month from mid-September to mid-October.

"Jake," she whispered, tilting her head, feeling his strong arms wrap around her. He bent over her, molding her to his marvelous length, kissing her till her thoughts spun away.

It was on a misty April night on his ranch two weeks later, when Melody was asleep and Samantha was curled on the sofa in Jake's arms, that he shifted her away. She looked at his thick dark curls, the navy cable-knit sweater, and she felt desire uncoil, spreading through her. She wanted to pull him to her and kiss him. He reached into his pocket and withdrew the box with the diamond ring and held out his hand.

"I think it's time we settle our future. I proposed in Akumal, and we've waited until we're back in our routines. What's your answer going to be, Samantha?"

## Chapter Thirteen

"I love you and I want you to be my wife," Jake said, his eyes revealing his love as much as his words. His dark gaze made her feel desired, cherished. She leaned forward to kiss him full on the mouth. His arms wrapped around her tightly, and he pulled her onto his lap.

"Samantha, I need you," Jake whispered, knowing he did badly. He hadn't had a peaceful night's sleep since returning from Akumal, and it was time she gave him an answer.

Samantha felt torn, knowing exactly what he was asking. Her career was at stake. How badly did she want Jake? How badly did she want a job? She thought of her salary and the independence it gave her. For the first time she could go out and buy a dress if she wanted. If one of the kids needed to go to the dentist, she didn't have to sit down and try to juggle every dime. Yet it wasn't the money, and she knew it. It was the challenge and the responsibility.

She looked at his black eyes and thick lashes,

knowing him intimately—the contours and planes of his body, the rough texture and hard muscles, knowing his moments of passion and moments of laughter. She had seen him in tender moments with his daughter, watched him fight and ride in a rodeo. And she'd spent hours and hours talking to him.

He framed her face with his large, rough hands. "Will you marry me?" His dark eyes probed, fanning fires, yet she felt she would never be happy living at the ranch and giving up her job.

"I want to say yes, but I want to keep working."

His jaw clamped shut, and the hard, shuttered look came to his features, and she could feel a chasm opening between them. His gaze went over her features, her eyes, her hair, her mouth. He shifted away and stood, dropping the ring and box into his pocket. He crossed the room to the fire and turned to face her, his back to the dancing flames, his lean body a dark silhouette against the bright glow.

"I love you, but I won't go into a marriage like that again."

"Jake, what would I do all day out here? All I've known is work since I was thirteen, when I started baby-sitting for people. I worked through high school and college and since then. This is an exciting job. Would you want to retire?"

"I'm asking you to be a mother to Melody, to have our own children, to run this household. It keeps Mrs. Latham busy. Get some job in Salido where you don't travel and you come home at night. Run Salido Sam's full-time, I don't care if you work. I just don't want your career to come before your family, and I don't want you gone for weeks at a time."

She felt a surge of anger, because he was going to be implacable. She stood up and faced him. "You know I can't get work here that would hold the responsibility and challenge I have. Where would I find something like this in Salido or Monroe or Sangley or any other town within a hundred miles?"

"Does it have to be that challenging, Samantha?"

"I love what I'm doing."

"Evidently far more than I realized," he snapped, and the words that stung like a lash.

"It looks as if we've reached an impasse." They were only yards apart, yet she felt on an ever-widening rift. They stared at each other, and she felt engulfed in pain. "You'll have to take me home," she replied stiffly, angry with him for demanding something *he* wouldn't want to do.

He crossed the room to get her jacket. He held it, his hands brushing her nape, his dark eyes flashing pinpoints of angry fire. "I want to let Mrs. Latham know that I'm driving you home," he said, walking down the hallway.

Samantha went to the back door, standing in the dusky light of the silent kitchen, looking at the house and knowing what he had offered and what she was turning down. In minutes he came striding through the room. His gaze locked with hers and her heart pounded. She ached to be in his arms, yet she wasn't giving up her life for his demands.

They stepped outside, a fine rain falling. She felt a constriction in her chest, wondering if he would take her home and tell her goodbye, and that would be the end of seeing him.

He held the door to the Bronco and she climbed inside. He started the engine and in minutes it was warm inside, the windshield wipers going with a steady click-clack as they drove off. She listened to them, wondering if she would forever associate the sound with pain.

"Are we saying goodbye?" she asked, turning toward him, hurting, because she loved him.

He glanced at her and pushed his hat to the back of his head, black curls springing forward around his face. "That's up to you, Samantha. This choice is yours."

"No, it's not mine alone."

"When and where is the next restaurant opening?"

She rubbed her hands together. "Seattle," she answered, thinking how many miles away Seattle was from Salido.

"And when is that?" he asked, his voice tinged with anger.

"May fifth."

"Coming up all too soon. Seattle is a beautiful city. You should like it."

"Jake, I don't think you're being reasonable."

His head snapped around, and then he turned

his attention back to the road. "Maybe I'm not, but I know what I want and what I want to avoid. Maybe I'm stubborn and inflexible."

"Can't you bend a little?"

"I figured I was giving a little when I told you to get another job. Where have you bent a little?"

She felt a surge of anger. "If I tell Mr. Kyriakos that I can't go to openings and can't travel, how long do you think I'd have the job as manager here?"

"Probably as long as you damn well want. Why wouldn't he want you here as manager? He'd be crazy not to. But that really isn't what you want."

"No, it isn't." She studied his profile that was rugged and handsome. She felt angry with him, because he was being stubborn.

On her driveway, Jake climbed out of the Bronco. She stepped out and looked up at him, her emotions in a turmoil.

"Jake, I love you," she said softly, hurting and tempted to say yes to his demands. Each time she reached that brink, she thought of what she was giving up, and she couldn't accept his proposal.

He reached out to take her arm and walk her to the door. They climbed the steps. He leaned forward, his mouth hard, insistent, his tongue thrusting across hers. Heat burst within her, longing and tension unraveling and spilling through her veins.

With a soft cry she clung to him and kissed him. Finally he released her, looking down at her.

"Goodbye, Samantha," he said gruffly.

"Jake, can't we work out something?"

He looked at her. "You know what you want, and I know what I want, and our plans and desires and dreams don't fit together."

He strode off the porch and across the yard to the Bronco, and she watched him go. Stunned, she stared as the lights flashed on. The Bronco swung around and then was gone down the street, the red taillights disappearing.

She hurt, an all-consuming pain that bound her heart and fanned out, seeming to fill her soul. How could he be so stubborn? So unreasonable?

Yet he knew what he wanted, and he'd had one bad marriage because of his wife's career. She stared at the silent street and wondered if she was going to have a quiet, empty life because of her decision.

Tears spilled over—hot, salty, reminding her of his saltwater kisses in Akumal. "Jake," she whispered. She wiped her eyes. She didn't want to discuss her breakup with Jake tonight with Aunt Phoebe.

She opened the door quietly, saw the glow from the television set in the living room. Taking a deep breath, she stepped to the doorway.

"I'm home. I'm going to bed."

"Oh, Samantha, this is the best show. Remember *A Place in the Sun?* You should come watch."

"I'm exhausted, Aunt Phoebe. I'll see you in the morning," she said, hurrying to the stairs and up to her room. She sat down by the window, thinking about Jake driving home. She hurt, clutching her fist against her middle. Jake . . .

Tears fell over her hand. No one would know she was crying, because she wouldn't see them until morning.

And how was she going to tell the family? Phoebe had had the wedding planned for months now. The kids liked him, and he had become part of the boys' lives, going to their games, talking to them. Myra would storm and rave and stir up the entire household. And Asa would be disappointed, although he should understand her answer. But it was going to hurt him, because he truly liked Jake and he wanted her happy. And he wanted her married. Phoebe and Asa both thought she should be married, so morning would bring a new set of problems.

And Melody . . . The thought of never seeing the little girl again hurt. Melody had won a place in her heart, and Samantha felt another wrench of loss. She thought about holding Melody, remembering the child's laughter, recalling how Melody would kiss her cheek, giving her love freely. She was precious, part of Jake, and Samantha's pain mushroomed.

She stared out the window, thinking about Eldon Kyriakos, her job and travel, Jake and Melody, her family. She moved closer to the window, looking at mist-shrouded trees and drops of water forming and running down the pane. Jake was still out in the storm, driving home, but he hadn't called and he wouldn't. He had severed their relationship after her answer, and he would say that she was the one to end it.

She dozed in the chair until morning and woke feeling lost and forlorn and hurting. And she dreaded facing the family. She showered and changed, dressing in a bright aqua sweater and slacks, trying to look as cheerful as possible. She heard Bernie and Tom yelling and doors banging, and she hurried. If she told them now, they wouldn't have time to ply her with endless questions. By the end of the school day, they would have accepted the breakup.

Everyone was in the kitchen. Asa was bundled in his brown robe, Bernie and Tom were in T-shirts and jeans, gulping down glasses of milk. Phoebe had the paper and sat in her pink robe and fuzzy slippers at the table. In a miniskirt of black leather and a tight red blouse, knee boots of black leather and dangling red earrings, enough makeup to last a week, Myra looked like anything but a fourteen-year-old school girl.

"At least your face isn't going to get cold, but your seat sure will," Bernie remarked.

Myra turned around, narrowing her eyes. "I won't be cold."

"Your legs will be blue when you get to school," Bernie said. "Long skinny blue legs like some old swamp bird."

"Nyaa. Look who's talking. You have enough holes in your jeans to get frostbite."

"Bernie's right. You've got on too much makeup," Tom added.

He set his glass in the sink and turned to go. "Tom," Samantha said, wanting to catch them all

266

now. "Before you go — while all of us are together — I want to tell you something."

"I gotta run," Tom said, heading toward the door.

"You got a raise?" Myra asked.

"You're going to Disney World to open a Salido Sam's?" Bernie asked.

"Tom!" she exclaimed as he reached the door. "Wait a minute. I've broken up with Jake and I wanted all of you to know it."

"Sorry," Tom said and was gone.

"Samantha!" Aunt Phoebe cried and clutched her heart while Myra shrieked.

"You did what? You broke up with him?" Myra cried. "Don't do that now, Samantha. Wait a few years."

"So you can try to get him?" Bernie sneered. "Dream on, twerp."

"Dork."

"You wanted to, or he wanted to?" Bernie asked, getting to the heart of the matter.

"Neither of us wanted to. He asked me to marry him, but I would have to give up my job."

Bernie studied her. "We won't see Melody, either, will we?"

"No."

"You gave Jake and Melody up for Salido Sam's?" Myra asked.

"You're going to be late for school," Asa said quietly and Myra fled the room. Samantha turned to look at Asa and see the worry in his expression.

"Samantha," Phoebe said. "You gave up getting

married to that nice, wealthy man for your job? I mean, we're well-fixed now. It isn't like it used to be. I don't think you gave his proposal enough thought. You need to be married. Women today are just too liberated to know what's good for them, and a man is definitely a necessity. And that sweet little girl—she needs you, Samantha."

"Aunt Phoebe, Jake is everything to Melody."

"You don't have a man, Phoebe, and you get along fine," Asa stated. "I'm going upstairs and I'll talk to you," he said to Samantha.

She knew he would be waiting upstairs to talk to her about it, reserving his comments until he was away from Phoebe.

"I may get along," Phoebe grumbled, "but it isn't fine, and I don't like it without a man. If I could just find a nice man who likes late night movies—" She broke off and studied Samantha, who drank a glass of orange juice. "Samantha, I think you should seriously reconsider. Oh, my, when I tell Wanda, she'll be fit to be tied. She already had a little shower gift for you."

"That was premature, Aunt Phoebe, and you know it. I'll be back down in a little while."

"Samantha, think it over. Jake Colby is the nicest fellow, and the little girl of his is a beautiful and sweet child. She needs a mother. I wouldn't ever urge you into a marriage I thought you couldn't handle, but that child seemed so sweet. You don't want to work all your life."

"Right now I feel like I do. I can't just sit and do nothing."

"If you would just get interested in the movies, you can't imagine what a difference that would make in your life. I shudder to think what my life would be like without them. Tonight *Don't Talk to the Aliens* will be on and it's a hoot. Matter of fact, watch it with us, because it'll cheer you up."

"Thanks, we'll see what time I get off work tonight."

"You work too hard. You're the manager, and they have all kinds of help now, so you come home. The movie starts at eleven o'clock. Samantha, you think about it before you do anything hasty with Jake. He's a wonderful man."

"Yes, ma'am. If you'll excuse me, I'm going up and brush my teeth and talk to Granddad a minute. Then I have to be on my way to the restaurant."

As she climbed the stairs, she hurt. The worst was coming, when she would have to talk to Asa — because he would be hurt, and he would worry about her choice. He was old-fashioned about some things, and she suspected he would like to see her married.

The door to her room was open, and he was seated in the rocker near the window. She closed the door and felt a knot come in her throat. "Granddad, he doesn't want me to work at all. He wanted me to quit my job."

"And you didn't want to quit?"

"No. I love this job and everything that goes with it, and the more I do it, the more I like it. I can't imagine sitting out on the ranch week after week. What would I do?"

He tilted his head to study her. "You don't want your own family?"

"Yes, someday, but right now I'm in the first months of this job. Maybe two or three years from now I'll feel entirely differently about the whole thing."

"Well, honey, I'm sorry." He sighed, running his hand over his forehead. "I like Jake Colby and think he'd make you a good husband, and I'd be happy to see you marry him. But if you have such doubts and want to do something else, then you did the right thing. Marriage ought to be something two people want with all their hearts. But you're going to hurt for a while, because I know how you are when you love someone. It took a while to get over Devon, and I don't think you were as much in love with him." He stood up and crossed the room to give her a hug and a pat.

"Cheer up. Time helps. Maybe it's best. If it wasn't right for you, you'll forget Jake before long just like you did Devon. You don't regret Devon, do you?"

"Good heavens, no."

"See? You may feel the same about Jake in two months and be thankful you chose the way you did. Don't let Phoebe get you riled up. She's an incurable romantic."

"I won't."

"It'll pass. You'll forget him if you did the right thing," Asa repeated as he left the room.

Would she ever forget Jake? How different this had been from Devon!

She brushed her hair and finished dressing, finally leaving to walk to the restaurant.

During the morning she lost three bills for customers, left someone on hold on the phone and forgot them and then forgot to call a repair man about the heater. She was exhausted when the day was over, and she went home missing Jake, hurting more than she had the night before.

It didn't improve as the next two weeks passed. The weather warmed and spring was in full bloom with magnolias and tulips and yellow jonquils. She hurt all the time. She wasn't sleeping; she wasn't hungry and had lost five pounds.

"Saw Jake today," Myra remarked one night at dinner, giving Samantha a glare. "He looked as if he is suffering," she added darkly.

"I'll bet you tried to get him to take you out," Bernie scoffed.

"Did not!"

"Good thing. He wouldn't take out a child."

"I'm not a child!"

"Cool it," Samantha said, glancing at Phoebe's freshly dyed hair. "You had your hair done today, didn't you?"

"Yes," she answered, smiling.

"Looks really great," Myra said with obvious envy. "I would like to get mine the same color."

"Not until you're older," Samantha interjected. "How's Ellie getting along?"

"She's selling the shop. Vernon wants her to live

271

on the farm and she wants to. This is Ellie's last month."

Samantha was quiet as talk swirled around her, thinking about Ellie moving to the farm with Vernon and not working in Salido any longer. Samantha glanced out the window and wondered where Jake was and what he was doing. She thought about him constantly; more, it seemed, than she used to.

Then it was time to leave for Seattle, and for the first time, Jake didn't fly her to Oklahoma City to take the plane. She drove and left the car parked at the airport, catching the flight to Denver and then on to Seattle. For once she didn't feel eager to visit a new city. She looked at Oklahoma City as the ground fell away, and she wanted to be home.

Seattle was gorgeous, with blue skies and spring flowers in full bloom. The restaurant was on Madison Street near Seattle University. Once she was in the restaurant, she was busy constantly trying to get things running smoothly for the opening. Each time she returned to the hotel, it seemed empty — so different from the times Jake had flown up to join her, or when he would call her, or the times he had sent flowers.

Opening night was chaotic, and the karaoke broke down halfway through the evening. She was exhausted by half past two in the morning when she returned to the hotel. Rain had fallen all day and she shook her raincoat and hung it in the bathroom to dry. She moved to the window to look out at the streets, the reflection of headlights and red taillights shimmering on the wet pavement as water pelted the windows. She leaned her forehead against the cool window and hurt. She missed Jake badly.

Why wasn't this opening exciting like the others? When Jake had gone out of her life, something had dulled. Was it just the hurt that took the excitement and joy out of the openings? The little she had seen of Seattle had been beautiful, but she didn't have much interest in seeing more of the town. She sank down on a chair and leaned her head back. Had she made a terrible mistake?

She returned home, feeling alone, missing him terribly on the drive from Oklahoma City. It had been six weeks now. Was he dating anyone? She had been asked out by the new manager in Seattle, and she had declined. Dating was the last thing she wanted to do, because all she would think about would be Jake.

It was late when she turned into the drive. Phoebe was watching a movie. She met Samantha at the door. "How was Seattle?"

"Busy. It's a very pretty city."

"Did you take pictures?" Phoebe asked, hugging Samantha and stepping back to look up at her.

"No, I didn't. Where's everyone?"

"Bernie and Tom are out. Myra's in bed, and Asa's in bed."

"It's a school night. Bernie and Tom should be home."

"They called and said something about some football players and a coach. They said they would be in by midnight."

"All right. Any calls?" she asked and held her breath.

"No, no calls. Want to watch the movie?"

"All right, Aunt Phoebe." She consented just to be with another person. She felt a disappointment that was ridiculous. She shouldn't expect Jake to call ever again, yet a faint hope existed that he would relent. Had he gotten over the breakup? Or did he hurt the way she did?

Tomorrow she would have to talk to Bernie and Tom and find out where they had been and what they had been doing.

The next Monday as she walked to the bank during the afternoon to make a deposit, she looked up as a pickup pulled to the curb and Jake climbed out.

Her heart lurched like a roller coaster over the first big drop. He had on his black Stetson, worn jeans, a blue chambray shirt with the sleeves rolled back. She realized she had stopped walking and people were moving around her.

"Hi, Samantha," Lori Foster said, passing her.

"Hi, Lori," she answered perfunctorily, taking a deep breath. His gaze swung to meet hers, and she felt as if a fist had squeezed her heart. Why was falling in love supposed to be so wonderful? She hadn't ever hurt as badly as she did now.

"Hi, Samantha," a man said.

"Hi," she answered without knowing who had

spoken. For an instant she thought Jake might go on his way without speaking, but he came forward slowly as if he was reluctant to talk to her.

"Hello."

"Hi, Jake." He was deeply tanned, handsome enough to make her feel faint. "How's Melody?"

Something flickered in his expression, so slight, and then it was gone. "She's fine. How's your family?"

"They're fine," she answered. How polite, how cool they sounded. Did he hurt as badly as she did? Would she ever stop feeling the loss? It was so good to see him. She locked the fingers of both hands together, suddenly feeling compelled to touch him and knowing she couldn't.

"How's the job?"

"Fine," she replied.

"Where are you going next?"

"Tulsa."

"Closer to home this time." They looked at each other, and she remembered how black his eyes were, the deep dark pools fringed with thick lashes. "I heard they're expanding the chain overseas."

"Yes. London is the first place. I'll be there next fall."

"So you'll get to see England."

"Mostly I see the inside of a kitchen and a hotel room."

"I've got some errands. It was nice to see you."

"It was good to see you."

He turned and disappeared inside an office

275

building. She felt as if she had just been run over by a truck. Dazed, she hurt and wanted to run back and tell him how much she had missed him and feel his arms around her again. He hadn't looked in agony or worried. Had he gotten over the hurt? Would she ever get over it? Would she feel this way every time she ran into him. And if she saw him with another woman—

She blinked and drew a deep breath and her hands shook. She glanced over her shoulder.

She couldn't get the encounter out of her mind. It was only a matter of time before she did run into him with another woman. When she did, it would hurt more than anything before.

The third week in June she drove to Tulsa from Salido, arriving in the middle of the afternoon. Two nights after the opening, she paced the motel room impatiently. She was in a smaller room, and she felt cooped up, restless, missing Jake more each day, dreaming about him when she did fall into a fitful sleep. She missed Melody and kept thinking about her. Phoebe's words that the child needed Samantha kept running through her thoughts. Did Melody miss and need her? The idea was a knife in her heart.

The excitement had gone out of the job. She had been having the most wonderful time in her life, but Jake had been a part of it. Now, without him, everything seemed hollow and empty. The money didn't seem that important. She stared at the blank wall and remembered when the restaurant was on the brink of ruin and bills were high, yet she was happy because she was dating Jake.

She looked at the empty motel room. If this was all she had to come home to for years, she had made a mistake. Her gaze slid to the phone again, and she looked at the clock. It was three in the morning, and Jake would be asleep.

The shrill ring of the phone made her jump. She blinked and stared at it in shock. It rang again, and she rushed to pick up the receiver.

"Samantha?" Jake's voice came over the line.

# Chapter Fourteen

She felt as if she had stepped off the earth and was tumbling through space. "Jake! Yes, I was just—"

"Sorry to call at this hour. I'm at the airport."

She blinked and realized his voice was solemn and he must be in Tulsa. "In Tulsa?" she asked, feeling dazed. He didn't talk like a man in love. He sounded like a man who was in trouble.

"Yes. I'm coming to get you."

"Jake, what's wrong?" she asked, suddenly terrified that something dreadful had happened to Asa or Bernie.

"Your family is okay," Jake reassured her swiftly, and she let out her breath. "The restaurant is burning. I thought you'd want to be there."

"Oh, my! Oh, yes. Is everyone out?"

"People are okay. Everyone got out. I just knew you'd want to get home. I can be at the motel in twenty minutes. I brought a ranch hand, Don Quinton. He'll drive your car back and park it at your house. He can get a ride home from there."

"I'll be ready. My room is 114."

"See you," he said and hung up.

She replaced the receiver and stared into space, imagining the restaurant going up in flames. All of Salido might burn if they didn't get more help from surrounding towns to fight the fire. She looked at the phone. Jake had come to get her and take her home. Jake was here. Coming to the motel. She would be with him all the way back to Salido.

She looked down at herself. Her linen skirt and blouse were wrinkled. She yanked them off and rushed to shower, going as fast as possible and dressing in fresh jeans, a pale blue knit shirt, socks and sneakers. She dried her hair, letting it go in soft curls while it was still partially damp. She was stuffing shoes into the shoulder bag when she heard a knock at the door.

She threw it open and looked up at Jake and was held, as if by invisible bonds, as tension curled between them, pulling on her emotions. He wore tight, faded jeans, a red knit shirt that showed his muscles, and he looked marvelous. Her heart hammered violently, and she noticed that a muscle worked in his jaw. Another man in a broad-brimmed hat and dusty jeans stood beside him.

"Sorry this is why I had to come."

"Come in. I'm almost packed up to go."

"Samantha, this is Don Quinton. Don, this is Samantha Bardwell," Jake said without taking his gaze from her.

"Hi." Don smiled. "I'll drive your car back for you."

"Thanks. Here are the keys."

"See you folks in Salido."

Jake closed the door behind him and turned to look at her. "I have to call Mrs. Latham. I told her I'd check in when I arrived in Tulsa."

He placed the call while she packed the last of her things, cramming them into the suitcase and zipping it closed.

"Mrs. Latham?" He turned his back to Samantha, and her gaze ran over him and she remembered in the tiniest detail the textures and smoothness of his naked body.

"I'm in Tulsa, and we'll start back to Salido within the hour." He paused to listen. "If she wakes before I get home, tell her I called and I'll be home in a few hours."

He replaced the receiver as Samantha picked up the shoulder bag. "I'm ready."

As he took the shoulder bag from her and her suitcase, she caught a scent of woodsy after-shave that tantalized her nerves, a subtle reminder of intimate moments with him that momentarily made a flush of warmth surge in her.

"I'll run over to the motel office and leave the key," she said, trying to think about what she should be doing. "They have the credit card number, and I'll put the room on my expense report."

"I'll drive you there. Get in." He opened the door to the back of a black rental car and dropped her things inside. He held a door for her, and she slid into the passenger seat.

"Jake, thank you for coming to get me."

He shrugged. "I knew you'd want to be there, and I know Asa needs you. Even though Salido Sam's

280

no longer belongs to your family, I know Asa will be sentimental about it." He stopped in front of the office and held out his hand. "Give me the key and I'll leave it."

She did, looking into his black eyes that made her weak with longing every time he focused on her like twin cannon ready to turn her into fodder. He rushed around the car, his long jeans-clad legs stretching out. The knit shirt hugged his broad chest. He was wearing dusty black boots that made him even taller. In seconds he slid back behind the wheel. He drove fast, the tires squealing as he swung onto the highway.

"How bad is the fire?"

"They're trying to get it under control," he said, not giving her an answer.

"That bad?"

"No, I'm not being evasive. Fires can look terrible and not be as bad as they appear, so I mean it. I don't know. It looks bad. Monroe and Sangley have firemen there to help."

"You really meant it when you said everyone was okay?"

"Yes, I did." He watched the road, passing a car and changing lanes to pass another one. Light from the dash gave a faint orange tint to his cheekbones. There was a dark stubble on his jaw.

"How's Melody?"

He glanced at her swiftly and back to the road. "She's fine."

"How did the fire start?"

"That's one reason you need to come home. Everyone who worked in the kitchen said it was an

281

accident, but the microwave shorted and Bernie had been using it earlier and I think he's taking this hard. When I left, he seemed to feel responsible, but all the others said he wasn't."

"I hope the insurance will cover everything."

"Don't worry. The building was old—worth a lot more now than a year ago, but it's not like the new places you've installed in fancy parts of big cities. If this had been San Francisco, the cost would have been astronomical."

"How did you know about it?"

"I was in the pool hall when it came on the air. I went to the house and got Asa. He was there with Bernie when I left. No one could find Tom. Myra went with us, but Phoebe stayed home. She said she couldn't bear to watch it. Wanda Mayfield came over to sit with her."

"Thank you, Jake, for getting Granddad and coming to get me."

"Sure," he answered quietly, and she thought how polite and distant they were and all she really wanted to do was throw herself into his arms.

"How's the Tulsa opening?"

"The usual. I suppose someone notified Mr. Kyriakos's office?"

"I don't know, Samantha. I didn't ask about that," he said, sounding indifferent to whether Kyriakos Enterprises knew about the fire or not.

They raced to the airport and were cleared for takeoff, and soon the twinkling lights of Tulsa spread below her. She turned to look at Jake, and emotions tugged at her. She worried about her family and the restaurant, Bernie and Asa, the two who would be most affected. She thought about the restaurant built so long ago. All her family had been involved with the building and now it was burning.

"Jake, I've missed you."

He turned his head and gave her a long, solemn look. "I've missed you, and so has Melody. I'm taking her to Disney World in August."

"That'll be fun for her," she said, longing to see Melody, needing Jake. She ached to reach out and touch him, but a barrier was between them, and his coolness held her back. He was concentrating on flying the plane. Did he date someone else now? Was tonight a charitable mission and nothing more, just as he said? Had he come because he felt sorry for Asa and knew Asa would want her home . . . or because he still cared? "Has Melody been to Disney World before?"

"No. We've made other trips. I've taken her to Six Flags and to Silver Dollar City. She's been with me on business when I've flown to Louisiana, and we went on to Akumal."

"So that wasn't the first time you'd been there?"

"No, I've been there before."

Had he taken another woman to Akumal? "Did you spend your honeymoon with Diantha somewhere tropical?"

"No," he answered tersely. "Paris. She wouldn't have gone to an isolated beach. She wanted to shop. There's your fire, Samantha. Down there, on the horizon."

She saw a glow and a spiral of gray curling into the night sky, and suddenly the fire seemed real and devastating. "Oh, Jake," she cried, gripping his arm. "We don't own it any longer, but that building has been as much a part of our family almost as the house." His fingers squeezed hers, continuing to hold her hand in his while she stared at the glow and the bright lights of Salido. "I'm afraid this will hurt Granddad terribly."

"He's tough, Samantha. He seemed to be doing all right. He's trying to console Bernie, so he's putting up a good front."

"I suppose I should just be thankful everyone got out, and not worry about an old building that a lot of people thought ought to be torn down, anyway."

"I imagine they can build it back to look just like it did before the fire."

"I hope the fire doesn't take all of the buildings on Main Street with it."

They flew over Sangley, then over Monroe. As they approached Salido, the fire became easier to see, changing from a glow on the horizon to flames leaping in the air and smoke billowing skyward.

"Jake they don't have it under control at all!"

"Doesn't look like it. Probably other buildings are burning."

She stared at it as he circled to avoid the smoke. She remembered the night she was locked in the pantry, and she became aware of his fingers curled around hers. He was looking below, and she felt another rush of longing to grab him and tell him how terribly she had missed him. Her gaze ran over the flat planes of his cheeks, his firm jaw, and she wondered how he felt now.

He released her hand as the blue runway lights rushed up to meet them and then they touched down smoothly.

Tension coiled tighter in her when they neared the fire in Jake's Bronco, and finally Jake stopped a block away. They climbed out, and he took her hand to rush toward the crowd. People stood in clusters, some on rooftops of houses or buildings in other blocks. Men shouted orders as hissing streams of water arced high in the air. Hoses were stretched across the ground like fat beige pipes. The fires crackled and burned. The smoke-filled air was acrid, burning her throat and stinging her eyes, and heat rolled over her as if it was blown from a furnace. Devastated, she stared at the flaming pool hall — the restaurant a charred hulk with the roof caved in.

"Oh, Jake!" She stared at it in horror, suddenly feeling weak in the knees and thankful everyone had gotten out safely. "I hope the firemen are all okay."

Trucks were parked at angles, blocking streets, men in slickers rushing around them. Jake shouldered her through the crowd while she looked at the disaster.

"There's Asa," he said, and she looked around. Asa stood with his arm around Bernie, whose white face was tear-streaked. Myra stood beside him.

"Granddad!" Samantha exclaimed, rushing to hug him.

"Thanks for bringing her home, Jake," Asa said over her head as he held her. She turned to hug Bernie.

"I don't know what happened," he stated in a voice that was a croak. "I was cooking, and I had used the microwave and then there was a fire."

285

"Bernie, everyone got out. That's what matters."
She hugged him tightly, realizing as she held him
how he had grown. She moved back to give Myra a
squeeze. "How's Aunt Phoebe?"

"She was crying, and she was upset," Myra answered. "But Miss Mayfield came over to sit with
her."

Samantha went back to stand beside Asa, and
Jake moved close, draping his arm across her shoulder as he stood with her. She was aware of the slight
contact with him, grateful for his strength now.

"They've got it contained," Asa said. "If they can
get it out, this will be over."

"Bernie," she asked, leaning around Asa, "did
anyone notify Kyriakos Enterprises?"

"Yes." He looked at Asa.

"I called Mr. Kyriakos," Asa stated. "He has some
men here now, and some insurance people have
shown up."

She shivered as she looked at the smoldering ruin
that had been the restaurant. She remembered old
times, times with Jake, the morning Eldon Kyriakos
had sat at the corner table and made her the offer
that had changed all their lives. She shivered, even
though heat radiated from the fire.

Jake's arm tightened around her, and she looked
up to see him watching her, and her breath caught as
she gazed into his dark eyes.

"It'll be rebuilt, Samantha," he said in a gruff
voice, and she felt a rush of warmth. He still cared!

"Sorry, Samantha," Wilson Yarrell said, moving
out of the crowd.

"Thanks, Mr. Yarrell," she replied, aware of him

286

going to speak to Asa. She glanced over the crowd and saw Ellie and Vernon. Ellie met her gaze and looked away, and Samantha realized there were people who didn't speak to her or offer sympathy, even during a catastrophe. She knew then that as long as she lived in Salido, she would probably never win back their friendship. Even so, this was home, and she wanted the restaurant rebuilt.

"There's Phoebe!" Asa exclaimed in surprise and Samantha turned her head.

Phoebe was wrapped in a pink shawl, and Wanda Mayfield held her arm as they moved through the crowd. Wanda looked worried and Phoebe's face was ashen, drained of all color, her lips a thin line, and Samantha hurt for her.

Phoebe rushed up to grasp Asa's hand. She looked at Samantha. "Thank heavens you're home, Samantha," she exclaimed, giving her arm a squeeze and turning to grasp Asa's arm again. "Dad, I just got a call from a Monroe policeman." She looked at Samantha. "He's at the Monroe Hospital, and he called because Tom has had a wreck and is at the Monroe Emergency and we need to get over there."

Samantha's senses reeled with the second shock. Bernie let out a high-pitched wail that sounded as filled with pain and shock as if he'd been stabbed. He clutched his head and spun around, stomping his foot, and Samantha stared at him.

"Bernie?"

He looked stricken as he met her gaze, and tears welled up in his eyes. "I'm sorry," he said, shaking his head.

"We all are." She was amazed by the intensity of

his reaction. Was it too much, coming on top of the restaurant burning?

Phoebe handed a sheet of paper to Asa. "Here's the number, and they said for you or Samantha to call as soon as possible."

Jake's arm moved from Samantha's shoulder to her waist, and he held her tightly as he shifted. "I can take all of you to Monroe. I've got the Bronco, and we can get everyone in it."

"Thanks," Samantha said in relief.

"I'd better find a phone," Asa said, looking around.

"I've got one in the car," Jake said. "It's this way." His fingers curved lightly around Samantha's arm.

She reached out to grasp Bernie's hand. "Bernie, are you all right?"

He wiped his eyes and stared at her, and she hugged him. He clung to her tightly. "Jeez, Samantha, I'm sorry."

"Let's not worry until we get there and see how he is."

He released her, and she looked up at him to see tears fill his eyes again. He swiped his hand across his eyes and frowned. "Samantha, he was riding my bike. I let him have it."

She closed her eyes, feeling a tight wrench. He was on the motorcycle when he'd had a wreck. Her worst fears about the bike had come true. Lord, please let him recover, she prayed swiftly.

"Let's go. The sooner Asa calls, the sooner you'll know," Jake said in her ear, taking her arm to steer her toward the Bronco.

Wanda told Phoebe goodbye. "I'll wait at the

house, and don't you worry too much."

They climbed in, and Jake started driving while Asa called the hospital and finally hung up. "He's got his leg torn up, and they need to do surgery to get it fixed. He's bruised and has a broken collarbone and a broken arm, but he's going to survive."

Bernie sobbed and Myra patted his shoulder, while Asa turned to talk quietly to him. Jake reached over to take Samantha's hand and hold it, looking at her as he drove out of town.

"All right?"

"Yes. Thanks for staying."

Within the hour, they arrived at the Monroe hospital. They waited through the surgery, Jake holding her hand part of the time, and then a doctor appeared.

"Mr. Bardwell?"

"Here," Asa answered. "I'm Asa Bardwell." He offered his hand. "This is my granddaughter, Samantha Bardwell, and a friend Jake Colby, my daughter Phoebe, and my other grandchildren Bernie and Myra."

"I'm Dr. Richard Faidly," he said. "Tom's going to be fine."

Samantha felt a surge of relief as she listened to what they had done in surgery.

"He'll be in recovery, so it'll still be a while before you can see him, but he came through just fine. We'll let you know when he's ready to go to his room. He's going to be groggy."

"Thank you, Dr. Faidly. We were at the fire in Salido and couldn't find Tom and still don't know much about what happened."

"From what we gathered from the Monroe police, a car struck his motorcycle on the highway. He must have been trying to get home. It'll be a while now before he's home, but at least he should get there eventually."

Samantha turned away, running her fingers across her forehead. "Bernie is going to suffer. He wasn't supposed to let Tom ride on the bike, much less let him take it to Monroe. Both of them may have learned lessons."

Jake touched her cheek. "You've had a rough time. When's the last time you ate?"

"I don't remember, but I'm not hungry."

"How about a cold drink? I saw a machine in the hall."

"That sounds good."

"Asa, I'll get some pop for everyone," Jake said, taking Samantha with him.

In the deserted hall he turned her to look at him and placed his hands on the rail along the wall on either side of her. "I know you just went through an opening night and you've been working long hours. With all this coming on top of that, you should be ready to drop."

"I'm not. I don't feel sleepy or tired." She gazed into his dark eyes that made her pulse race. Longing billowed like the columns of smoke she had seen. "I'm relieved about Tom and sad about the fire. And I know Bernie is going to have problems."

"Stop worrying tonight," Jake replied quietly. "I can get motel rooms for everyone who wants to stay here, and I can drive anybody who wants to go back to Salido."

She looked up at Jake, her thoughts spinning about where she should be. She wanted to stay to see Tom and be with him when he came out of recovery.

And Jake was standing so close, looking at her intently, making her heart beat faster and making it more difficult for her to think about what she should do. She tried to forget that he was only inches away and he had spent the evening taking care of her and her family. He was concerned, or he wouldn't be here. Yet she didn't know for sure, because he would be considerate even if he'd lost interest. He would do the same for Diantha, even though he didn't have any love left for her.

"You need to get back to Melody."

"I will, but she's asleep now, anyway."

"I want to be with Tom."

"Let Bernie and Asa stay tonight. You've had a rough night and a long day. I'll bring you back tomorrow, because he'll be coming out of the anesthesia fully then, and you'll be needed more than you will tonight. We can wait until he's in his room and talks to you. I'll take you back."

"Bernie may be needed since he was at the restaurant."

"There are plenty of other people who were at the restaurant. Leave him here, Samantha, so he can see that Tom is going to be all right, and let *him* help Tom. The first few days after surgery are rough."

"All right," she agreed, seeing the wisdom in his suggestion. "The rest of us will go back to Salido with you. Jake, aren't you exhausted?"

"I'm fine," he reassured her, his voice becoming soft. For a moment they studied each other, and she felt the spring of tension that made her forget all the problems except that she had lost Jake.

"We'll get that pop," he said, straightening up. She walked down the hall with him, the sound of his boots and the faint swish of her sneakers against the polished floor the only sound. Jake dropped coins into the machine and handed her a cold can of pop and another to take to Asa.

"Take this, Bernie," Jake said, handing him a can. "I'll get some more. "Here, Phoebe," he said, giving her the other can and taking one from Samantha to give Myra.

"I want to stay with Tom when he comes out of recovery," Bernie said. "Samantha, I'm sorry," he added, raking his fingers through his hair. "Can I stay here with him?"

"Yes. Jake and I have already talked about it. He suggested you and Granddad stay, and Jake will take the rest of us to Salido. I'll come back tomorrow and bring the car so you'll have transportation." She squeezed his arm. "Bernie, stop worrying. He's doing okay. You can't blame yourself."

"I shouldn't have let him have the bike. You told me not to."

"It's over now. Sooner or later he would have wanted one too." She patted his arm.

It was dawn when they left Tom's room. He was groggy, beginning to make sense, and the nurse had given him something for pain. Jake took Asa to a motel and left Bernie with Tom. As they stopped in front of the motel room, Jake turned back to Asa.

"I'll follow Samantha over tomorrow and she can leave a car for you and Bernie."

292

"Thanks, Jake. See you folks tomorrow. Let's hope nothing else happens." He climbed out and ' disappeared into the motel room, closing the door behind him.

They drove home, and by the time they reached Salido, dawn was spilling over the earth, pink rays shooting up from the eastern sky. Main Street was charred ruins, with firemen milling around, a couple of wisps of smoke still rising.

"How long do the firemen have to stay?"

"They probably have to check on it for hours to make sure it doesn't flare back up again."

At the house everyone climbed out, mumbling sleepy thanks to Jake. "Want to come in and call Mrs. Latham?" Samantha asked Jake.

"No, I called her from the Monroe hospital," he said to her. Samantha sat alone with him in the Bronco, and she placed her hand on his arm.

"Thank you for all you've done for us tonight. It would have been so much worse without your help."

"It was nothing." He ran his fingers along her cheek, and she fought the urge to turn her head and kiss his hand. "Melody has missed you, and she'll know I was with you last night. Want to come out to the ranch soon for dinner with her?"

"Yes," she accepted softly, feeling her heart lurch. "I'll have to see what kind of schedule we keep with Tom, because someone will need to be with him."

"Sure, we can talk."

"Jake, thank you for tonight," she said, kissing his cheek lightly, turning to climb out of the Bronco. He was at her side, and she looked at her feet as she walked to the porch. Emotions overwhelmed her, and she knew she was exhausted and emotionally drained.

At the porch steps, she faced him. "I don't know what we would have done without you. Always to the rescue," she murmured softly, touching his knit collar lightly, aware of his hard collarbone beneath her finger. "Saving me from locked pantries, taking me home when I'm needed, getting all of us to Tom at the hospital. Thank you so much."

"Anytime. I'd do it all again if the need arose. Including the locked pantry. Good night, Samantha."

He turned and walked away in quick, long strides, and she felt her heart twist. I love you, Jake Colby. More than I knew, more than I've told you.

Because of Tom and driving back and forth between Monroe and Salido, it was the following week on Monday night the twenty-sixth of June, before she had a date with Jake.

Jake came at six to pick her up, and she stood at the front window upstairs and watched him turn in the drive and stride up the porch. Her heart pounded violently as she scooped up her purse and hurried downstairs.

# Chapter Fifteen

She felt excitement surge when she sat in the living room while Jake visited with Phoebe. He had brought Melody with him, and she sat on Myra's lap, but when Samantha entered the room, she slid off Myra's lap and ran across the room. Samantha picked her up and gave her a squeeze.

"How are you?" she asked, looking into Melody's dark twinkling eyes that were so much like her father's.

"Fine. You're coming to our house to dinner tonight."

"I know I am."

"I have a new doll, and her name is Samantha."

"You gave her my name?" she asked, aware Jake was watching them. Melody smelled like roses, and she wore a plaid dress. Her hair was caught up behind her head with a grosgrain bow. She wriggled, and Samantha set her down, watching her as she ran to pick up a rag doll with long yellow braids.

"Here's Samantha."

Samantha smiled as she took the doll with long

skinny rag arms and legs, blue button eyes and a smiling mouth. "She's a very nice doll. And special if she has my name."

Melody tugged on a lock of Samantha's hair. "I missed you."

"I've missed you, too," Samantha said softly as Melody hugged her. She gave the child a squeeze, feeling a tight knot in her throat. She couldn't look at Jake, and she squeezed her eyes shut.

She leaned back and smiled at Melody. "I'll read to you tonight."

Melody smiled in return, and Samantha stood up. Jake was beside them, studying her and looking solemn. He took Melody's hand. "Tell everyone goodbye and to come see us."

She waved. "Come see us."

He took Samantha's arm with his free hand, and they went to the Bronco where they buckled Melody between them.

Conversation revolved around Melody through the drive and dinner, and after dinner Samantha read three stories to her. Melody sat on her lap and wound a curl of Samantha's hair in her fingers while she read. As Samantha turned a page, Melody looked up. "You haven't come to see me for a long time."

"I missed you," she said, without looking at Jake.

"Daddy said you were gone far away. That you are going to England, too, and it's farther away than anywhere."

"It is far away, but it'll be a long time before I go to England."

"Will you come back and see me soon?"

"I'd like that, Melody." Samantha leaned forward to give the child a hug. Melody's thin arms wrapped around her neck and squeezed.

"I love you, Samantha."

Samantha felt as if she were being torn in two. "I love you, too," she said softly, closing her eyes and holding Melody. She hurt, and she felt a rush of love for the child who was open and sweet and loving, knowing Jake was fortunate in having Melody.

Melody snuggled back in Samantha's arms and pointed to the book. "Read."

As Samantha read, she glanced across the room. Jake sat quietly, his dark eyes intent on her. One long leg was slightly bent, the other booted foot on his knee, while he held a cold beer in his hand.

She looked down to continue reading, but her heart was beating swiftly, and she felt her emotions churning.

When they finished the book, Melody wiggled around, trying to reach another book, but Jake scooped her up from Samantha. "Mrs. Latham is waiting, and it's way past your bedtime."

"One more story, please."

"Not tonight." He held her with one arm and brushed her hair away from her face. "Samantha has already read three. It's bedtime."

"Good night, Samantha." Melody blew Samantha a kiss.

" 'Night, Melody." Samantha leaned close, intending to brush Melody's cheek with a kiss. Melody twisted forward so one arm was around Samantha's neck.

"I want you to stay here with Daddy and me."

"Thank you." Samantha's voice became weak, and her heart thudded. "I'd like that, too, but I have a job, Melody, and I have to be in certain places, just like your Daddy has to go to work." She felt her mouth go dry as she looked into Jake's black eyes that blazed with longing. There was no mistaking the look for a moment, and then it was gone.

"Bedtime," he announced, turning away. "I'll be right back." He disappeared down the hall with Melody.

Suddenly Samantha felt out of place; she shouldn't be here unless she wanted to conform to his demands. He hadn't changed, and she still couldn't face quitting her job. When he returned, she stood up and picked up her purse. "Maybe I should go home now."

He nodded, striding down the hall.

At the door he paused to face her. "Melody missed you so much," he said in a tight voice. "I thought after being with you the night of the fire and the next day, that I could bring you out here and it would make her happy, and I could keep control of my feelings. But it didn't work that way, and I won't do it again. Why did you come with me tonight?"

The question hung in the air, and she thought of all she had gone through, the questions in her mind, the longing.

"I've missed you terribly," she whispered, and his eyes narrowed a fraction. He caught her chin roughly and tilted her face up.

"Are you quitting your job?" he asked bluntly in a

harsh voice, and she stared at him, the question echoing in her heart and mind.

"I haven't, Jake."

He turned and opened the door and she went outside. Was this what she wanted? Couldn't he compromise? Suddenly she turned to him.

"You won't make any kind of compromise?" she asked stiffly, feeling her breath catch and her heart beat swiftly as she waited.

"I know it must sound unreasonable to you, Samantha, to want my wife home, but I do. I've had the other kind of marriage. No, I don't want to compromise, as much as I love you and want you."

His answer cut like the slash of a blade and she drew a deep breath, locking her hands together and heading for the Bronco and fighting tears. Why had she put herself through this again?

He drove fast back to town, and they were quiet. Finally they talked about the fire.

"Have you talked to Kyriakos?"

"Yes, and he's going to build it all back to look like it did. It'll be in keeping with the rest of the town, which should make other merchants happy," she answered perfunctorily. She felt as if she were crumbling into a thousand pieces inside.

"How was Tom today?"

"Much better, and he gets to come home tomorrow. Bernie will bring him home, and Myra is going with him in the morning. This has hurt Bernie. The bike was totaled, but he said he won't own another one. He's looking for a car."

"Sounds as if he's learned something."

How calm Jake's conversation sounded! He

wasn't going to compromise. She would have to give up all in order to conform to his wishes, and it didn't seem fair. And whether it was the wrong thing or the right thing to do, it was the only course open, because that was all he would accept.

"That's one worry you won't have then," he said as they turned into her driveway.

"Good night, Jake," she said, climbing out of the Bronco.

He came around and walked in silence beside her to the door. His fingers touching her arm lightly was a sizzling contact that made her ache for more. She loved him and she didn't want to tell him goodbye and watch him walk out of her life.

At the top of the steps he paused. "Goodbye, Samantha," he said tersely and turned and left, striding across the yard. She watched him go through a shimmering blur of tears. Was this really what she wanted?

She hurried up to her room, calling a greeting to Phoebe as she rushed past the living room. She closed her door and leaned against it, placing her hand against her heart. She felt as if it had been torn out. She hurt, and she wanted him and her job. But she didn't want a career as much as she wanted Jake. She thought of the lonely nights, the tedious hours, the empty motel rooms that were beginning to look alike. The airports were no longer distinctive in memory, just places to rush through on her way to somewhere else. They all looked similar, with glass and tile and dark carpets and desks and monitors.

"Jake," she whispered, knowing she didn't want to give him up for that. There had to be some other

300

job she could do. He would accept her working in Salido at the restaurant. She faced the fact that she didn't want to lose Jake.

She wanted to rush and grab the phone up and call him and ask him to come back, but she hesitated, because she had to be so sure. She couldn't give everything up and then find out she'd made a terrible mistake . . . and then hurt Jake and Melody by wanting out of a marriage.

And yet the thought of calling him, of telling him she had changed her mind, was the first bit of happiness she had experienced since the breakup. She had missed him every day and every night, and no job and no amount of money was worth losing him.

She crossed the darkened room to the window as she had done so many times when she'd come home from dates with him. She looked over the treetops and imagined him heading home.

"Jake, I love you . . ." she whispered, knowing she did and she always would and it wouldn't change. Instead of lessening with time, the hurt over losing him had deepened until it was all consuming. And he must feel the same, from the things he had said and done this week. He still was in love with her. And all she could do was either give him up or do things his way. And right now, his way seemed the way to happiness.

"Jake . . ." she whispered again, thinking she would give herself time — one week — to think about changing jobs, to see what she could try to find, to make absolutely sure, and then she would call him.

# *Chapter Sixteen*

Beneath a clear, blue June sky Jake shifted restlessly in the saddle, leaning forward as his horse wound up a steep hillside to search for a lost steer. Riding usually relaxed him, but today he felt impatient and irritable, with his nerves raw. He tried to keep his thoughts on what he was doing.

The swish of high grass and the clop of hooves mingled with the creak of his saddle. He hadn't slept at all last night and not much the night before. He loved Samantha, Melody loved her, he missed Samantha and he wanted her desperately. Hell, he missed all of them, Asa, Phoebe, Myra, the boys. Yet every time he thought it all over, he came back to the same conclusion.

And he knew she must still love him. But not as much as her job.

"Dammit," he said, and the bay's ears flicked back and forth as if he were listening. There had to be some way to work out a compromise, yet when he thought of her going to England to open a restaurant, he knew that he couldn't compromise.

He wouldn't have her out to the ranch again, because it hurt too badly and it hurt Melody. She had asked for Samantha every day since then, and now she wanted to go into town to see her.

He stared into space, looking at his ranch that he loved. It provided a serene contentment. But even that seemed gone now. He closed his eyes in pain, his hands tightening into fists.

He could see laughing blue eyes, see her in moments of passion, lips swollen, body arching beneath his, her hips moving wildly. He remembered her reading to Melody and telling her stories. He surveyed the sprawling land from the vantage point of the hillside. He looked at the meandering river that bordered the land. All this was his, but now it seemed empty without her. And Melody was drooping over Samantha's absence.

If he sold the ranch and moved into a city—he rejected that idea the moment it came. He loved the land and he wasn't going to give it up. It was his heritage, his lifeblood and Melody's heritage.

In the distance he saw one of the oil wells on the land, the pump rising and falling steadily. His investments now were going into stocks and mutual funds and bonds instead of land, but it was all beginning to seem empty.

If *he* owned the damned restaurant in town, he could let her work there when she wanted to. His eyes narrowed as he thought about the possibility of buying back Salido Sam's. Now, because of the fire, it might make it a more difficult deal, or it might make it easier, depending on the insurance payments to Kyriakos. Or he might not listen, no matter what kind of deal Jake would make.

Jake sat in the saddle, letting the horse make his own way, while he thought about buying the restaurant.

His pulse began to drum, because he felt as if he'd found a nugget of gold. He turned the horse. Suddenly he wanted to find the steers and ride back to the house and make some calls to his accountant and his attorney.

Samantha watched Tom ease down on the sofa, where they had set up a temporary bed for him. Since he was on crutches and wore a cast, he didn't think he could manage going up and down the stairs yet. Myra brought him a heaping bowl of chocolate ice cream, while Phoebe placed get-well cards on the end table.

As Myra crossed the room to him, Samantha studied her, realizing Tom's wreck had made a big change in Myra as well as in Bernie. Myra wore jeans and a T-shirt and the thick makeup was gone. Samantha suspected she had Bernie to thank for the change as much as the accident, because she knew Bernie had talked to Myra.

She didn't know how long Myra would remain subdued, but so far, it was a refreshing change and a relief. As the first day passed, it was Tom's Salido high school friends who came to see him.

There wasn't one person from Monroe, and she wondered about his new set of friends.

Friday morning, as she was getting ready to leave to meet with Eldon Kyriakos at the new hotel in town, she paused and looked at Tom. He was reclining on the sofa and staring into space.

"Want anything before I go?"

"No, thank you. Samantha," he said solemnly, studying her. "I'm sorry I was on the bike, because you told me not to ride it. I won't again."

"Okay, Tom."

"Jeez, it felt as if an express train going full-speed hit me, and then I didn't remember anything. And I missed the fire. I can't believe that I missed the fire and the whole block burned. It must have taken hours."

"It did. It was still burning when we went to Monroe to see about you."

"They said Jake came to get you."

"Yes."

"That's a nice guy. I wouldn't have gone to get someone if I had broken up with them."

"Jake is very nice," she said, smiling.

"Yeah? You going back to him?"

"Maybe so."

The phone rang and she rushed to pick it up, knowing some of the family still asleep upstairs.

"Samantha?" Jake's voice made her breath catch.

"Yes," she said, gripping the phone and carrying it into the dining room and closing the door so

305

she could have some privacy. She looked out the window at the green lawn and Aunt Phoebe's roses in bloom in two rows of rainbow colors.

"I'd like to talk to you. Can I pick you up tomorrow afternoon about four? Will you come out here for dinner, so we can talk where we won't be disturbed?"

"Yes," she answered, her heart drumming.

"Good. I'll come by the house then. Bye, love."

"Goodbye, Jake," she said quietly, hanging up the receiver and thinking about what she needed to do during the day, thinking about what she wanted to tell Jake.


Her pulse raced as she entered the office temporarily set up by Kyriakos Enterprises. Eldon Kyriakos rose from behind a desk and came around to shake her hand. His gaze ran over her swiftly and impartially as he smiled.

She wore a tailored navy silk dress with a white collar, and her hair was in the pageboy, and she felt confident about what she wanted to discuss.

"Come have a seat," he said. "We've talked to the architectural firm, and he'd like to borrow your pictures of the restaurant while he draws up the plans."

"Of course."

"You've done a good job with the restaurants, Samantha. A really nice job."

"Thank you," she said, surprised at the warmth in his voice. His eyes twinkled, and she wondered if a raise was coming. Working there for less than a year, she couldn't imagine it, yet he looked as if he had something special he was about to say.

"I talked to Ed in Tulsa, and there's no need for you to go back there. They're doing fine."

"Good. I thought they would be. Mr. Kyriakos, I asked for this appointment because I wanted to talk to you."

"Of course."

"This has been a wonderful job. I've loved it enormously and felt it was very challenging."

"You've done a good job, and you've become more confident, Samantha. It's always interesting to watch people change."

"Thank you. It's with regrets and for personal reasons that I have to turn in my resignation."

For just a moment his eyes widened a fraction as if in surprise. Then the look was gone and he smiled. "I'll hate to lose you. Do you have another offer?"

"I want to get married, and I don't want to travel. I want to be home with my husband and our family," she said, holding her breath. She wondered if he would offer a job staying at Salido Sam's in her hometown and tell her he could hire someone else for the openings. Instead, he merely shook his head.

"Regrettable, but the fellow is fortunate, and I give you my best wishes and hope I get invited to the wedding. It's Jake Colby, isn't it?"

She felt a ripple of disappointment that there would be no connection with the restaurant she had started, yet Jake was more important. "Yes, it's Jake. Of course I'll send you an invitation."

His eyes twinkled. "It'll give me an excuse to fish at Lake Lewiston more often."

She smiled and suddenly felt as if a burden had lifted. "I'm going to miss this job and miss the restaurant. It's been such a part of my life." She stood up, and he rose to his feet.

"Best wishes to you, Samantha."

"Thank you." She turned to offer her hand.

He took hers in both of his. "I knew that first morning I met you that you would do a good job for me. I hate to lose you, but I wish you well."

"Thank you."

He held the door. "Don't forget the wedding invitation."

"I won't," she said, glancing back to see him smiling.

She stepped outside and felt as if the whole world was sparkling. She glanced at her watch to see it was hours until time for Jake. Ahead she saw Ellie and she smiled at her.

"Hi, Ellie."

Ellie nodded and crossed the street, walking on the opposite side. Samantha sighed, realizing that some things wouldn't change. Yet she knew she wasn't going to be staying alone in empty motel rooms any longer. She walked home, stopping to talk to friends, not quite so stung by the people who no longer would speak.

She soaked in a hot tub for thirty minutes and then took her time dressing, changing three times before she decided on her old blue sundress that Jake had always liked. She washed and dried her hair and let it fall loosely on her shoulders in curls.

And finally he was here, talking to Tom when she entered the living room. He turned, his dark gaze drifting over her. Her pulse raced and she felt more certain than ever she had made the right decision.

He walked across the room to her. "Hi."

"Tom's doing better."

"Sounds like it. Are you ready?" When she nodded, he glanced at Tom. "See you, Tom."

Tom waved at them and turned his attention back to television as Jake took her arm. "Melody is in Dallas now, and I'll go get her Thursday."

"I'll miss her," she said, realizing they would be alone when she told him her news.

"How was the trip to Dallas?"

"Fine," he answered as they climbed into the Bronco. When he turned down the drive, he talked about the ranch. She studied him, her heart racing with excitement. Dressed in jeans and a plaid cotton shirt and boots, he looked masculine, appealing, and every inch the man she loved.

She wanted to blurt out now what she'd done, but she knew she had to wait until they were at the ranch and he didn't have to concentrate on his driving.

"You look like you did on one of our first dates."

"And you like that?"

"Yes, you look delicious and gorgeous," he answered, and she realized he was happy and more like his old self, and she wondered what had brought about the change when she hadn't told him her surprise yet.

"You're easy to please, Jake Colby."

"We'll see how easy when I quit driving. This is one time the miles to the ranch seem to stretch without end."

"What's brought about this jolly mood?"

He glanced at her. "You have to ask?" he drawled, his gaze lowering and she felt her nipples tighten beneath his gaze and her body respond to his heated look.

"Jake! Watch the road."

"You asked, so I gave you my answer. It's summer and I'm with you for the evening," he answered. "That's enough reason to bring on a jolly mood, Samantha."

"I agree," she said solemnly, thinking of the heartache they had been through and thankful it was over. "Oh, Jake, hurry and let's get there. I want out of the Bronco and—"

"Don't stop! And what?"

She turned to look out the window and get her attention off him before he wrecked the Bronco. "I think we'd better get onto a safe subject."

"You name it."

"Aunt Phoebe took a tour to the cemetery yesterday and told them she was a descendant of the Draytons. A man in the group is a member of the Sons and Daughters of Old West Outlaws and he asked her to join. She seems real taken with this fellow. But if she joins the organization, she's going to have to write down the family tree."

He laughed. "Phoebe will work it out."

"Granddad said she might as well claim being related to an outlaw, because she's robbing people when she charges ten dollars a head to show them around the Salido Cemetery."

"I talked to Asa this morning. He's entering the bass tournament on Lake Lewiston this year."

"Granddad? He didn't tell me that, but I'm glad, because I know he's always wanted to enter it. He thinks he knows where to catch the biggest bass in the lake. I think Mr. Kyriakos has tried to worm it out of him, but he hasn't been able to."

She felt bubbly, tingling with excitement that grew with each mile. She couldn't wait to tell Jake about her resignation. When he turned into the ranch road, she became quiet, suddenly hoping everything worked out like she expected. He drove the first quarter mile and pulled off on a rise to park beneath an oak.

He got out and came around the Bronco and opened her door. "Get out, Samantha."

Her brows arched and she stared at him. "Jake—"

He reached in and hauled her out, picking her up in his arms to carry her to the peak of the hill, where he set her on her feet. "This is one of the loves of my life," he said, waving his hand. And she looked at the sprawling ranch that was the deep emerald-green of summer. Easy, rolling land

311

stretched to meet a blue horizon. Fields were dotted with trees and cut through by streams and ribbons of roads. The land was vast, and she knew he loved it and that it was a part of him.

He turned her to face him and he was solemn, his black eyes tugging on her. Her heart thudded as she looked at the longing in his expression, and there was no mistaking what he felt.

"I love you, Samantha, and I want you for my wife. I met with Eldon Kyriakos today and I offered to buy the Salido Sam's from him. I'll own them," he said tensely, his voice becoming gruff and his eyes dark shards of marble. "And then you can work where you want to work and where I want you to work. We'll cancel the overseas operations—"

Stunned, she stared at him. "Jake, how could you buy all those restaurants? Did you sell the ranch?"

"No, I didn't," he said, suddenly sounding tough and determined. "I used my ranch for collateral. I have land and oil and I came up with the money to make Kyriakos a damned fine offer he couldn't refuse!"

Shocked, she stared at him. "You borrowed on the ranch—all this—for me?"

"Yes, dammit. I love you—" Suddenly she saw his eyes darken like storm clouds gathering, and he pulled her to him. His mouth covered hers, his tongue thrust over hers, sliding over her teeth, setting off a gush of warmth in her. She wrapped her arms around him, moaning with need, thrusting her hips against him. She was overwhelmed by Jake, by what he had done. And he was here, holding her, kissing her.

He bent over her, kissing her passionately. His hands fumbled with her zipper, yanking it down and pushing away the sundress to bare her breasts. She stood in a lacy garter belt and blue bikinis as he cupped her soft fullness, his thumbs caressing her nipples in easy circles that made her tremble.

Samantha's heart felt as if it would burst with desire and joy. She tugged at his belt, pulling up his shirt. He yanked it away and yanked down his jeans and briefs, pushing her to the ground.

"Jake, it's been so long since—"

"Too damned long," he said gruffly.

She felt an urgency as her hands fluttered over his hard body, over his broad chest and flat belly down to his narrow thighs, to his stiff rod that was ready.

He moved between her legs, his eyes dark, demanding and promising at the same time. He lowered himself into her, slowly, making her arch and swell against him and then tighten around him as they both moved.

Wild with joy, she clung to him, knowing this is what she wanted and all she wanted. He drove into her until she felt filled with him, impaled, wanting him and melting with release.

"Samantha," he said hoarsely, turning his head to kiss her—a hot, hungry kiss that drove her over another brink. And she moved with him, a rapture finally bursting over her that was both physical

313

and emotional.

He was heavy on her, both of them gasping for breath as she stroked his smooth bare back. "That wasn't exactly the way I planned the evening," he said. "But I couldn't wait." He rolled them both over as he gazed at her. "Will you marry me?"

"Yes," she gasped, squeezing against him and hearing him chuckle softly.

"I was beginning to wonder what I'd have to do to win you, babe."

"You didn't have to do as much as you did." She raised up. "Jake, you don't have to buy Salido Sam's. I quit today."

"You what?" he asked, his eyes narrowing.

"We shouldn't have tried to surprise each other. I quit."

He stared at her so long that she wondered if he'd gone into shock.

"Jake?"

Suddenly a slow grin spread across his face and he yanked her down against him. "Damn, woman, you love me enough to toss aside that career?"

"Oh, Jake, yes!" She rose up and slanted him a look, lowering her voice to a sultry level. "Want me to show you how much?" she asked, running her hand between his legs along his thigh.

His eyes darkened and he pulled her down to kiss her. When he raised himself up to look at her, she stroked his jaw. "Jake, it was so bad. I've missed you, and the job wasn't the same. Nothing was the same. All the magic went out of life."

He kissed her throat, trailing kisses to her ear.

"I know."

Framing his face with her hands, she studied him. "You don't have to buy the restaurants."

"I've already made a commitment."

"Oh, no! Jake, it will cost a fortune—"

He laughed. "Stop worrying." He kissed her lightly. "I've had some people look into it. It's a good investment. There won't be any foreign restaurants until these ones are really solid. He was opening them too fast for me. We'll keep all of them except Seattle, simply because it's the farthest away. Dallas, New Orleans, Chicago are easy to get to."

"San Francisco?"

He grinned. "It's showing a tidy profit already. We keep it unless it begins to lose money. You can work at the one in Salido if you want, or you can stay home if you want."

She gazed up at him. "When they rebuild the restaurant, I hope they put in a big pantry with a tiny window."

He grinned and stroked the curve of her hip. "You have some decisions to make . . . like when can we have a wedding?"

"I seem to remember a very beautiful ring—"

"Oh!" He sat up, his jeans around his ankles. He dug into his pocket and pulled out a plastic bag and unwrapped it. "I got tired of carrying the box around." He took her hand and slid it on her finger.

"Jake, it's beautiful!" she said, waving her fingers and turning to kiss him, and then she was lost. He stroked her until finally she pushed at him. "I'm getting poked with sticks and rocks."

He grinned and sat up. "Softie. There's something about being part of nature this way."

"Then we reverse where we are, buster, and you lie on the ground—"

He swung her over him, as he kissed her and wrapped his arms around her.


The last Saturday in July, dressed in white satin and lace, Samantha walked down the aisle. All she could see waiting for her was Jake, looking darkly handsome in the tuxedo. Asa would give her away, so she had her arm linked with his. Myra and Nedra and Lori were bridesmaids with Bernie and Tom and Ryan Cain as groomsmen and Melody as flower girl.

Before they left for a honeymoon, taking Samantha with him, Jake scooped up Melody and carried her into an office in the church building to tell her goodbye. "We're leaving, sweetie, and we'll be back in five days and get you and then we'll all go on a trip together to Disney World. All nine of us," he said, giving Samantha a wink.

Melody grinned and hugged him and turned to Samantha, holding out her arms as Samantha picked her up for a hug.

"You look pretty," Melody said, touching the white veil that framed Samantha's face.

"Thank you. You do, too, Melody."

"Daddy said I can call you Mommie if I want

to."

"That's right, you can. I'd like that, Melody, if you'd like to."

She smiled. "I get to stay at your house with Myra and Aunt Phoebe and Granddad."

"Yes, you do."

Jake took Melody and set her on her feet and held her hand. "Let's find Asa for some last-minute words and goodbyes. My daughter just adopted seven people as her family."

"They're happy to have her adopt them."

They found Asa, and he took Melody's hand. "I'll call every day," Jake promised, giving Melody another hug and kiss. Samantha kissed her again and then stood up to look at Asa.

"We'll be back soon."

"I'm happy for you, honey. The restaurant brought us a lot of good things, but the best was Jake."

"I think so, too." She kissed Asa and blew kisses to the others as they left.


Four hours later Jake closed the door at the villa in Akumal and turned to take her into his arms. "Mrs. Colby, you could have gone anywhere in the world. Switzerland, Australia—"

"This was my choice, and you said it was fine with you," she said, wrapping her arms around his neck and thinking she was the luckiest woman on earth. She turned her face up, looking into his dark eyes that were filled with love.

"Samantha, it should be so good," he said softly, his hands sliding down the zipper of her turquoise dress and pushing it away as he leaned forward to kiss her.

She clung to him, her heart racing with joy, knowing she had found a love to last forever.

# DISCOVER DEANA JAMES!

**CAPTIVE ANGEL** (2524, $4.50/$5.50)
Abandoned, penniless, and suddenly responsible for the biggest tobacco plantation in Colleton County, distraught Caroline Gillard had no time to dissolve into tears. By day the willowy redhead labored to exhaustion beside her slaves . . . but each night left her restless with longing for her wayward husband. She'd make the sea captain regret his betrayal until he begged her to take him back!

**MASQUE OF SAPPHIRE** (2885, $4.50/$5.50)
Judith Talbot-Harrow left England with a heavy heart. She was going to America to join a father she despised and a sister she distrusted. She was certainly in no mood to put up with the insulting actions of the arrogant Yankee privateer who boarded her ship, ransacked her things, then "apologized" with an indecent, brazen kiss! She vowed that someday he'd pay dearly for the liberties he had taken and the desires he had awakened.

**SPEAK ONLY LOVE** (3439, $4.95/$5.95)
Long ago, the shock of her mother's death had robbed Vivian Marleigh of the power of speech. Now she was being forced to marry a bitter man with brandy on his breath. But she could not say what was in her heart. It was up to the viscount to spark the fires that would melt her icy reserve.

**WILD TEXAS HEART** (3205, $4.95/$5.95)
Fan Breckenridge was terrified when the stranger found her near-naked and shivering beneath the Texas stars. Unable to remember who she was or what had happened, all she had in the world was the deed to a patch of land that might yield oil . . . and the fierce loving of this wildcatter who called himself Irons.

*Available wherever paperbacks are sold, or order direct from the Publisher. Send cover price plus 50¢ per copy for mailing and handling to Zebra Books, Dept. 4052, 475 Park Avenue South, New York, N.Y. 10016. Residents of New York and Tennessee must include sales tax. DO NOT SEND CASH. For a free Zebra/ Pinnacle catalog please write to the above address.*